RAVES FOR
JAMES PATTERSON

"Patterson knows where our deepest fears are buried...There's no stopping his imagination."
—*New York Times Book Review*

"James Patterson writes his thrillers as if he were building roller coasters."
—Associated Press

"No one gets this big without natural storytelling talent—which is what James Patterson has, in spades."
—Lee Child, #1 *New York Times* bestselling author of the Jack Reacher series

"James Patterson knows how to sell thrills and suspense in clear, unwavering prose."
—*People*

"Patterson boils a scene down to a single, telling detail, the element that defines a character or moves a plot along. It's what fires off the movie projector in the reader's mind."
—Michael Connelly

"James Patterson is the boss. End of."
—Ian Rankin, *New York Times* bestselling author of the Inspector Rebus series

THE MIDWIFE MURDERS

For a complete list of books, visit
JamesPatterson.com.

THE
MIDWIFE
MURDERS

JAMES PATTERSON
AND RICHARD DiLALLO

GRAND
CENTRAL
PUBLISHING
New York   Boston

Copyright © 2020 by James Patterson
Preview of *The President's Daughter* copyright © 2021 by James Patterson and William Jefferson Clinton

Hachette Book Group supports the right to free expression and the value of copyright. The purpose of copyright is to encourage writers and artists to produce the creative works that enrich our culture.

The scanning, uploading, and distribution of this book without permission is a theft of the author's intellectual property. If you would like permission to use material from the book (other than for review purposes), please contact permissions@hbgusa.com. Thank you for your support of the author's rights.

Grand Central Publishing
Hachette Book Group
1290 Avenue of the Americas, New York, NY 10104
grandcentralpublishing.com
twitter.com/grandcentralpub

Originally published in trade paperback and ebook in August 2020
First oversize mass market edition: April 2021

Grand Central Publishing is a division of Hachette Book Group, Inc. The Grand Central Publishing name and logo is a trademark of Hachette Book Group, Inc.

The publisher is not responsible for websites (or their content) that are not owned by the publisher.

The Hachette Speakers Bureau provides a wide range of authors for speaking events. To find out more, go to hachettespeakersbureau.com or call (866) 376-6591.

ISBNs: 978-1-5387-0368-7 (oversize mass market), 978-1-5387-0366-3 (ebook)

Printed in the United States of America

OPM

10 9 8 7 6 5 4 3 2 1

For Bob DiLallo and Ed Petrillo
—R.D.

THE MIDWIFE MURDERS

PROLOGUE

IT'S MONDAY. IT'S AUGUST. And it's one of those days that's already so hot at 6 a.m. that they tell you to check on your elderly neighbors and please don't go outside if you don't have to. So of course I'm jogging through the stifling, smelly streets of Crown Heights, Brooklyn, with a dog—a dog named The Duke. Yes. Not Duke, but *The* Duke. That's his name. That's what my son, Willie, who was four years old when The Duke was a puppy, wanted. So that's what we did.

The Duke is a terrific dog, a mixed breed German shepherd, terrier, and God knows what else from the Brooklyn Animal Resource Coalition—BARC—animal shelter. He's cuter than any guy I ever dated, and Willie was instinctively right about the dog's name. He's The Duke. The Duke is snooty and snobby and slow. He actually seems to think he's royalty. His Highness belongs to Willie, but for forty-five minutes a day, The Duke condescends to be my running buddy.

The Duke doesn't seem to know or care that I've got places to be. I'm a certified nurse-midwife, so I do my work by the schedules of a lot of pregnant women. On a normal day like today, I've got only a small window of time to exercise before getting breakfast on the table, because although Willie is now nine years old, he still needs a lot of looking after by me, his single mom. Then it's a half-hour subway ride into midtown Manhattan. Back to work, although I'm tired as hell from delivering a preterm last night. (Emma Rose, the infant, is doing just fine, I'm relieved to say.) Yeah, I'm beat, but I love my job as much as I hate running.

Get away from that rotten piece of melon, The Duke. Those pigeons got there first!

I tug hard on the leash. It takes The Duke a full city block to forget about the melon. Don't feel bad for the dog; he'll find some other rotten food to run after. If not, there's a big bowl of Purina and some cold Chinese takeout beef and broccoli waiting for him at home.

I turn up the volume in my headphones. Okay, it's the same playlist I listened to when I was a teenager, but Motörhead's *Ace of Spades* never gets old, does it? Willie says that every band I like—Motörhead, Korn, Cake—is *"definitely old school."* He's right. But, hey, you like what you like, right? And, hey, old school isn't so awful. At least not for me.

No, no, no. We're not stopping to talk to Marty… "Hey, Marty, how ya doing, man?" *No, no, The Duke, we don't need any cocaine today. Keep moving. Keep moving.*

Pep talk to self: *Come on, Lucy Ryuan, you can do it. Keep moving. Even on just four hours' sleep, you can do it. A little bit more. One more block. Then one more block.*

And now we're moving into Grand Army Plaza, into Prospect Park with all the other runners. God bless them. They're all an annoying inspiration.

I'm strangely and amazingly awake on so little sleep. Now I'm into a running groove, and every-thing feels good, until the music suddenly stops. My cell is ringing. It's one of my assistants, Tracy Anne Cavanaugh, a smart, energetic young woman.

"Lucy, I'm sorry, really sorry, to bother you. I know you must be—"

"What's up, Tracy Anne?"

"Valerina Gomez is here at the hospital. Her brother brought her in. She's at eight centimeters…"

I roll my eyes at The Duke, for God's sake. Valerina Gomez has been trouble from the get-go. A druggie, a smoker, a drinker, and I'm afraid to think how she makes her living. Plus, just her luck, she's carrying twins.

"Handle her till I get there. You can do that, Tracy Anne." And, yes, there's a very impatient tone to my voice. But Tracy Anne's great. Tracy Anne can handle her just fine.

"I will, I will," she says. "But there's something else…"

"Okay, what?"

"A newborn baby has gone missing."

I ask the question that every shocked person asks: "Are you kidding me?"

Tracy Anne doesn't even bother to say no. Instead she says, "The hospital is going crazy. The cops. Detectives. They're all over the place. They say this has never happened here before. I mean…I've heard once or twice somebody got the wrong baby to take home. And I know that—"

"Listen, don't you go crazy, too, Tracy Anne. Just cooperate, do your job, and—"

"Lucy, what are we gonna do?"

Then, with my head aching, sweat dropping from me like rain, my stomach churning, I say something absolutely stupid.

"What are we gonna do, Tracy Anne? We're gonna help them find the baby."

CHAPTER 1

SHOCKINGLY, THE DOG SEEMS to know that this is an emergency. He runs with me at an unusually un-The-Duke-like pace. Once inside our little building, he takes the stairs to our third-floor apartment two steps at a time. *I'll show him who's boss.* I take the steps three at a time. When we hit the third-floor landing it's a close call as to which of us is sweatier and smellier.

Willie sleeps in our one tiny bedroom. The living room with the foldout sofa is mine. This is particularly convenient today because there is a large selection of my clothes on both my unfolded foldout and the steamer trunk that doubles as a toy box and a coffee table.

I now begin trying to do three things at once. One, I start to get dressed. No time for a shower. A wet washcloth under my arms, a few swipes of deodorant, and a generous helping of Johnson's Baby Powder will compensate. Two, I try to find information about the missing baby on my laptop. Nothing. *Where are you, Twitter, when I need you?* Three, I keep yelling toward the bedroom, "Willie, wake up!"

Within a few seconds I'm slipping into a pair

of slightly stained jeans and a less-than-glamorous turquoise V-neck T-shirt, also slightly stained. Both are victims of the Chinese beef and broccoli, which The Duke is noisily eating right now.

I try searching an all-news website.

Great. I guess.

Missing baby NYC and *missing baby hospital news info* brings me one news brief that "an underage patient at Gramatan University Hospital (GUH) has been reported missing."

Underage? The freaking baby is one day old. That's PR for you.

I head back into Willie's room. He is snoring like a three-hundred-pound drunk. I'm surprised he doesn't wake the neighbors, and I've got to wonder how somebody that little can make a noise so loud.

"Willie, get up. Come on. You've gotta get down to Sabryna's. Right! Now!" *Well, that sure didn't work.*

I stand in the little bedroom, and then I waste a few seconds just staring at my fine-looking son, asleep on Bart Simpson sheets. I tousle his hair. No reaction. I tousle it somewhat harder. One eye opens. Then a mouth.

"You've got a really huge stain on that T-shirt, Mom."

"I know," I say. "I haven't had time to do laundry. And the stain is not huge. It's medium."

Willie now has both eyes closed again. He's gone back to sleep. I move into very-loud-but-still-not-yelling volume.

"You're going down to Sabryna's in your underwear if you don't get up right this minute. I repeat: Right. This. Minute."

Sabryna and her thirteen-year-old son, Devan, are our downstairs neighbors. She is originally from

Jamaica, and her voice still has the beautiful island lilt to it. That lilt, which Sabryna can turn on and off like a faucet, also adds a note of authenticity to the small Caribbean grocery store she runs on the ground floor. The store is a jumble of goods: baskets of plantains and bunches of callaloo greens, as well as Pringles, Skittles, cigarettes, and New York Lottery tickets.

Sabryna's store is open from five in the morning until seven at night. She works hard, and she works alone, except for some reluctant help from Devan. Sabryna, who is hands down my best friend, also is my go-to babysitter when I'm called out suddenly.

A buzz, a beep, a phone text from Tracy Anne: R u on way? Hosp nurse about 2 interfere.

Let me explain something here about how things operate in my professional world. The nurse-midwives are entirely separate from the medical staff at Gramatan University Hospital. We've trained for three years—intensely, some of us at the best teaching hospitals in the world: Johns Hopkins, University of Chicago, Yale. I honestly believe we're only a few steps away from being doctors. I say that with just a touch of arrogance. I don't want you to think we're a bunch of former hippies who stand and sing over a screaming woman giving birth on a kitchen table. The hospital setting is around us only in case of an emergency. So when Tracy Anne uses the word *interfere,* my blood starts to boil.

"Okay, Willie. You're going downstairs in your tighty-whities," I yell. I toss a pair of khaki cargo shorts on top of him.

"Wait. I need a shirt, and I need to go to the bath-room, and I need—"

"And I need to help a woman give birth to twins. Downstairs! Right now, buddy boy. Right now!"

CHAPTER 2

WHAT'S GOING ON IN my world this morning is really *not* at all unusual. My life seems to always be a great big blur of chaos. It's the collision of my very intense job, my adorable but somewhat demanding kid, my unbearably messy home, and my dog. Yes, of course I love my son. He is smart and charming and usually quite cooperative. Yes, of course I hate my life. I don't have enough time, and I don't have enough money. I often think if had more of either of those things I'd be able to manage, but I'm smart enough to know that isn't true.

As Sabryna says, "Money is a necessity, but it never is a solution." *I guess.* Sabryna's folk wisdom catch-phrases always sound right, but I've never really put them to the test. Like the one that she loves about raising children: "Don't pester your children with lots of discipline. Allow room for the good Lord to raise them." Okay, sounds good, but I'm not buying it. And I'm certainly not going to test it out on Willie.

"Where you off to, Lucy?" Sabryna asks as she stacks cans of gungo peas. I can smell the frying of onions and goat meat coming from the tiny kitchen in the back. Devan is stacking cigarette packages on the shelf slowly...very, very slowly. His face lights with a smile, however, when he sees Willie. They exchange one of those complicated handshakes that only young people seem to know how to do.

"I'm sorry. I have an emergency," I say.

"No worries, girl. We always got use for an extra pair of working hands, no matter the size of the hands," says Sabryna.

Now it's Willie's turn to roll his eyes.

"Didn't I hear you coming up the stairs early this morning?" Sabryna asks.

"Yeah, I went out running with the dog and then I got a call about an emergency," I say.

"Some lady-mama is ready to pop?" she asks.

"That's one way of putting it."

"You might as well live at that hospital of yours," says Sabryna. Then she adds, "Well, you practically do. Pretty soon Willie-boy's gonna think that *I'm* his mama."

I laugh at the joke, but a part of me, just for a second, is sad at even the funny truth of it.

My own slightly bossy mother, who should be canonized a saint, lives a long, long car ride away, down in West Virginia, so I can't lean on her for help. I've read all the online advice for the single mother, the working mother, the single mother with two jobs, the single mother with two children, the single mother with no family, the single mother with a bossy mother of her own. With all this advice available, why does it usually feel like I'm making it up as I go along?

"The Duke's up in the apartment. I'm not sure he did his stuff when we were out. I've lost my memory completely," I say.

"Not a worry. I'll get the boys to take him out later."

My cell phone buzzes. I know it will be the frantic Tracy Anne. I don't even bother to look at the screen. Instead I stoop down and hug Willie. "Do whatever you can to help Sabryna," I say.

Sabryna jumps in immediately. "You can start by unpacking that sack of Scotch Bonnet chili peppers."

"A Scotch Bonnet. What's that?" Willie asks.

"Not some rich lady's hat. They're the hottest peppers on earth, just about. You touch your eyes after handling the Scotch Bonnets, you'll be blind for three days or maybe even forever."

I kiss Willie on his forehead, what we call a *head kiss*.

"See you later," Willie says. Then he glances at the small burlap sack of peppers and adds, "At least I sure hope so."

CHAPTER 3

TWO NEW YORK CITY police officers are at the employees' entrance of GUH.

What the hell is going on? And then, of course, I start to think about the missing baby. I'd been so focused on getting here for the birth of Val's babies that I'd managed to forget the horrible news.

It takes a full minute of plowing through my bag to find my employee ID card. Both officers glance back and forth a few times between my face and my card. One of the guards says, "Okay. Go to second check."

I walk about ten yards and run into Caspar, the hospital guard who usually sits weekdays at the employees' entrance.

"Morning, Caspar," I say. But this is serious business.

Caspar, who is usually full of jokes and smiles and weather predictions, is stern. "May I please see your identification card, Ms. Ryuan?" He usually would have just called me Lucy, but these are clearly dangerous times.

I smile. Caspar does not. I realize that Caspar's only doing what he's been told to do, and that it makes no difference that fifteen seconds ago I presented my ID to two New York City police officers.

Caspar looks at my ID. He says, "Thank you, ma'am."

"'Thank you, ma'am'?" I ask. "Caspar, it's me. Lucy."

"Sorry, orders from Dr. Katz. We gotta do it all by the book."

I walk a few more yards and...*Hold on, what the hell is this?*

At the end of the entrance corridor stands Dr. Barrett Katz himself, the pompous, self-important, arrogant, despicable—Am I making my feelings clear?—CEO of Gramatan University Hospital. Katz has been called the Invisible CEO. He is almost always *in a meeting, in conference, with an important donor, out of town*. Right now he is flanked by two other physicians: Dr. Rudra Sarkar, one of the hospital's few male ob-gyn doctors, and Dr. Maureen Mahrlig, a radiologist who may or may not be on track to becoming the fourth Mrs. Katz.

A short line has formed in front of this gang of three. The line moves quickly, and whatever Katz is telling each individual brings a serious expression and a strong nod of the head from each person. Most of us never see Dr. Katz regularly, and until today, none of us, I venture, has ever been greeted by him on our way into work.

My turn.

"Ms. Ryuan," Katz says. "I'm telling every employee that it's very important that there be no communication with the press about the absent patient."

I can't resist. "You mean the missing baby or are you referring to the 'absent patient' that somebody kidnapped?"

"Do not try to corral me into an angry, sarcastic

discussion, Ms. Ryuan, and in the future, I'd ask you to leave your bad attitude in the parking lot. Whatever the circumstances," he says, his eyes filled with the irritation that always shows up during our very rare encounters. "Discretion is very important while the police investigate the absence."

Again, I can't resist. But this time I'm serious. So serious that I ignore my buzzing cell phone. "I'm no expert, Dr. Katz, but I'd think the more information that's out there, names and photos and facts, then the better the chances of somebody who knows something coming forward and helping us find—"

"Thank you for your thoughts, Ms. Ryuan, but as I just said, there's no need for a discussion. Right now everything is in the very capable hands of—"

"Lucy!" I hear someone shout. Then almost immediately again, even louder, "Lucy!"

Within seconds Tracy Anne Cavanaugh is standing next to me. Young and blond and almost too perfectly pretty, Tracy Anne completely ignores Katz.

"I've been trying to reach you. I've been calling and calling. Val is ready to go. And Troy is with her. But there's a problem, a real problem, with Val."

Great. Now my problem is that Val has a problem.

Tracy Anne and I take off. If we had left a cloud of dust, Barrett Katz would be covered with it.

CHAPTER 4

"WHAT THE HELL IS this?" I shout as Tracy Anne and I rush into Valerina Gomez's birthing room. I am truly struck by the horror of what I see before me. Val has been shackled with wrist and ankle restraints. She looks like a woman forced into admission at a mental hospital during Victorian times. Val is screaming, sweating, struggling. Her wrists and ankles are red from the shackles. Her hospital gown is way up above her breasts.

I look at Troy Jackson. He's a strong, hefty African American guy, and both my assistant *and* one of the best midwives I've ever worked with. He's efficient, organized, and kind, and he can be as tough as a large pit bull when he decides to.

"How the hell could you let them do this, Troy?" I yell at him.

The tone of his voice matches the anger in mine. "You think I let this happen? Don't you think I did everything but punch them to prevent it? And by 'them' I mean that nurse over there. She said if we didn't restrain the patient, she'd call Security. You sure as hell didn't think this was my idea, didja?"

Troy is pointing at floor supervisor Nurse Deborah Franklin.

"Get her undone. Get my patient undone," I yell. "Hurry up. Jesus, leave someone alone with general hospital staff and this is what happens."

Troy and Tracy Anne begin removing Val's restraints. They know the nurse isn't going to mess with me.

Val is yelling with delivery pain. I take two giant steps toward Deborah Franklin, who stands with her arms folded.

"What the hell were you thinking?" I say to her. I practically spit the question out.

"I ordered the restraints as a precaution," Franklin says.

"GUH staff should not be anywhere near midwife services unless they are requested. What are you even doing in here? Get out. Just get the hell out," I yell.

Franklin doesn't move. I could continue my battle with Franklin or I could shut up and work with my patient. That's an easy decision for me. If the decision is easy, the execution takes a lot of willpower on my part. *Okay, get strong, Lucy. Be the best there is.* From this moment on my concern is completely aimed at Val.

"Let's relax, Val. Let's just relax," I say. I take Val's hand. She's shaking, not quite uncontrollably but way more than a woman in labor should be. Tracy Anne dabs at Val's face with a damp lavender-scented cloth. Lavender is about as hippie as we get at GUH Midwifery.

Then, through barely clenched teeth, Troy speaks to me softly, "Lucy, I did everything to stop Franklin."

"I'm sure you did, Troy," I say. And I mean it. "Let's stay focused now. This is going to be tough, and we are off to a very bad start."

Tracy Anne pulls up a screenshot of Val's most recent sonogram on the bedside PC. Nothing new. Twins. The second baby is in complete breech position. That means the feet want to come out first, and the head wants to come out last. We knew this for the past two months. There was not much we could do except fight off anyone who said we should perform a C-section. But any discussion and planning are in the past. Now the difficult circumstances are nonnegotiable. Now we've got to deal with them in real time. First things first: I need to have a very intense discussion with the very screwed-up mother-to-be.

Tracy Anne is helping Val with her breathing and her counting. The tremors from Val's hands have spread to her arms and shoulders. She is shaking even worse than before. All the lavender cloths in the world are not going to absorb the perspiration that's streaming out of her.

I hear Deborah Franklin say, "Now perhaps you can see why I ordered restraints. Your patient is going through withdrawal. She should be delivering under general anesthesia. I'm going to call OB for help."

"You call OB, lady, and you better call orthopedics, too. You're gonna have some broken bones to tend to," Troy says.

"Ditto," I say.

Honestly, I don't think Nurse Franklin is frightened of me. But Troy, one of the nicest, gentlest people I know, can look absolutely terrifying, weighing in at just under three hundred pounds, and with steely eyes that look as if they could flash fire if he wanted them to blaze.

"You people are living in another world," says Franklin. She can rant all she wants. All I know is that she's not moving to call OB. And I wouldn't put it past Troy to try to stop her physically.

From here on in, I just ignore Franklin. I kneel on the delivery bed and hold down Val's shoulders.

"Listen," I say firmly but not unkindly to Val. "Like it or not, you're about to have two babies right now. It's going to be tough."

Val screams.

Okay. Yelling back at this frail mother will get me nowhere. I move into *soft* gear.

"Just stay calm. Concentrate. Just do what I say. We're in this together. I'll do my job. And you do yours."

CHAPTER 5

PUSHING. SCREAMING. HOWLING. "Everything's looking good with the first baby," I say to Troy. "But once we start with the second one, we're gonna need—"

Troy finishes my sentence, "I know…an on-call doc in case we need a C-section with the breech. I already notified OB surgery. Thought I'd best get them ready rather than count on that crazy-ball Nurse Franklin."

"Good man," I say.

Deborah Franklin, who has yet to leave the room, says, "C-section, huh? I thought you guys never did those."

"We hate 'em, but we hate dead babies even more," Troy says.

Then I speak. "And now, once and for all, Deborah, get the hell out of this birthing room. I will not hesitate to call Security to have you removed from a restricted area."

Deborah Franklin leaves.

Troy smiles and turns to me. "You've got such a nice way with words."

My voice goes loud as I say, "The mother is at

nine centimeters, and..." I pause. I watch. "And now she's ready."

Val screams out, "I need one of those epidemics."

Troy and I, of course, know what she means, and I'm hoping Troy will take on the job of telling her that it's way too late in the process to even consider an epidural.

"This game is in the final inning, baby doll," Troy says. "You just breathe some quick breaths and push when Lucy tells you. You're with us. We're all a team."

Val speaks through her tears. "But I need some painkillers. I can't—"

"Val," I say. "Let me ask you something. Why do you think everybody always disagrees with me?"

"How would I know? All's I know is that I can't go on with all this pain," she says.

"Val," says Troy. "Nobody in God's green world can stop you from going on with it. This isn't in your hands now. This is no longer your decision. Your babies coming out is part of the good Lord's plan. So...big push."

The word *push* is barely out of Troy's mouth when a baby comes sliding out of Val.

That's right—sliding like a Snickers bar out of a candy machine. I don't know whether it's the quickest and easiest delivery I've ever helped with, but it's in the running.

Even more spectacular is this: we are holding a remarkably healthy baby girl. Cord gets cut. Eyes get cleaned. Blanket tucked in and around the infant girl. On the scale: five pounds, three ounces. That's a nice size for a twin, a very nice size. It's especially, miraculously fine for a mom who's a serious drug user.

Pediatrics will test the baby for infant addiction, but the signs so far are showing that we've got a normal, healthy, bouncing baby girl on our hands.

"Gimme. Gimme. Gimme my baby," Val is yelling.

When there are multiple births, the firstborn baby is placed on the mother's shoulder as the next baby is delivered. It's comfortable and safe for the baby and the mama. It also leaves a nice twin-size place for the second baby. Troy moves to rest the first baby on Val's shoulder. She has an idea of her own.

"Let's rest a few minutes while I get to know this one. Let's not go get the new baby right away," Val says.

Troy's face—and I guess my own—clearly looks like he's thinking, *Is this woman just plain insane?*

"I hurt too much," she sobs. "I have to stop. I'll spend the time learning to know my baby."

"We don't have time for a discussion, Val. There's a baby inside you who's got to come out."

This conversation takes place while I am wrist-deep inside Val.

Troy has now handed the first baby off to Tracy Anne.

Meanwhile, I notice three ob-gyn residents have arrived in the room. A motley crew, as they say: one black, one white, one Indian. Surprisingly, the white resident is a man. That's fairly unusual these days— a male ob-gyn—but now's not the time to start a discussion about it. The group of doctors-to-be is quiet. I warn them to hold all their questions until *after* the delivery. Actually, I'd like to ask them to leave. But I don't. I just warn them to keep very, very quiet. The mom and the babies are starring in this production.

Troy begins massaging Val's belly. She has one

fewer baby inside her, but her belly remains large and hard. We've never been sure that this belly massage has an effect on a patient, but it's become almost like a good-luck gesture. We've just got to do it.

"Go easy, Troy. Go easy," I say.

He shoots a look at me. It's gentle, yes, but it says, *I don't need directions, Lucy.*

Tracy Anne has returned from depositing Baby Number One in the nursery. She approaches me, stands close to me, then whispers, "They've already got a social worker waiting to see Val when she's well enough. They know she's a user."

"I never filed a warning with the city," I say. Then I realize what must have happened.

"I bet that bitch Franklin notified Social Services," I say. "We can't worry about it now. Damn it. Give us a hand here."

Tracy Anne nods and begins wiping Val's head and lips and throat with our endless supply of moist lavender cloths. I keep trying unsuccessfully to gently manipulate the fetus into a more "benign" delivery position. To be honest, this procedure rarely works. And this time is no exception. What's more, there is a small but steady stream of blood beginning to cover my gloved hands.

"I'll call surgery," says Troy. "She needs a section."

"Wait," I say. "I've got an idea."

"I've got an idea, too," Troy says. "My idea is, let's get someone in to do a C-section."

I ignore him. I need to give it one more try. Not to worry, I don't ever object to calling in an OB person if necessary. But I know when to make that call.

"Help me move her," I say. I remove my bloody gloves and pull on a new pair. "Come on. You take one side. I'll take the other. Let's get her into the bathroom. Tracy Anne, go inside the bathroom and turn the shower on full blast, very hot, as hot as someone can stand it."

"But she's bleeding, Lucy," Troy says, his voice full of alarm with a touch of outrage.

"Just do what I tell you to do, for Chrissake," I snap back at him. "Tracy Anne, go into the bathroom and blast the shower water up as hot as it'll go."

Tracy Anne rushes into the adjacent bathroom. Troy and I begin lifting the screaming, weeping Val.

"Lucy, have you ever done this before?" Troy says.

I don't answer him.

CHAPTER 6

VAL IS ALTERNATELY SCREAMING and sobbing. I test the shower water with my hand. Tracy Anne has, as always, followed instructions. It is full-blast hot. I lower it to a still very hot, but not scalding, temperature. Then I slip Val's hospital gown up and over and off.

No, I have never used this method before. But my mama was a practicing midwife in West Virginia, in a place and at a time when there wasn't always a doc to do a C-section. Sometimes you've got to do whatever it takes to get the baby moving.

Val vomits on the bathroom floor as we try, as gently as possible, to get her into the shower stall. We three midwives are wearing disposable paper slippers. The soles of these slippers are so well engineered that you could walk on a frozen lake and not fall.

I ask Val to lean against the wall. She doesn't move. I realize that one of us is going to have to get in there with her. It certainly won't be Troy; he's way too big. I step into the shower myself. I move Val's hands onto the tiled shower wall.

"The shower helps with the pain," I say.

"No, it don't," Val yells. Frankly, I bet she's right

about that. She is yelling a string of other nasty, angry sentences. Her outrage is aimed at us three midwives, and a man by the name of Alonso. Alonso seems to be married, and it is Val's hope that Alonso and his "fucking wife" will die and burn in "fucking hell."

Troy steps in. In his incredibly soothing voice, he says over and over, "Move with the contractions. Just move with the contractions." The hot water is steaming up the bathroom, like it's a bad day in the Amazon rainy season.

The contractions are coming much faster now, and Val is not cooperating with my directions or Troy's directions. She is *not* moving with the contractions.

"She's ready," I yell, and I pitch my voice louder than Val's. Then I tell her to kneel on the shower floor. She doesn't move. So, very firmly, and as smoothly as possible, I ease her down to a kneeling position. I kneel next to her. I bend her over. I urge her to give "a really big push." Amazingly she cooperates.

After the big push, and equally amazingly, two infant legs appear. *Please, God, let this go well. Please, come on.*

God must have heard me—this is not always the case—because with one more push the baby's torso slides out.

Now the most dangerous part of all: we need the head. And the head is refusing to make an appearance. I cannot even see the neck or chin section. I am afraid that whatever flesh I think is emerging is actually the umbilical cord twisted around the infant's neck. I know that in a moment we'll have to call an OB surgeon in for a C-section. Tracy Anne is holding her phone in her hand. She's ready to make the call as soon as I give the signal.

"One more breath. And one more push," I say.

And then it happens. The baby comes out. I immediately create the metaphor that I will use when I tell the story of this delivery: *"The baby popped out like the cork from a bottle of champagne."*

Champagne bottle or not, this second baby, another girl, is in serious distress. This baby girl is tiny, really tiny. A guesstimate weight? Three pounds. What's as worrisome is the baby's skin—a horrid purplish color, deep purple.

Troy cuts and clips the umbilical cord.

My stethoscope says the baby is breathing normally, but that important first scream of life has yet to emerge.

Val is yelling, "What is it? What is it?" as I hand the baby to Tracy Anne, who places Baby Number Two in a portable incubator and rushes her to Neonatal ICU.

"It's another girl," I say. "She needs help. Don't worry. We're going to get her all fixed up for you."

"What's wrong?" Val yells.

"Nothing that we can't take care of." I hope. God, I hope.

Troy slowly, carefully, lovingly helps Val to a bed. I remain in the bathroom to blot and shake off as much water as I can. I remove my shirt. I wring it out. I'm a mess. I look like a mess. I feel like a mess. But I've got to keep moving.

CHAPTER 7

A FEW MINUTES LATER—maybe five minutes—
I step out of the bathroom and into the patient room.

The room is totally empty. No Troy. No Tracy
Anne. Most upsetting, no Val.

I rush into the corridor. It's crazier than usual.
Along with the rolling gurneys and rolling wheel-
chairs, along with the patients walking with dangling
IV packs, along with doctors and nurses and flower
deliveries and meal deliveries, there are uniformed and
plainclothes police officers, and right in front of me is
the head of ob-gyn, Dr. Rudra Sarkar. *Rudi,* but I have
never called him by that name. I have never seen Dr.
Sarkar flustered or angry. Today is no exception.

Sarkar smiles at me and says, "I hope you don't
mind that I looked in on your birthing procedure
today, Ms. Ryuan."

Along with his good looks, his accent is seductive—
slightly British with the tiniest Indian inflection. But
I put myself on hold. I'm one of those women who is
highly suspicious when a guy is extremely handsome.
No foolish schoolgirl am I when it comes to men, but
there is something fairly enticing about Rudi.

Before I can respond, he says, "I have not seen that

old-fashioned water breech procedure since I was in Doctors Without Borders in Kolkata."

He says *Kolkata,* not *Calcutta*. Cool. Cool until I realize his warm observation may actually be veiled criticism.

"Well, it seemed worth a try," I say.

"And it was surely a try worth taking. Sometimes the oldest methods are the best, when used properly. That's what you did."

Damn it. Now I am feeling a little like a schoolgirl. "Thank you. It seems to have worked."

"Yes, indeed. You are living proof that in a decade or two all obstetricians will be replaced by midwives. And perhaps that is the way it should evolve."

That flattery had the annoying scent of bullshit to it. The schoolgirl in me is now vanishing fast. In fact, it is not only vanishing but being quickly replaced by the chief midwife, who hates any sort of main hospital interference.

"Can I ask you something, Dr. Sarkar?" Big smile from Sarkar, big nod also. I continue: "Why would a hospital staff member like you, the chairman of the department, even *look in on* a midwife birthing?"

"Well, I was passing by, and I thought—"

"And you thought you'd take a look and report back to our CEO, Barrett Katz, about how things were going in the crazy midwife world," I say.

"Not at all. Paranoia aside, Ms. Ryuan, I simply—"

How many times do I have to interrupt before he stops smiling?

"Look, it's no secret that our CEO has nothing but utter disrespect for the midwife practice, and I know that I am a midwife who particularly sets him off. He's used to having people kiss his ass—"

"Now I must interrupt you, ma'am. Perhaps some people court him. I am not one of them. My lack of, as you say, ass kissing has not hurt me."

I tell him that I'd really like to continue this discussion, but I need to locate the patient, Valerina Gomez, whose twins' births he just praised. I add that with the current missing baby crisis, nothing unusual can pass unnoticed.

"A wise objective on your part. However, I can put your mind at ease. I thought your patient would be better off in the Addiction Recovery Center. I suggested that to your man, Troy."

I explode.

"Let's start with this. Troy is not *my man*. He is a trusted and professional midwife. Further, you should not even have made that suggestion. It was not a wrong decision. But it was none of your business. It should have been my decision."

The guy smiles at me. Yes, I could spit.

"Enough," I say. "Now that you've put my mind at ease about Val, I've got to get over to Neonatal ICU and see how the second twin is doing."

Sarkar takes a small step and moves to his side. He stands very close and directly opposite me. "There's no need for you to go to the ICU," he says.

"What have you done? Transferred Gomez Baby Number Two to another unit, the way you did with her mother?" I am all-out angry.

Then he hits me with it.

"Please, Ms. Ryuan. Listen to me. Your visit is unnecessary for the saddest of reasons. Gomez Baby Number Two died within minutes of being taken to Neonatal."

"No!" I yell, and it takes a few seconds to realize

that Rudi Sarkar is holding both my hands in his. Then I do what I can't help but do. I begin to cry.

I look away from the doctor. He speaks.

"Do not be ashamed to cry, Lucy. It's a sign that you are a very good midwife."

CHAPTER 8

YOU KNOW HOW WHEN you're tired and the tiredness is so tremendous, so achy, that all your mind's eye can see is...a bed? A big bed, a soft bed, any freaking bed in the world? That's the tiredness I'm feeling when I walk into my apartment at six o'clock.

The sight of Willie, and a big hug from Willie, revives me for a few seconds. Well, it doesn't quite *revive* me; it just really, really comforts me. But it also reminds me that I've got to fix some supper for the boy.

Yeah, I could send him downstairs to Sabryna's for a meal. But how many variations on Jamaican goat stew can a kid handle? He loves Sabryna, but her cooking is sometimes another matter.

"What's for dinner, Mom?" he asks. I do notice that his question sounds a little too formal, a little too staged. He's been practicing that question, and he's up to something.

"Oh, the usual," I say. "Lobster, roast beef, and Baked Alaska."

"You know, you're not too far from the truth," he says with a smile that could light most of Brooklyn. He walks a few steps to the cluttered yellow Formica table, the one that had been in my mother's kitchenette when I was a kid. He sweeps away two paper napkins and reveals two dinner plates, each with a scoop of tuna-mayonnaise salad, a wedge of iceberg lettuce covered in a bright pink sauce—Russian dressing...or did he injure himself cutting the lettuce? —and neatly buttered slices of toast with the crusts removed.

"You are an amazing *sous chef,* Willie. Just amazing," I say.

"No, Mom. A *sous chef* is an assistant. I'm the guy in charge of the cold food course. I'm the *chef garde manger.*"

When you've got a nine-year-old who knows what a *chef garde manger* is, you've got a perfect kid or a future Emeril Lagasse...or both.

Everything about this little supper is perfect. It even erases my incredible tiredness. At least for a minute. But when the first forkful of tuna feels heavy in my hand, and when the first gulp of apple juice nauseates me, I hallucinate about the bed once more.

"Häagen-Dazs chocolate for dessert, Mom," he says.

I smile, too exhausted to talk.

And then, the phone.

"Lemme get it," Willie says.

"Only if you know how to deliver babies," I say weakly.

"I'm a quick learner," he says. He hands me my cell phone.

"Lucy, it's Troy," comes Troy's voice.

"What's up, buddy?" I ask. "I'm tired top to bottom. I'm about to pass out."

"I just wanted you to know...Well, it can wait."

"Don't mess with me, Troy. Why'd you call?"

Then he spits it out: "Another baby's gone missing."

I don't scream. I don't speak. I don't move. Instead, I cry. That's it. I just start to cry.

Why? Why the hell? What's happening? I should go in. I will go in. I'll call an Uber. I'll expense it. But I'm still crying.

"Lucy, you okay?" Troy says.

"No, I'm not okay," I say quietly. "But I will come in."

I glance over at the folded-out foldout couch. Then I look down at the crazy pink river of Russian dressing. Then I look at Willie, who's staring intently at me.

"Mom, you gotta choose the right thing," he says.

Like I said, he might just be perfect.

"You're right," I say. I stand up from the table.

Then I walk to the foldout and almost fall onto it.

Willie smiles. "Good choice, Mom."

CHAPTER 9

I'M BACK AT GRAMATAN University Hospital the next morning. Early. The chaos and crowds on the sidewalks and entrance roads are overwhelming. It looks as if every newsperson in New York City has shown up to cover the scene. Yep, I guess my boss, Dr. Barrett Katz, could not keep news of the second missing baby under wraps.

"Are you on staff here at the hospital?" asks a preppy-looking guy outside the employees' entrance to GUH. I assume he's a reporter.

"Sure am," I say.

Then, as I begin to walk away, he calls out loud and nasty, "Just hold it, lady. I need ID."

I hand the preppy-looking guy my ID. He studies it.

"Your department?" he asks.

"I work in the cafeteria. I make the baloney sandwiches for lunch. One-third of them with mayo, one-third with mustard, one-third plain."

A few other Gramatan employees are backed up behind me.

"Your attitude isn't helping the situation, ma'am," the guy says. And you know what? He's right. I'm acting exactly like the kind of asshole I'd hate to be talking to.

"Sorry, man. I'm just cranky." A pause. "I'm with the Midwifery Division."

It's a good thing I changed my tune. As I slip my ID back inside my wallet, I notice that two NYPD officers are standing on either side of me. They've been taking in my whole act.

"Sorry," I say.

Then I see the all-too-familiar sight of Dr. Katz and Dr. Sarkar. They're precisely where I saw them yesterday, doing their usual job: stopping hospital staff and giving them instructions.

My turn.

"Ms. Ryuan, I'll be perfectly happy if you give out absolutely no information to the media," says the very harassed Dr. Katz.

"Your happiness is always my goal, Doctor," I say. I see that a small smile has invaded Sarkar's lips. Katz ignores the sarcasm. He's become very good at ignoring me.

"I noticed that you couldn't even check in without making a scene, Ms. Ryuan. The time has come for you to learn a little respect," Katz says.

"And I guess you'll be the one to teach me respect?" I say.

Katz storms off.

I'm sure this is doing wonders for my career. The hell with it. If he ever touches me, I'll have ten lawyers, all women.

Now Dr. Sarkar decides to speak. But of course before he talks, he, too, does the traditional eye roll. "Lucy, Dr. Katz is under a lot of pressure. Be nice."

"To whom? To him? Obviously his solution to this horrendous, heartbreaking, terrible problem is to hire a lot more security people and warn us not to talk to the media. The media—for God's sake—can be helpful. People go online. People watch TV. The people—those folks out there—might have information to help us."

"Of course you're right. I understand. I agree. There's going to be a directors' meeting in a half hour. I'm sure some of the directors will get Dr. Katz to cool down a bit. He's been awake for twenty-four hours."

I shake my head gently, and once again I try to find the kind-and-helpful me inside the rude-and-impatient me. "Okay, okay. What can I do to help?" I ask.

"Do what you usually do—just do a great job."

"Dr. Sarkar, I—"

"Rudi," he says.

Okay, he calls me Lucy. I should call him Rudi.

"Look. I get it. I really do get it. Katz is thinking about the hospital, its reputation, the bad PR. But you know what I'm thinking about?"

"Yes, I do. You're thinking about the missing babies," he says.

Hmmm. Bingo. Sarkar apparently has a good brain on top of that handsome face of his.

"That's it. Rudi, there are two stolen babies out there—alone, starting life with who knows what kind of maniacs. There are two mothers right here, in this hospital, crying, aching, ready to die for their babies, ready to do anything to get them back."

Sarkar nods. He's grim. Then he says, "There's a police and detective setup down in the residents' cafeteria. It's pretty impressive—computers, a lead detective, a few assistant detectives, a big group. NYPD is taking this very seriously."

"Great, so am I," I say. "In fact, I think I'll pay a visit later to this in-house police unit."

"They don't know what they're in for," Sarkar says with a smile.

I begin to walk away and he calls after me, "Lucy. Speaking of paying a visit, is it okay if I pop by your office later? I have a little favor to ask."

"Pop away, Rudi. I'm around all day," I say. "Unless Dr. Katz fires me before then."

"I hope not, Lucy," he says. "We need you around here."

CHAPTER 10

MOST PEOPLE HAVE A good idea of what midwives do. We help deliver babies. But that is only a very small part of the story. Sure, maybe it's the most dramatic part, maybe even the most important part, but about 20 percent of our time is spent helping bring babies into the world. And we don't spend the rest of the time waiting around for our moms to go into labor.

So what else do we do? We help women in many other ways, at every stage of their lives. Lots of women find us for prenatal care, but others come for urinary-tract infections, Pap smears, breast exams, IUD fittings—any traditional gynecological procedures. Some pregnant women come to discuss drug abuse, alcohol abuse, physical abuse. In our hospital, we get plenty of those. It's challenging, but in a weird way it's rewarding. A lot of women, especially the young ones and the ones with addiction problems, are scared about taking their baby home. So we talk, and we're never in a hurry. I'll listen to them until they're talked out.

I've dealt with abused women, and I've dealt with couples who come to every appointment together. I've

helped poor women find the right social services, and
I've worked with two famous actresses, two famous
authors, and a circus performer who makes her living
as a bareback rider. (In her sixth month of pregnancy,
she switched to being a clown.)

Today I've got a classy Upper East Side gal, as if
where you're from makes anything different in giving
birth. This woman, one of my overeducated pregnant
patients, is here to discuss the torment of a cyst on her
ovary. I know that an ovarian cyst during pregnancy
is one of life's extraordinary tortures. I am truly sympathetic. But there's not a lot I can do to help. Telling
her to feast on binge-worthy TV episodes doesn't
seem like much of a help. I can almost actually feel
the woman's pain.

Sheila Gross talks with tears in her eyes. That's
how much it hurts. "It's like I swallowed a razor
blade. It's got to be more than a cyst, Lucy. I know
it is. I think it's probably kidney cancer. I was on the
internet…"

Ah. The magical phrases: *I was on the internet* and
I was on WebMD and *My cousin told* her *gynecologist
about it*.

I hold Sheila's hand. "Listen. I told you before,
and I'll tell you again. It's a cyst. We have the x-rays
to prove it. Yes, it's just about the most painful thing
that can happen during a pregnancy, except for the
birth itself. But there's not a damn thing we can do
about it. You could take Tylenol, but that won't help a
whole lot. And it's actually better that you don't. Now,
eventually—"

Sheila interrupts. "It's kidney cancer. I don't want
to sound like a crazy lady, but I'm really sure."

"No. It's not kidney cancer."

"I'm sure that it's kidney cancer. The pain in the back, right where the kidneys are…"

Okay. It's time to play tough. "Stop it. It is not kidney cancer. It's a cyst. It's excruciating. All I can give you for it is my sympathy. And my sympathy is real."

Five minutes later, Sheila says that she understands, but I know she doesn't believe me. Or at the very least she thinks I've misdiagnosed her. I have to face it. Sheila's going to spend the rest of her life believing that she had kidney cancer and that it miraculously disappeared after she gave birth.

Funny how arrogant people always think they're smart people.

By lunchtime, I realize how hungry I am. I had no breakfast. I should eat an apple, a few whole-grain crackers, and a salad with just a disgusting, unsatisfying dash of red wine vinegar.

"Never balsamic vinegar," Tracy Anne always reminds me. *"That has a ton of sugar in it."*

I think it over carefully and then decide I will go down to the cafeteria and pick up a frosted doughnut, a bag of Fritos, and a special Lucy Ryuan dipping sauce: mayo, ketchup, mustard, and extra salt. As I'm convincing myself that I've worked hard enough to have such a deliciously stupid lunch, there is a knock on the door. Before I can say *"Come in,"* the door opens.

It's Sarkar, of course. I had actually forgotten that he said he might come by.

He smiles. He speaks. "Is this the right office for my internal exam?"

"No," I say. "We're only doing bleeding hemorrhoids today. Come in and bend over."

He laughs. I think I've used that joke only a thousand times.

"I am here to beg for my favor," he says.

For this favor-asking visit, Sarkar has ditched his white coat. He's spruced up quite a bit. He wears a blue linen blazer with slightly pegged gray khakis. Okay, there's no point in lying to myself: he looks pretty good. Not hot, just pretty good.

"Hit me with the favor request," I say.

"I have a patient who is near-term. You may have heard of her. Greta Moss."

Heard of her? After Melania Trump, Greta Moss is quite simply the most famous model in the world. As a mainstream celebrity, she ranks somewhere between Beyoncé and Jennifer Lawrence on sites like TMZ, Dlisted, and People.com. Greta has fifteen million followers on Twitter, because, after all, what woman doesn't want to know what kind of two-hundred-dollar seaweed-based cleansing cream should be used to remove your three-hundred-dollar Provençal organic avocado foundation?

"Yes, I think I've heard of her," I say casually. Then, as if I wasn't sure, I casually ask, "She's married to that football player guy, right? Plays for the Bears."

"Hank Waldren. He's a wide receiver for the Giants."

Not only is Waldren the male equivalent of his wife in the ridiculously good looks department, but also those hands...only Michelangelo could have sculpted them. Well, he is a wide receiver.

"Anyway," Sarkar says. "Here comes the favor request. Greta Moss has suddenly decided that she wants to deliver with a midwife, not an ob-gyn. She told me that she wants her baby to be born the way she herself was born: on a kitchen table in Copenhagen."

"We're all out of kitchen tables," I say. "And look out the window. It sure isn't Copenhagen out there."

"Come on, Lucy. Please. Greta really wants this," he says. "And I think the publicity for the hospital, for you, for the midwives, would be great."

"Well, yeah, maybe, but it would not be good for *my* schedule or *Troy's* schedule or *Tracy Anne's* schedule. We are booked solid. When is Greta Moss due?"

"Any moment," he says.

"As in *any* moment, even this very moment?"

"I'm afraid so."

"Forget it," I say. "It can't be done." I'm also thinking, *Damn it, this guy thinks he can waltz in here, ask for a favor, and I'll do it. He thinks that just because he's charming and just because I'm a midwife that—*

A knock on the door. Tracy Anne's head appears.

"Katra Kovac has gone into labor. Birthing room 3," she says.

Rudi Sarkar squints his eyes in a fake-funny evil pose. "Did you have your colleague poised to come in here to show me just how busy you are?"

"Sure. Tracy Anne was listening at the door. There's really no Katra Kovac. There's really no scared, unmarried seventeen-year-old girl who's going to give birth. No, there are only big shots like Greta Moss and Hank Waldren. Sorry, Rudi."

"Oh, come on, Lucy. For me?"

But before he can say something like *"Aw, c'mon, sweetie pie. Pretty please with sugar on it?"* I say, "Gotta run. New member of the human race is on the way."

CHAPTER 11

FENDING OFF RUDI SARKAR'S arrogant request was a small challenge compared to the problem waiting for me in birthing room 3. Tracy Anne and I move quickly toward the room. Even after years of delivering babies, I still always feel the happy anticipation when a mother is about to bring a new life into this world.

Katra Kovac has quite a few obstacles facing her in the next few hours—a young, first-time mother and recent immigrant, I think from Eastern Europe, and there's no sign of the baby's father. But Katra is strong, healthy, and enthusiastic, with the full support of her mother and father.

I follow Tracy Anne into the room. It's empty. *What the hell?* No nurse, no other midwives, most alarmingly, no Katra Kovac.

"Tracy Anne, is this the wrong room number?"

"No, I'm sure this is the right room. We were assigned to birthing 3. Emergency Registration was bringing her up when I went out to get you."

"Well, there's some screwup," I say, and I'm hoping that's all it is—a simple screwup.

Tracy Anne and I head quickly toward the nurses'

station. I'm certain we're both thinking the worst: have we escalated from missing babies to missing mothers?

My usual good luck: Nurse Charming, Deborah Franklin, is on duty at the central desk.

"Where's the patient who's supposed to be in birthing room 3, Katra Kovac? I can't find her," I say.

"Did you look in the bed?" Franklin says.

I'm in no mood for Franklin's sarcasm right now. "Do you know where Katra Kovac is?" I say slowly and loudly. "Did you see her brought up from Registration?"

"I surely did. She was there a few minutes ago. In fact, one of *your* people was with her."

"Who was it?"

"I wasn't watching," says Nurse Franklin.

I don't have time for bullshit. I spring into action. "Let's start looking, Trace," I say.

Tracy Anne and I each take a side of the hospital corridor. We scurry unannounced into patients' rooms, bathrooms, visitors' lounges, even an archaic room with a small brass sign on it that says FATHERS' WAITING ROOM. We look in custodian closets and the food storage rooms that hold the thousands of packets of peanut-butter crackers, Jell-O cups, and apple juice.

Now I'm a bit frightened. Okay, I'm really frightened.

"What should we do?" Tracy Anne asks.

"What do you think? We keep looking, and we call for backup."

We rush to the nurses' station. I tell Nurse Franklin to call Security.

"I already have," she says. "They're on their way."

Two men from GUH Security appear almost instantaneously. I know these two guys, but I certainly do not know the other two people with them: a uniformed NYC female cop and a grumpy-looking guy in a rumpled gray suit. The woman looks ready to work. The guy looks just the opposite: sullen, tired. He has one of those slightly paunchy dad bods. He's got to be the detective.

"I'm Detective Leon Blumenthal, NYPD." *Was I right or was I right?* "This is Officer Cindy Hazard. Let's get started."

Apparently he doesn't care to know our names. I don't even try.

"Missing person is seventeen, dark blond hair, wearing hospital gown," he says. "Let's search this floor first."

"We've already done that," I say.

"And you are…?"

I guess he's changed his mind. He does want an intro. "Midwife Lucy Ryuan."

"And you found nothing and no one?"

"Well, we certainly didn't find Katra Kovac."

"Well, why don't we just take one more crack at it. I already have a team moving hard through the hospital," he says. "Let's go."

Forget paunchy and tired. I'll call him *arrogant as shit.*

CHAPTER 12

WITHIN MINUTES, TRACY ANNE and I have joined the search with Blumenthal and his colleagues, or maybe they even forgot we were there with them. Either way, we're tagging along with the crew through Adult Neurosurgery and ICU. I don't exactly know what Blumenthal and company are doing that's so different from what Tracy Anne and I were doing fifteen minutes ago. They pull open drawers and look under beds. They go into bathrooms and knock on stall doors. Could it be that their flashlights make them seem professional?

There aren't many good places to hide in a hospital—no matter what you've seen on television. Sure, a supply closet, a visitors' bathroom, an occasional doctor's vacant office. But for the most part, the spaces are all very wide corridors and lots of rooms for patients.

"That's a janitor's closet," I say as NYPD officer Cindy Hazard opens a janitor's closet, the same one I'd opened fifteen minutes ago. Hazard and Blumenthal step into the closet.

Okay, moving right along.

We finish searching Adult Neurosurgery and ICU.

We head for the Darlow Pavilion, a fancy area of the hospital with marble floors and dark wood-paneled private rooms. I explain to Blumenthal that the Darlow Pavilion was designed for super-rich patients willing to pay a lot of money for being sick in absolute privacy and luxury. Darlow is a cash cow for Gramatan, and most patients in Darlow are not used to being disturbed by anyone except their masseurs and stockbrokers. Blumenthal and his gang don't seem to care. We look in. We move on. Now we're running out of places to look.

We are walking toward the huge physiotherapy rehab room when Blumenthal gets a message on his cell phone. He reports that another police search group thinks they may have located the "possible MP Kovac." He says, "The victim is in a basement storage room."

Why did he use the word victim?

Now I'm nervous as shit. This isn't a game. This is real.

We run for the elevator. Blumenthal tells us we're headed for Mechanical Storage and Lab. It's an area of the hospital I know nothing about. As we run, Blumenthal gets another text. They report that MP Kovac is seriously injured.

During the brief elevator ride, Blumenthal speaks directly to me. "My team says that this storage room is pretty grim. Have you ever been down there?"

"No," I tell him. "I think it's probably just where they keep old equipment like out-of-date x-ray machines, filing cabinets, that sort of stuff."

The elevator arrives in the basement. We exit and quickly survey the area. The basement is vast. Its ceiling is low, and the very tall Detective Blumenthal has to tip his head forward to avoid lighting fixtures. Long corridors crisscross one another. Two NYPD officers quickly escort us to an open door.

Grim? They said the room was grim?

The harsh lighting, the putrid odors. The room sure is *grim*. But that's only the beginning.

CHAPTER 13

OUR EYES BURN. OUR throats gag. The storage room is filled with three or four more cops and two men I recognize from GUH Security. We enter a miserable scene: small puddles of filthy, stinky liquid on the floor, dripping, oozing pipes running along the ceiling. The smell is an overpowering mixture of bathroom antiseptic and human or animal feces. Handkerchiefs go to faces, and a tough-looking NYPD officer vomits almost immediately. It is totally out of keeping with the high standards of you-can-eat-off-the-floor cleanliness practiced by GUH.

Two huge MRI machines are pushed up against big old-fashioned x-ray units, twenty-foot-long chunks of steel with worn leather and dirty plastic. Someone more creative than me might see this mash-up as a fascinating art installation, the absurd landscape of a foul medical junkyard, or props from a horror movie.

The sickening odor in the air is accompanied by a nerve-racking soundtrack: squeaking, squawking, screeching sounds. A million birds gone crazy? Then suddenly an answer from many feet away…a woman's voice…

"Rats! They've got cages and cages of goddamn rats!" she screams.

We move toward her voice.

"A lot of rats, maybe hundreds of them," the same woman's voice shouts.

Once we know that the squealing and smell are coming from rats—not pigs or birds or even cute little white mice—it all seems even more disgusting, more frightening.

The lights flicker. We see a mountain of desk chairs and examination tables. We turn the mountain's corner and see yet another pile, a traffic jam of cabinets. We make another turn, and there it is: ten cages packed with rats. Rats scampering over one another. Rats packed tightly together. White, black, brown rats. Some as large as raccoons. Some as small as mice. Fat rats nibble on dead rats.

One of the GUH Security people explains. "This is some sort of goddamn private place for raising lab rats. I've got an idea who's doing it. They grab a few rats brought into the med school for research, and the assholes mate them and raise them down here. Dr. Katz is going to have a shit fit when he finds out."

My instincts tell me the security guy might know more about this illegal rat farm if we only let him keep on talking. But then suddenly a loud yell erupts from deeper in the pile of abandoned equipment.

"Over here. Detective B, over here."

The group seems to follow in some sort of order of seniority, Blumenthal at the lead.

The hell with it. I'm on this case, too. I'm the one who knows how to deliver babies.

I push my way to the front of the pack. We make our way, stumbling through a jungle of broken desk chairs, cartons of old glass syringes, office clipboards. The smell. Jesus Christ, the smell.

Another yells, "Hurry up, for Chrissake. Will you just hurry up?"

Blumenthal and I look quickly at each other. We keep moving. We are like a crazy lunatic parade wending its way through the disgusting basement room. We should ignore the smells, the screeching, the filthy floors.

My instincts kick in again. I have a miserable feeling that the nightmare is just beginning.

CHAPTER 14

KATRA KOVAC IS SPREAD unconscious on the narrow bed of another discarded MRI machine. She is a dead or near-dead body in a deserted tunnel. She is almost naked. Only a bloodstained hospital gown is scrunched up around her neck.

"Jesus Christ!" says one of the police officers. He took the words out of everyone's mouths.

Some of the group turn away. Tracy Anne checks Katra's neck for a pulse. She's got one.

I look at the blood-covered belly of the motionless woman. Blood is still seeping in small rivulets down over her sides, puddling on the floor.

Alarms ring. Sirens sound. Somewhere in the distance we can hear loud, fast clattering feet. Nurses and doctors appear in the basement. The goddamn rats won't shut up; it's as if they know something terrible has happened. We're in a hospital, but no one has brought a medical emergency kit. One police officer rips off his shirt to staunch the blood. Orderlies and two doctors rush in with padding and surgical staplers. Hands covered in plastic gloves reach in and slip an IV needle into Katra's arm. An oxygen tube is now dangling from her nose.

"Don't transfer her to a gurney," a voice yells. It is unmistakably Sarkar's voice.

"Move her on the bed of the machine. Move the bed *with* her," I yell.

Now I suddenly think that Sarkar, Tracy Anne, and I are most likely the only ones present who can tell exactly what has happened: Katra Kovac, nine months pregnant, has been slit open. Her baby has been taken.

The procedure—it's a disgusting lie to confuse this butchery with the term *C-section*—has left the mother barely clinging to life. And the baby? Who in hell knows what has become of the baby, this baby who was literally ripped from its mother's womb.

Two GUH maintenance men and two residents begin to attack the ancient MRI machine with screwdrivers and electric saws, to detach the bed from its base, while Dr. Sarkar is literally on top of the machine's bed with Katra, straddling her knees and pushing down on her stomach. If this was not all so horrible, it would look almost ridiculous—a grown man on top of a woman in a blood-drenched hospital gown, surrounded by a highly agitated crowd.

Then a gurney appears. Someone has—perhaps wisely—vetoed my suggestion that Katra not be moved.

"Lucy, you hold her neck," Sarkar says as he climbs off the MRI bed. ER staff slide Katra onto what is called a *sponge gurney,* a stretcher thick with a great deal of absorption material. It's used a lot at accident scenes. Right now it's ready to suck up Katra's blood. It's been a few million hours, but Katra is now quickly being wheeled toward the elevator. Sarkar hurries along beside the gurney, his hands red and slimy with blood.

I am shaking.

I remember what my mother always told herself when a procedure wasn't going smoothly. *"We must rise to the occasion, Lucy. We must rise to the occasion."*

Five minutes later, Dr. Sarkar, along with two surgeons—one general, one gynecologic—begins trying to put Katra Kovac back together.

And two rooms away, with a muted CNN report on the television and a stack of old *Good Housekeeping* magazines on a table nearby, sits a trio brought together by unlucky chance: Detective Leon Blumenthal, CEO Dr. Barrett Katz, and me. Blumenthal and I are sick, scared, and spattered with blood. Katz looks rich, beautifully groomed, and very much on edge.

CHAPTER 15

SIMPLY PUT, DR. BARRETT Katz is a big mess of crazy nerves at the moment. I should not take pleasure in his pain, especially at an awful time like this, but I can't help it. I watch him closely. The guy just can't sit still. Every few minutes he moves from his chair to the thick glass window that separates our room from the pre-surgical scrub room. The next room over from the scrub room is the operating room itself. Katz squints each time he looks through the glass, as if he believes that if he tries hard enough, he will get x-ray vision and then actually see through and into the operating room. But no one, not even the hospital CEO, is ever allowed an unscheduled visit to the operating room. In fact, so cautious is NYPD now about the discovery of near-dead Katra and her brutal delivery that a detective and two officers have had an antiseptic shower, changed into scrubs, and joined the surgical team in the OR.

The only thing we all know is that Katra Kovac's condition is dire.

I am not lightly tossing around the phrase *near-dead*. Sarkar and his team are great, but as my mother used to say, *"You can never be sure of the future. Only the Lord Jesus knows the end of the story."*

I sit and play with my phone. I text Willie. His response is, Hey, Mom. Busy with Mike. Love u. Mike, a decent kid from down the street. I text Sabryna. No response. I read some news on CNN.com. I text Troy. I text Tracy Anne. I read my email. On the floor near me is the *Daily News*. It is opened to a page of comic strips and the jumble puzzle. Yes, it seems disrespectful, but I pick up the newspaper and look at the puzzle. I can't un-jumble the first word…or the second. So I toss the paper back on the floor.

I close my eyes and recite the prayer my mother always prayed. The prayer begins, *Lord, make me an instrument of thy peace.* Who can argue with that? I'm thinking a lot about my mother today. A crisis will do that to my brain.

NYPD officers and GUH personnel come in and out of our waiting room to confer with Leon Blumenthal. It's clear that wherever Blumenthal is, then that's where his central investigation office is. His laptop might just as well be actually attached to his lap. Whatever the reason, whoever the visitor, Blumenthal keeps tapping on that computer. I don't believe multitasking is for real, but this guy might prove me wrong.

Dr. Katz lights one of his signature Tareyton cigarettes. Yes, the CEO lit a cigarette in his own hospital.

"I don't think you want to be smoking in here, Doctor," I say to him. He looks at me with silent displeasure. This look of displeasure is followed by an unquestionable look of disgust. Katz is looking and acting like a spoiled little brat. Further proof, he then draws on his cigarette and lets out the smoke with a big satisfied-sounding exhale.

Let's not even discuss the idea of a medical person smoking! In a group! In a hospital! Should you still doubt that Katz is a nutcase.

"I didn't know they even made Tareytons anymore," I say. "When my friends in high school smoked, they always smoked Marlboro Lights. I don't really remember Tareytons."

"It's hard to find Tareytons in New York these days," says Katz as he emits a big puff of smoke. "I'm lucky enough to have a supplier in London who sends them to me by the case."

Color me impressed. The asshole is known for his finicky tastes—a framed collection of presidential autographs in his office, custom-made shirts with "exclusive" patterns (whatever that means; they all look light blue to me), English flannel driving caps, which, despite their quality, still make Katz look like a London cabby. *'Op on in, guv-nor.*

I say to Katz, "In any case…you should put the cigarette out."

"In any case," Katz says, "I'm the CEO in this room, and I want to smoke."

Blumenthal is seated on the one uncomfortable-looking steel folding chair in the room. I think he's oblivious to the scene around him. But I turn out to be wrong about that. The detective suddenly looks up—suspiciously perhaps—from his laptop.

"And I'm the cop in this room," Blumenthal says as he stands up. "Put out the cigarette, Doc."

There is an unpleasant pause. Then Katz drops the cigarette onto the linoleum floor and begins furiously grinding it out.

Almost immediately the door to the OR opens. A woman dressed in full surgical garb—head covering, surgical mask, protective eyeglasses, gloves, green scrubs—comes into our waiting area. She pushes the eyeglasses to her forehead and unsnaps her mask, then removes it.

I recognize her immediately: she's a GUH surgeon, one of the best.

She addresses us. "I'm Helen Whall."

She is as modest as she is talented, so I tell everyone else in the room that Helen Whall is the finest plastic surgeon at GUH, possibly in all of New York City. When a seven-year-old boy in the Bronx had his ear almost severed by a stray bullet, Whall reattached it perfectly. When the mayor had a melanoma on his shiny bald head, Whall was called in to remove and patch it. There really is no one remotely like her.

"Helen, what the hell is happening in there?" Katz asks.

"Please, stay calm, sir. That's why I'm here. I've got an update."

Why do I feel that things are not going well?

Helen reports, "The patient's condition is dangerous. Very dangerous. We all suspected that. Turns out that Katra has a small rupture in the uterine wall. Dr. Sarkar is working on that. And, as you no doubt noticed, there's been a significant loss of blood."

Katz is growing impatient. "Yes, as we 'no doubt noticed,' she's lost a lot of blood. But is this patient going to live? I'm the one who will have to face the goddamn media."

Dr. Whall doesn't answer.

"I asked you a question, Doctor," Katz says.

Helen Whall looks at Katz with a face that clearly registers restrained anger. Then she returns to her update. "They're draining the amniotic fluid. They've got the placenta out. They need to evaluate the extent of the liver damage. But one thing is clear…" Then she pauses.

"For Chrissake, what the hell is that?" Katz yells.

"The incision they used to take the baby out…is neat and elegant, a traditional bikini-cut C-section."

"And that means what?" Blumenthal asks.

I decide that I'll answer the question. "It means the C-section was probably done by a professional."

"A professional?" Blumenthal asks, only slightly confused.

"Yeah, it was done by a trained professional, *a real live doctor.* He, or she, cut the mother, delivered the baby, and then left Katra to bleed out and die."

Dr. Whall waits for us to register the horror of the information. After a few seconds, she says, "Dr. Sarkar and his team are still guardedly optimistic. Thanks, everyone," and she leaves.

Leon Blumenthal walks over to me. "Tell me," he says. "Is the use of the phrase 'guardedly optimistic' just hospital speak for 'not at all optimistic'?"

"It could be. But you never know until the operation's over."

Blumenthal nods. "Good answer," he says.

Then I say, "Only the Lord Jesus knows the end of the story."

"Amen," says Blumenthal.

I think he smiled slightly. I'm not sure.

CHAPTER 16

TWO HOURS LATER, LEON Blumenthal, two NYPD assistant detectives, and myself are seated around a banged-up metal lunch table in the residents' cafeteria. This room is no longer a cafeteria. The area has been clumsily transformed into a law enforcement investigation center at Gramatan University Hospital. Clusters of plastic forks and squeeze bottles of ketchup and cafeteria trays have been replaced by computers and wires and files and cameras and TV screens. Eager young residents have been replaced by eager young assistant detectives and NYPD officers.

Blumenthal is talking to NYPD personnel as they stream in and out. I am on my laptop giving updates and fielding questions from Troy and Tracy Anne and other midwife staffers. Katz walks nervously in and out of the conference area. We are all nervous, tired, and essentially ignoring one another. Then, into this insane police center, comes a very important visitor, Dr. Rudra Sarkar.

At this moment Rudi Sarkar is not his usual calm and dapper self. To put it bluntly, Sarkar looks like shit. He is exhausted, sweaty, red-eyed. He practically limps toward the table. His scrubs are splattered with blood. There is blood on his bare upper arms and the V-shaped exposed area of his chest. His disposable paper slippers are bloody.

We all reflexively stand when we see the doctor.

Sarkar says, "I am happy to tell you that Katra Kovac has come through this event very, very well." He adds, "I think that perhaps the patient's condition appeared much worse than it actually was."

I think Sarkar is being modest. Or he's being crazy. A C-section performed viciously, under unsanitary conditions, without anesthesia…*Come on, Rudi, it was a horror show, and this is a miracle.* For a moment I think I will say something, but somehow cheerleading and praise seem inappropriate at this moment.

I can hardly wait to get to the recovery room and see Katra Kovac. I know Katz wants to get his PR people churning out their brand of blather to the media. I can only imagine the gangs of reporters roaming outside the hospital.

But one thing I predict is this: Blumenthal must, of course, have his own agenda for continuing the investigation as quickly as possible.

The usually quiet detective spins around like an athlete and faces the group.

And I'm right.

"I…want…your…attention!" Blumenthal is just a decibel short of shouting. Suddenly he moves to his right and looks fiercely at Katz. "Get off the phone…now!"

Katz looks both startled and scared. I don't think the CEO is going to try to play the CEO card again. He quickly whispers into the phone, "I'll call you right back."

Blumenthal lowers his voice just a bit. But

the energy and anger are still there. "Listen. This is a double-barreled investigation. The challenges are…there's no other word…overwhelming. Okay, our victim lives. Super thanks and congratulations to Dr. Sarkar. That's number one. That's great, but it also means that we've got a person or persons who need to be brought in for attempted murder, some fucker or fuckers who butchered a pregnant woman. I know everyone is as disgusted and angry as I am. But as you all know, part two of the case is this, and it's just as bad: there's another brand-new stolen baby out there. The same pervert who slit open the baby's mother has that mother's baby.

"And now I've got to tell you just one more thing, one more thing you may already have figured out, and many of you know. Because these are kidnappings, we're dealing with a federal crime. That means the FBI is already crawling up our butts. A few members of their CARD team, the Child Abduction Response Deployment folks, have already been brought up to speed. They could be a help. They could be a hindrance. But whatever it turns out to be, it *is* a fact. They'll join us here. And we'd be idiots not to welcome their help. So there's no need to speak any further on that subject.

"This is my last thing. Then I'll shut up. I want to give you what else we're doing here in New York City. FYI, there are NYPD detectives and soon FBI agents at every hospital—*every* hospital—in every borough in New York. Lenox Hill. Beth Israel. Bellevue. This goes from Richmond Med Center on Staten Island to Montefiore in the Bronx, and everything in between. They're assigned to walk-in clinics, to fancy-ass private cosmetic surgery places. Hell, the commissioner is so into this, I think he'd stick police guards at every doctor's office in New York City if he could. On and on. He's with us every inch of the way. There's no need to go into everything else, but we have all the police labs open. We've interviewed anyone who might have seen something. The entrance and exit security was extremely tight. So it could have been an inside job."

He pauses for a few seconds. He looks at the ceiling, then quickly around the room. Now when he starts to speak, he sounds somber and sad.

"Look. We just don't know enough. I'll be here for the next twenty-four hours. At least."

He pauses again. Then, "Go about your business. Except for you two…" Blumenthal is looking directly at me and Dr. Sarkar. "I need to talk to you two. Everyone else, thank you. And, Dr. Katz, if you need a cigarette, go outside and smoke."

CHAPTER 17

"LISTEN, YOU TWO. I don't have a helluva lot of time," says Leon Blumenthal, "so you'll have to forgive me if I put my nice-guy personality on ice."

Sarkar, who looks like he could collapse from exhaustion at any moment, nods.

I say, "Sure," and I try to remember a time in my short relationship with Blumenthal when I ever witnessed that "nice-guy personality."

We sit, and Blumenthal leans in toward us from the other side of the cafeteria table.

This is the closest I've been to him physically. His hazel eyes are rimmed with red. He needs a shave, and his haircut looks like one of those ten-dollar jobs you get out in my neighborhood.

He's also—and I'm surprised and embarrassed to be thinking this—cute as hell…in that grumpy dad-bod way.

Blumenthal looks directly at Dr. Sarkar and speaks. "Is there anything, anything at all, anything you remember—any little thing that was slightly out of the usual during the surgical procedure on the victim, on Kovac?"

Without hesitation, Sarkar says, "No. Absolutely

not. It was difficult. But I have dealt many times before with people who were assaulted—stabbings, domestic violence, slashings, vehicular accidents. This one was particularly brutal, and the fact that it was immediately postnatal didn't make it easier. But I cannot supply you with any further information."

I decide that my opinion is needed here. "I don't think Dr. Sarkar can minimize the seriousness of working on a patient who was in her ninth month. The uterine wall...the...What else, Rudi?"

I don't know why I spoke the name "Rudi," but as soon as I say the word, Blumenthal's eyes widen, for a split second. He looks back and forth once between Dr. Sarkar and myself, clearly trying to evaluate what the deal is—personal, professional, friendly, romantic—between the two of us.

Sarkar must sense it, too. The doctor brings the conversation right back to business. "With the exception of the uterine-wall damage, it is all very typical—muscle damage, arterial damage, blood loss." Sarkar is starting to sound as if he is bored. It is clear to me that he just wants the interrogation to be over. All he wants is an icy martini and a nice long nap.

Blumenthal, however, is not yet finished. "Going back to the operation itself for a moment. Was there anyone's behavior that you would call unusual? For example, did anyone excuse herself, or himself—in other words, did anyone leave the room?"

I decide once again to jump in. I guess *butt in* is the right expression. "Well, of course. People often leave the room, re-scrub, and then come back. People have to use the bathroom or they don't feel good or they're tired and need a short break—"

"Thanks for the clarification, Ms. Ryuan, and, yes,

that's what I mean by unusual. Now maybe you can allow Dr. Sarkar to answer."

"My answer is no," Sarkar says. "One of the nurses became fatigued. So she left, and a few minutes later a sub came in for her. A few minutes after that a sub came in for the gas man."

Blumenthal looks up from his laptop. "The gas man?"

"The anesthesiologist," I explain.

Blumenthal gives a minuscule smile, then says, "Is there anything else? Even the tiniest thing. Someone made a passing comment. Someone had something to say about the victim. Someone had something that, damn it, we could honestly call a clue."

The devil in me surfaces for a second. This might be an opportunity to implicate Nurse Franklin, but that's just my own petty irritation. And making up lies is not my biggest talent.

"Please think, Dr. Sarkar," Blumenthal says.

Sarkar is starting to show some of his annoyance at the constant prodding.

So of course I speak. To no one in particular I say, "What about Helen Whall?"

"Helen Whall?" Sarkar asks.

"Yes, the plastic surgeon," I say.

With a speck of anger in his voice, Sarkar says, "I *know* who Helen Whall is, Lucy. What about her?"

Blumenthal reads from his computer screen. "Helen Whall, respected surgeon, GUH staff member, enters 4:17. Says Sarkar and team guardedly optimistic. Adds—"

Rudi perks up considerably. He says, "I don't recall Dr. Whall leaving the OR, and I certainly don't recall asking her to update anybody on my patient's condition."

"Rudi," I say, "Helen Whall implied that you asked her to let us know what was going on, that she was out there because you wanted her to tell us how Katra was doing."

"Possibly you simply don't remember doing this, Doctor?" asks Blumenthal. "You were under a great deal of stress."

"No," he says, and he is firm in his answer. "I would have remembered asking Dr. Whall to do that. She was standing by primarily for the wrap, the suturing. As it turns out, we didn't need her. But I'm still glad I brought her in."

"We'll talk to Dr. Whall," says Blumenthal. Then he adds, "And my guys are also doing follow-up investigations of everyone who was involved with the surgery."

Sarkar barely nods, and then Blumenthal says, "So I guess that's it for now."

I can't help it. I say very loudly, "That's it? You've got to be kidding, Detective."

"Lucy, please don't start," says Sarkar.

If I had a dollar for every time a man said to me, *"Lucy, please don't start,"* I'd be the richest woman in New York.

But Blumenthal's casual attitude is, in fact, making me crazy-angry, and I just can't hold it inside me. I raise my voice. "A baby is missing, stolen, kidnapped, maybe murdered, Detective Blumenthal. A woman is practically murdered, left for dead. And you say, 'that's it for now.'"

"Thanks for your opinion, Ms. Ryuan," Blumenthal says. "But I don't think you're precisely qualified to advise on a New York City crime."

"Yeah, I think I am," I say. "My uncle was a

policeman, a damned good policeman. He brought energy and courage to his work—"

Blumenthal interrupts. "Your uncle, was he with the NYPD?"

"No, my family is from West Virginia," I say.

With a touch of mild sarcasm, Blumenthal says, "I see…*West Virginia*."

"Yeah, that's right. West Virginia has more opioid problems than any place in America." As I say the words, I realize that, even though it's true, it has nothing to do with the case at hand, in this hospital, in this city.

Am I turning into a crazy lady? I'm as tired as Sarkar looks. And Sarkar performed dangerous surgery. All I did was fail at doing the *Daily News* jumble. I give myself some advice. *Shut up, Lucy,* I think. *Just shut up.* But it doesn't matter. Blumenthal puts a definite end to the conversation. He simply nods and says, "Okay, we'll stay in touch. And I've already texted two of my people to follow up immediately with Helen Whall."

Sarkar rubs his face and then says, "Thank you, Detective."

"Thank you, Doctor," says Blumenthal.

Next thing you know these two will be going out dancing.

Blumenthal has one final good-bye line: "And really, I appreciate your help, both of you. Like I said, we'll stay in touch. My cafeteria door is always open."

The three of us laugh softly, then exchange another quiet round of thank-yous.

As we walk to the exit of the cafeteria-office, Sarkar asks, "Are you going home now?"

"Yeah. If I don't go home, I may just fall asleep standing up right here."

"Let me give you a ride to your house," he says.

"No way. You live all the way on the Upper East Side, and I'm out in Brooklyn," I say. "Plus, you look like a guy who's just completed a marathon."

The fact is I just want to be alone, to get one of those end seats on the train, to listen to my music mix.

"I insist," Sarkar says.

A series of "No, really," followed by a series of "I insist, really," eventually ends with Sarkar saying, "Okay, meet you in ten minutes in the doctors' parking lot. Look for a handsome man driving a blue Lexus."

"I'll just look for a blue Lexus. That'll be enough," I say.

CHAPTER 18

HERE'S THE THING ABOUT modern luxury cars: When you see the commercials, the cars look really stupid and cheesy. And the commercials themselves are really annoying. They all look like they could have been shown on television in 1970. But once you get inside one of those luxury cars—the big seats, the complicated control system, the absolute quiet—you wonder how you can ever get back inside your 2008 Hyundai again.

Sarkar's Lexus has something called an ignition fob. To me it looks like a small remote control for a television, but as soon as he touches that fob, the big blue Lexus starts purring like...well, like a big blue Lexus is supposed to purr.

"The best way to get to my place is to take—" I start to say.

"Yes, I know," he says with a smile.

"Sorry," I say. "Not everybody knows how to get out of Manhattan and into Brooklyn. Or if they do know, they usually don't know how to get to Crown Heights."

"I only know Brooklyn because of two events," he says. "The first event is the invention of the GPS system, so I rarely get lost. The second event is my divorce."

"Uh, okay," I say. "The GPS I get. On the other thing, the divorce, well, would you like to explain what you mean by 'the second event is my divorce'?"

He laughs. "Of course. Obviously I was trying to be provocative," he says. "Instead I ended up just being confusing. And possibly quite irritating." Then he turns a bit more somber. He talks as if he is almost telling a story about someone else, not him.

"When my wife, Priya, and I first married, it was, as they say, heaven on earth. She was younger than I, but, also as they say, she was wise beyond her years. Plus, she was so beautiful. A perfect shape, magnificent skin, a smile that…" He pauses, as if he is recalling the shape, the skin, and the smile. "And then, merely a few months into the marriage, while I was an ob-gyn intern at Long Island Jewish Medical Center, she became pregnant. Could there be better news for a couple who loved each other so much? We were joyful. A baby girl. We named her Devangi, a goddess."

Sarkar slows down his driving, and he completely stops his story.

I feel that he wants me to ask the question that I ask: "So what happened?"

He pauses, then, "I returned one morning—three o'clock, after a difficult delivery. My wife and Devangi were missing, gone."

"My God. Where to?" I ask.

"The police in New York were totally not interested in the case. I think they believed we were just peculiar foreigners. So then I thought maybe Priya had gone back to her mother's. I hired two different investigators in Northeast India. A waste of money. The most and the best that I have heard is that my wife and child have crossed the border into Nepal." Sarkar spits the word out again: "Nepal! Nepal! Of all places. That bitch Priya might as well have gone to the moon. Or she might as well have taken the baby into hell itself. That is how impenetrable Nepal is."

Sarkar is once again silent. I have noticed that he ignored some of the GPS suggestions, and I think we are driving somewhere in Brooklyn's East Flatbush section, an area as impenetrable to me as Nepal is to Sarkar.

When Sarkar speaks again, he speaks quickly and honestly. "I traveled to India. I hired detectives. Nothing. My wife and my baby have left the face of the earth, at least they have disappeared from my part of it."

I now speak as slowly as he has spoken fast. "I am truly sorry for your problem and your loss."

"Thank you, Lucy. And I know you well enough that I suspect you mean what you say."

Suspect? He suspects? He's not certain? WTF?

I say nothing, and Dr. Sarkar moves on to the story's wrap-up.

"So…when my wife and daughter vanished, I would wake up very early, and most usually I was waking up all alone. Most days I was, of course, going to the hospital, going to work. But on Sunday mornings I felt terribly lonely, and for some reason I would drive into Brooklyn. Brooklyn seemed to lift my spirits. I don't know why. I'd buy a buttered bagel and black coffee and park near the Botanic Garden and relax. It worked like magic."

He looks at me, and we both smile.

"Well, at least can we stop and get a few of those magical bagels?" I ask.

"I am certain the bakery has since closed."

For some reason the fact that the bakery has closed makes me feel incredibly sad. We drive in silence for a few minutes. *What's wrong with me? Why am I fighting back tears?*

"That's it. That's the story. It's not much, I know. A lonely guy wakes up, decides to hide out in Brooklyn, smokes cigarettes in a beautiful garden, drives around interesting places—Park Slope, Bed-Stuy, sometimes as far as the Atlantic Ocean itself, down at Brighton Beach. But the ride through Brooklyn usually calmed me down. Plus, I learned a lot. I was an eyewitness to the gentrification of Williamsburg. I watched weekly progress on the construction of Barclays Center. And I discovered a great deli in Mill Basin. And…I think I've talked enough."

I only say, "Thank you for sharing."

And Sarkar says, "I'm very glad I told you about my wandering Sundays, and I'm very glad you at least pretended to care."

That certainly pisses me off. "I was not pretending!"

CHAPTER 19

WE RIDE SILENTLY FOR a few minutes. For blocks and blocks and miles and miles, the only sound is the classical music coming from the speakers. He turns up the volume. Someone is sitting in my ear playing a cello.

As you might guess, I have absolutely no idea what the pieces are. Who wrote them? Who is playing them? My musical knowledge goes back no further than Michael Jackson and Phil Collins.

As Dr. Sarkar turns onto Roebling Street, far to the north, he shouts very loudly, "Back!"

I twist my neck slightly and try to look behind me.

"Back!" he shouts again.

I'm confused. For a moment.

Then he says, "Listen, Lucy. Cello Suite Number One in G Major."

Mercifully, I finally figure out what he's saying. "Oh. *Bach!*" I say. "Now I get it. Bach."

Sarkar smiles, and we drive south again, now along Nostrand Avenue, as Yo-Yo Ma's cello comes pouring out of the speakers and into the car.

As we get closer to my neighborhood, Dr. Sarkar slows the car significantly. Then he suddenly pulls the car over and parks in front of Family Dollar.

"Are we going to go in and buy some polyester pillows?" I say.

"No. We are going to talk." He is not smiling. He is not being his usual charming self. Sarkar looks quite serious.

My late grandmother had an expression: *"I was so scared that I thought a flower was opening up in my stomach."* Right now, I'm feeling that a whole garden is opening up in mine. What are we going to talk about? Romance? Sex? Life? Death? Medicine? The hospital? No. Those subjects don't seem, well, I don't know, appropriate to the place we're in right now.

"Okay, Lucy. I have an important question for you. What in hell are we going to do about this goddamn Detective Blumenthal?"

Phew! I guess. I am a little scared that Blumenthal is the subject, but I'm pleased at the question. It mirrors my own concern.

"You mean, what are we going to do about Blumenthal dragging his ass on this case?"

Sarkar's response is fast and eager. *"You said it earlier.* Child snatching. Kidnapping. Attempted murder. This is not a stolen bicycle or a purse snatching. This is the horror of horrors."

This passion from Sarkar is pretty unusual. All I've ever known is his joking, teasing.

"It's all I could think about while I was stitching up that poor woman," he says.

"That's all *I* could think about while you were stitching up that poor woman."

"By the way," he says. "I got a text message from Blumenthal's assistant, some detective type, Bobby somebody or other. Two of the surgical nurses during the op do remember my asking Helen Whall to leave the room during the procedure. I apologize for not having remembered properly."

"Pressure. Tired. A million things," I say. "I can't remember what I had for breakfast." As a joke, I add, "Oh, wait, it was nothing. But yesterday it was Honey Bunches of Oats with Almonds."

His smile is small but warm. He leans toward me—no, not for a kiss, just for closeness. Secret. He's going to tell me secrets. Or so I hope, but I have to admit, as he moves closer to me, I am not unaware of the fact that he has the cleanest, sharpest features I've ever seen, that the bronze color of his skin is completely irresistible, that... *God damn you, Lucy, get back into the conversation*. Blumenthal. Katra. Babies. Blood. *Shift gears, Lucy*.

Sarkar starts the car up again as I begin to talk. "I don't know. One thing is, Blumenthal seems very slow and unconcerned, but I think that could just be his style."

Sarkar gives a little shrug and his eyes widen. "I don't know, either. I should tell you that I have checked him out." When we pull up in front of Sabryna's little store on Nostrand, the GPS announces, "You have reached your destination."

Before I say thank you, I say, "Rudi, did I give you my address?"

"No," he says. "I confess, I looked it up. I was hoping I would use it someday."

I am flattered—and not a little bit turned on—but it also makes me a tiny bit nervous.

"Lucy," he says. "How about we continue our conversation about Detective Blumenthal right now, over drinks, or even dinner?"

I tell him the truth. "My son, Willie, is waiting for

me. I've got to feed him, and I need to spend some time with him...I *want* to spend some time with him."

"He can join us," says Rudi.

"No. It's what Willie and I call *alone time*. He needs it. We both need it."

When Rudi speaks again, his voice is fast, crisp, and downright unfriendly. "Very well. Whatever you care to do. But I must tell you that I'm quite disappointed."

For a moment I think he's putting me on, faking the anger.

"Please get out of the car," he says.

"Rudi, come on, enough teasing..." I begin.

"Damn it, Lucy. Get out of the car."

He's not teasing.

CHAPTER 20

THE NEXT DAY BEGINS like any other. I'm taking the number 3 subway train from Crown Heights into midtown Manhattan, and of course my cell phone is not getting service. Everyone around me on the train is listening to music or playing games, but I'm sitting there reliving my ride home with Dr. Sarkar. The ride, and the oddly unpleasant ending.

As soon as I get aboveground, two blocks from the hospital, I go to my cell and check the hospital page labeled "Daily Staff Locations." I look first to see what's up with Troy and Tracy Anne. Troy is "on call, in hospital." Tracy Anne is "in hospital after 5 p.m."

Then I click on what I really want to see. Is Rudi Sarkar in today? Here it is: "SARKAR A/D GUH GC." This means that he's spending all day (A/D) at the Gramatan University Hospital (GUH) clinic on the Grand Concourse (GC) in the Bronx.

Like most other New York City assholes who use their cell phones while they're walking on the street, I bump into someone who reminds me that *I* am an asshole.

I make my way through the employees' entrance security. This time, I don't get into an argument with anyone.

Then I head straight for Katra's room. She's out of recovery and in a maternity patient room adjacent to the midwife area. The first thing I notice is this: a two-officer police team is standing outside Katra's door. And a plainclothes female detective sits on a folding chair very close to the NYPD officers. The detective seems to know who I am. She says, "Go right in. One of your guys is in there, and the patient's parents have been here overnight."

Katra is in bed. Quiet, scared, teary, but not bad, considering she had her body sliced open and stitched back up less than twenty-four hours ago. She's even had some time and energy to apply a little very pale pink lipstick.

"Katra's doing good, by my evaluation," Troy says, "really good, Lucy, but she's not in the mood for talking." He positions himself in such a way that I'm the only one who can see his eyes roll and his eyebrows arch up.

I look at Katra and then say to Troy, "I'm not surprised that she's doing so well. She's a strong woman." I say it loud enough so I can clearly be heard by Katra and her parents.

Then more directly to Katra I say, "Everything should be okay, sweetie. Everything. The police are all over it."

Katra turns away from me. Troy hands her a tissue and a plastic cup filled with ice water.

Then I hear a woman's voice. It is hesitant, with a foreign accent, "And the baby. What of the baby?"

I look at the slim blond woman, carrying a ripped-off version of a red Hermès Birkin bag. She must be Katra's mother. It is clear where Katra got her good looks. The parents really can't be a helluva lot older than myself. They both wear jeans and have kinda hip haircuts.

Then the man speaks. "My wife ask you about baby. What you will say?"

"I don't know what to say. I'm sorry. I don't know."

"The cops, they tell us nothing. 'Not their department,' they tell us," Mr. Kovac says.

Before I can answer, before I can even give the standard *"Everybody's concerned and everybody's working on it,"* a giant scream comes from Katra.

She is facing away from us. She is raised on one elbow. She holds a fistful of hair in her right hand.

"She pull the hair," Katra's mother says.

We all move in toward the bed. One of the officer guards enters the room. Katra screams again, and she pulls out another small chunk of hair. I unclench her hand from the new cluster of hair she's holding.

For a second, I consider calling for additional help or restraints or both.

But now Katra suddenly turns calm. She begins sobbing gently.

I pull up her chart on the bedside computer. "They didn't load her with any special meds," I say.

"I don't know what's happening," Troy says. "The lady's calm for about fifteen or twenty minutes. Then she goes to sleep for about ten minutes. Then she wakes up and gets all riled up again."

"Get a post-op doc in here. Let's see what he or she can tell us," I tell him.

"But what of the baby?" asks Mr. Kovac. "We must learn of the baby."

"We are all trying to find the baby. We are also trying to find the person who hurt your daughter. We will do everything in our power."

Katra turns onto her back and looks toward her father. Her eyes are filled with fear and frustration.

I say the only thing that comes to my mind. "Really, Mr. Kovac. We *will try*."

Yes, I'm speaking the truth, but it's also a delaying tactic, and I don't think the handsome Mr. Kovac is buying it.

Kovac says something to his daughter in a language I don't understand. Serbian? Hungarian?

Katra keeps nodding as her father speaks. Then she decides apparently to speak to me.

"Lucy, my papa says that you say you will try. Try. Try. Try. He understands your heart is big. But he says that *trying* is good, but is not good enough."

I nod. I tell her that I understand.

Troy walks toward me. He holds his iPad in my line of vision. "Take a look. The news media is all over us," he says.

I look down at the screen.

"Let me borrow your iPad," I say to Troy. "I'm going to visit our leader."

CHAPTER 21

Five years ago

ONLY TWO PASSENGERS FLEW on the private plane that left Saratov, Russia. They were a man and a woman, each about forty years old. They were not linked romantically. In fact, they did not particularly enjoy each other's company. But their supervisors had put them together. They would work as a team.

Fifteen hours later, they landed on a small airstrip somewhere just west of the Jersey shore. Two cars then brought them to a very small cottage—a shack, really—in Cranbury, New Jersey. One of the cars, a decrepit 1998 Toyota, was left with them.

After a week in Cranbury, the man told the woman that their "patrons" in Russia had emailed him. She was to take a job they had arranged for her. She would be clearing tables at the Molly Pitcher Service Area on the New Jersey Turnpike.

The woman was outraged. "I am a trained pediatrician. Now they want me to watch people eat hamburgers and cinnamon buns and then clean up their shit. No."

The man responded quietly but firmly. "They have told me that if you don't take some kind of job, we will be sent out of the country. Or even worse, sent to prison. And listen, *Doctor,* you will not be working any harder than myself. My job is terrible."

That was true, and the woman knew it. Almost every day the man drove into the city of Trenton and talked his way into homeless shelters or women's shelters. He went to the areas behind the railroad station and near the transient hotels where prostitutes gathered to meet clients, to shoot up, and often to perform their services right on the streets.

It was at those places the man searched for pregnant women, women who might be persuaded to sell their babies when they were born. The women—often addled by fear or drugs, or both—usually accepted his proposal.

So his partner angrily agreed to take the job. Every night after he worked in Trenton, he would pick her up at the Molly Pitcher Service Area. They would sit in the 1998 Toyota and dine on the food she had sneaked from the fast-food restaurants—cold, chewy shish kebabs, Coca-Colas without fizz, hot dogs without buns.

This happened every night of the week except Wednesday. Wednesday was delivery night. That night he would come screeching into the parking lot, she would jump into the Toyota, and then she would pick up the swaddled bundle on the back seat.

The bundle always contained an infant. Sometimes there were two infants.

The woman would take a stethoscope and examination light from her purse and carefully examine the babies. Then she would write careful notes.

"Less than four pounds."

"Enlarged rear head."

"Jaundice."

"Atrial fibrillation."

But most often her notation was "Perfect."

These notes were attached to the swaddling cloth around each infant.

Then the man and the woman and the baby, or babies, would travel along the back roads of northeastern New Jersey. Eventually the car brought them to the William T. Davis Wildlife Refuge on Staten Island. There they would meet a man and a woman driving a small white van. The back of this van was outfitted with emergency medical supplies and oxygen tanks.

The people from the van took the infants, changed their diapers, powdered them, wrapped them again carefully, and read the doctor's notes. Then the white van drove off.

This ritual occurred every Wednesday evening for eight months until one night when the man pulled into the Molly Pitcher parking lot and said to the woman, "No more Trenton. We've been transferred."

"To where? What happened? Tell me!"

He smiled. "They're moving us to Manhattan."

She exclaimed in surprise.

"Yep. Like they say in America, this is the big time, baby."

CHAPTER 22

"I WANT YOU TO take a look at CNN *and* NY1 on-line." I am now practically screaming at Dr. Katz.

He holds out his hand like a traffic cop. "Who the hell allowed you into my office?" he yells.

I ignore the question. I yell just as loudly at the man: "Take a look at what's going on in the news, Dr. Katz."

"I've already seen it, Ms. Ryuan. I don't depend on you for my news. Now answer my question. How did you—"

I continue to ignore him and begin to read out loud the report from the internet:

The very place that people go to get healed has turned into a place where people go to get kid-napped, even killed. Gramatan University Hospital is now being called the Hospital of Death. In the past forty-eight hours, three newborn infants have been kidnapped from the hospital's maternity ward. What's more, the mother of one of the kidnapped infants was viciously attacked and left for dead in a basement storage room. CEO Dr. Barrett Katz issued a statement saying the hospital was cooperating

fully with the FBI and NYPD. Chairperson of the
hospital's maternity division, Dr. Rudra Sarkar, was
away from the hospital and unavailable for comment.
Leon Blumenthal, the NYPD detective heading up
this shocking criminal investigation, would say only
that the inquiry was ongoing. Further—

"Enough, Ms. Ryuan," Katz says. "Are you here to
tell me what I already know?"

"No, I'm here to tell you that sooner, rather than
later, we won't have a functioning maternity ward, or
more importantly, we won't have a viable Midwifery
Division. No pregnant woman in her right mind will
want to come here to deliver."

Katz sits at his handsome steel-and-glass desk,
more of a dining table than a piece of office furniture.
He folds his hands, and it is obvious to me that he is
struggling to stay calm.

"The statements that we issued are completely ac-
curate. There's not much more we can do. You've seen
the security. It's like the Pentagon around here."

He could have chosen a better security compari-
son than the Pentagon—Fort Knox, maybe—but I
decide to say nothing about that.

I do still have a lot to say.

"I think we could have twice as much security. I
think we could have more cops. I think this Blumenthal character could move more aggressively. I think a
lot of things."

Katz now speaks quietly. "I know you do. And here's
what I think. I think you should be back in your office
or in one of your hippie-dippie birthing rooms."

He is almost scarlet from trying to suppress his
anger.

As for me, now I'm determined to get more involved in everything. I'm not quite sure how, but I will figure out something. Troy is smart as hell, and when it comes to passion and energy, he's got unlimited resources. If Sarkar and I ever reconnect and "make nice" with each other, he might be of some help. He might be able to light a fire under Blumenthal.

"Now, if you'll please leave, Ms. Ryuan," I hear Katz say.

Oh, right. My mind wandered. I'm standing in the big boss's office. *Oh, who the hell cares?* I look at him as if he is just some annoying stranger. And in a way, he is.

"Thanks, as always, for your help," I say sweetly. Then I walk out.

CHAPTER 23

TROY IS THE MAN!

At 10 a.m. I ask him to join me in my office.

I am crazy-angry with Barrett Katz's lazy, self-serving attitude and the investigative team's stupid, slow-as-a-freaking-snail pace. Three kidnappings, a vicious stabbing—something has to be done. Okay, I am not the person to do it, but I am often the person who is never afraid of trying to do it.

"So you need me to light a BFF under him," Troy says.

"Huh? A Best Friends Forever?"

"No, no, Lucy honey. A BFF is a Big Fucking Fire."

An hour later, Troy and I are huddled together in a small meeting room watching the screen of my laptop, hypnotized by the hours of video unfurling in front of us: uninterrupted footage from a GUH surveillance camera trained on the corridor that connects the maternity area with the midwife birthing section.

I am afraid to blink, afraid to lift the can of Diet Pepsi to my lips. I've gotta stay glued to the computer screen for that one second when the possible clue shows up, that wonderful moment when the TV detective yells, *"Hold it. Go back a little. Yeah, right there."*

The viewing is a combination of the hypnotically fascinating and the numbingly boring at the same time. We watch it on a higher speed than normal, but not so high that we can't catch virtually everything that's going on—quite a few very pregnant women, a few postnatal women walking with portable IVs, doctors walking with an entourage of residents, visitors laughing, visitors crying. It's an interminable film of doctors and nurses and orderlies and janitors and visitors and patients and security guards and gurneys and janitor carts. The surveillance camera records life on the corridor in fuzzy black and white some of the time and fuzzy color at other times. The camera placement gives a strange angle to anyone captured by its lens. The camera is positioned on the ceiling, so high up that each person's head is large and their body is much smaller, narrowing down to very teeny-tiny feet. Everyone on camera is either walking toward or away from the vanishing point.

"Okay," I say to Troy, neither of us looking away from the screen. "While we're here watching this fabulous movie, I really would like to know how you managed to get your hands on these surveillance DVDs."

"I have my secret ways," says Troy. He speaks so seriously that I'm actually a little creeped out. He's not being sarcastic. He's not being funny. He's telling the truth.

"Did you steal them?"

"Not really. Let's just say I have some tight connections."

"Could you be a little clearer?" I ask. "C'mon. How'd you get these?"

"I just act my charming self. The ladies like me.

The gentlemen who are so inclined also like me. Could it be my professionally whitened teeth, the cut of my Zegna jeans, or—" Troy, who has not stopped studying the monitor while carrying on jokingly about his good looks and charm, suddenly shouts, "Hold the video, Lucy!"

I freeze the image on the screen and dial the speed down to normal. We watch a man in a cheesy-looking navy-blue warm-up suit pause, then bend over at the waist. He hangs in that bent-over position, his hands almost touching the floor. Then a nurse approaches him and speaks to him. The man stands up straight. The nurse looks concerned, but the man waves her away. It must be the nurse's lucky day, because as soon as she's a few feet away the man vomits what looks like a week's worth of meals.

"Mount Vesuvius blows!" Troy yells and laughs.

I click a control button and we watch the continuing segment at a faster speed: the man walks into a visitors' bathroom and the nurse returns. She leaves frame. Then she returns again. This time she carries with her an antiseptic foam spray.

"So far this has been the most exciting part of the recordings," says Troy. Then he adds, "And, by the way, I am *not* trying to avoid the question of how I managed to secure these."

"Okay, and so…"

"So have you ever noticed that young security guy Jonah?" Troy asks.

"Well, no…I don't think so."

"Tall. Latino. Part-timer. He's usually at the ER entrance on the dead-man's shift."

"Can't say as I know him," I say.

"Sometimes, when it's real cold, he wears a black

satin jacket with the logo from the *Jersey Boys* musical on it and a baseball cap with the logo from *Hamilton* on it."

"Okay, now I know who it is," I say. Then I add, just so I can be entirely unprofessional, "He's got a nice little butt."

"Well, Jonah is trying to be an actor, and let me just say that he and I have grown pretty close."

"*Pretty* close?" I ask skeptically.

"Okay, Lucy, *very* close."

"*Very* close?" I ask.

"And lucky for you, Lucy, that we are, because sometimes Jonah gets assigned to the video archives room when other folks are taking their break, and we do each other favors. We are close friends, very close friends. I have visited the video archives room a fair number of times."

"Stop right there," I say.

"No, it's nothing like you're thinking," Troy says.

"No, *stop the video.*"

This section of recording has flipped into blurry color.

Troy freezes the frame: a woman. Nurse's uniform. Looks like she's got blond hair. Because the image quality is so bad it's hard to tell for sure. The woman is walking toward the camera. But her head is bent downward. Her time on camera is less than five seconds.

"Okay, Troy. What was wrong with that picture?"

Troy doesn't skip a beat. "She's wearing high heels."

Troy is the man!

"When was the last time you saw a nurse wearing high-heeled shoes?" I ask.

"Only once, but that was a drag show in the Poconos."

The fact is that nurses wear sneakers and clogs. I turn to Troy and say, "A nurse would never wear heels."

"And such ugly ones," he says. But neither of us laughs. We both know we might be onto something. We both know we might be looking at the baby-napper...or at least looking at the baby-napper's possibly blond hair and probably black heels.

We watch the very brief scene a few times. We determine by mutual agreement that the shoes are red, possibly purple.

During the fifth viewing, my phone sounds with a text.

I click, and the screen says, Birthing rm 4. ASAP. G. Leonard.

I show the screen to Troy.

"Do we have a mama called G. Leonard?" Troy asks.

"Never heard of her," I say. "But it sounds like she's in birthing room 4, and she's about to have a baby."

CHAPTER 24

TROY PUSHES THE PAUSE button on the surveillance video, ejects the disc from my laptop, and we both rush toward birthing room 4.

"Who *sent* the alert about this G. Leonard woman?" Troy asks as we walk-run down the hallway.

"It was unsigned," I said. "No name. It's probably from ER. We'll find out soon enough."

Outside birthing room 4 is an unusually large group, even for these crazy times: two NYPD officers and two GUH Security people, plus two people in plain clothes. The cheap gray suits give them away as private security, Secret Service types. One woman with two cameras around her neck stands talking quietly to a guy who has a microphone attached to a fairly bulky recording apparatus. Nobody stops us from entering the room.

Standing around a birthing cot I see Dr. Lia Alba, a senior pediatrician. With her is Dr. Steve Swanbeck, a research neurologist. There is a third person—Dr. Rudra Sarkar. My eyes widen a bit as I look at the woman in the bed. Son of a bitch, it's none other than internationally insanely famous Greta Moss, apparently now using the alias G. Leonard.

I should have known.

"You tricked me, goddamnit," I say to Sarkar. "Your call sheet said you were up in the Bronx clinic all day."

He smiles at me—boyish, charming, handsome—but it doesn't work at all this time. I am way beyond furious.

"Forget it, Dr. Sarkar. Just forget it," I say.

"You're not going to leave us out here to dry, are you?" he asks.

"You bet your ass that I'm going to leave you out here to dry," I say.

"But Ms. Moss is about to deliver," Sarkar says.

Sarkar is head of the department. I'm sure he's correct, but, almost reflexively, I place both my hands on Greta Moss's taut stomach. Yep, Greta's ready to go. I look closely at Greta's face. She's squinting with the beginning of labor pains. I'm ashamed to admit—*even to myself*—that all I can think is *My God, this woman is beautiful!*

I also can't help but notice that she's wearing full makeup: eyeliner, mascara, even a little foundation.

"Somebody get her jewelry removed," I say.

"Absolutely not," Greta yells.

Troy speaks firmly. He's not in the mood to charm the patient. He tells her, "This is standard procedure, ma'am, in case surgery becomes necessary. This isn't a fashion show, lady."

"Do you know how valuable these earrings are? I'm not taking them off," says Greta.

Now it's time for my special touch. "That's fine," I say. "In that case, then, you can deliver your own baby. Or they can wheel you right down the corridor to obstetrics."

"Very well," Greta says.

Then Troy begins advising Greta on simple breathing. Greta seems uninterested.

"You gotta do some short breaths with me, ma'am," Troy says. "You took the natural childbirth class, didn't you?"

She looks at him blankly. It dawns on me that chances are great that our patient did not attend any natural childbirth classes. Perhaps she expected customer service from Chanel or Bergdorf to show up in her hospital room with a newborn in a shopping bag.

Suddenly a voice comes from behind me. "You can do this, Greta. I'll coach you." I turn around and I see football star and all-American heartthrob Hank Waldren. The guy can only be described as *annoyingly handsome*. I do not go weak in the knees.

Sarkar moves close to me. "I see you have everything under control," he whispers. Then he adds, "Thank you," and leaves.

I'm pissed off enough to give him a punch, but I've got my diva patient to take care of.

Greta's knees are bent, pointing up. Her chin is pushing hard into her sternum. Troy is still advising on breathing. Every thirty seconds he says, "Everything's looking good down below."

I know that the labor pains are intense, but Greta doesn't yell, doesn't cry. Her face is contorted, but that's it.

I wipe the perspiration from her head. I feel compelled to say, "You're doing well, Greta. You're doing just fine." Then I turn and look at her husband standing behind me.

"Why don't you hold her hand?" I say to Waldren. He nods quickly and reaches for his wife's hand.

"No," Greta says as she pulls her hand away from him. "I'm good. I'm doing good."

I move into the firm-strong-angry mode, the tone I've perfected over the years. "Listen, Greta. This is a two-person job. You and Hank are in this together. Take his hand."

The model holds out her elegant model hand—the slim fingers, the perfect skin, the tapered nails. The football player takes that hand into his own very big hand. The couple look at each other.

"Good," I say. "Let's have a baby."

CHAPTER 25

IF EVER SOMEONE NEEDED actual living proof that the Lord is consistently kind and generous to the rich and the beautiful, Greta Moss's delivery is that proof. Her eight-and-a-half-pound—*You heard that right, eight and a half pounds. The baby almost weighs the same as the mother*—baby boy arrives quickly, happily, and looking camera ready. It was a traditional vaginal birth, but amazingly he came out wrinkle-free. I could swear that he actually smelled of Johnson's Baby Powder when he arrived.

The photographers descend, and Hank and Greta's "people" allow the media—"Two at a time, please!"—into the room for photos. *People, Vogue, Football Weekly.*

Troy looks at me and whispers, "Ya know, this sort of reminds me of something I read about that happened in Bethlehem two thousand years ago."

Meanwhile, I am busting to make my way to Dr. Rudi Sarkar's office. I am so damned ready to lace into him about tricking me into assisting with Greta Moss's birth. Of course the moment he sees me, he knows why I've come, and his charm defense is in high gear. His head is tilted to one side. His precious phony smile is that of a little boy who's broken his mommy's favorite vase.

"Okay. Okay. Okay. Mea culpa."

My response? "You son of a bitch!"

"Look," he says. "I tried to talk Greta out of relying on your services. But she insisted."

"But you didn't care to remember that I insisted I didn't want to do it," I say, just a few decibels away from a scream. "Your trying to talk her out of it came way too late in the game."

"Listen. Greta Moss and Hank Waldren are extremely important people in New York. Right? It didn't hurt."

I raise my voice a little higher. "No, now you listen. I don't give a shit. I'm extremely *un*important, but you asked. I said no, and then you...then you..."

Sarkar now says what I've actually been holding back from saying. "And then I tricked you."

"You took the words right out of my mouth."

"Yes. I suspect I did."

I walk toward the door. He follows me and holds the door closed.

"Look, Lucy. The Waldrens and their new baby will be all over the papers and the internet and tonight's TV. Smiling. Happy. Most important for us, safe. It will be wonderful publicity for the hospital. And we sure can use it."

"But you tricked me. You lied to me," I say. My voice is only a shade softer.

He moves back to his desk and turns to thrust a laptop screen in my face. "Look at this," he says. He scrolls upward. He holds the screen even closer to my face, and I read the *New York Post* headline:

HANK IS HAPPY. GRETA IS GREAT. A NEW BABY BOY.

This is followed by typical corny copy:

Fashion celeb Greta Moss scored her own winning touchdown today. She delivered Hank Waldren Jr. to Hank Waldren Sr. Mother and Baby and Giant are doing great.

"You see, this is perfect news for Gramatan University Hospital," says Sarkar. Then he scrolls again. This time he shows me a page on AOL News. An adorable photo of Greta—her full makeup miraculously undisturbed by the ordeal of delivery—and the cute new baby with the equally cute new father holding the little one. The cute caption is:

THE LITTLEST GIANT

If I wasn't so angry, I'd be willing to admit that it's a really irresistible picture. These three should model as a family. *Hold on, Lucy. You've got to stay angry.*

"Admit it. It's really good for the hospital," says Sarkar.

"Okay, I admit it, but what would really be perfect is this: you and your NYPD and FBI buddies actually find the *missing* babies instead of helping to feed a media blitz all about a celebrity baby. Like this: The cops find the madman who tried to kill Katra. The cops do their job. Possibly you can get in touch with your pal Blumenthal and tell him to wake the hell up."

"I think Detective Blumenthal and his people are doing all they can do. I think they are doing their absolute best," he says. He moves closer to me.

Oh, God, why am I thinking what I'm thinking? I am suddenly certain that Dr. Sarkar may lean in and kiss me. I'm frightened. I should have a plan. Will I kiss him? Will I turn away? Will he—

Instead he speaks, his face close to mine. "I am truly sorry for the deception." His voice is almost a whisper.

I believe Sarkar is being sincere. I'm tough, but I'm not an idiot. Even I can only stay angry for so long.

"Yeah, okay. But don't do it again," I say. *Damn it.* Am I sounding like a nursery school teacher?

The moment has become intimate, close, warm. I think it might be a good idea to tell him about the video that Troy and I saw earlier—the blond woman in the high heels. This is perhaps the only real clue we have so far. All of a sudden I'm longing to share this knowledge.

The small smile on Sarkar's face seems to broadcast friendship and trust. Yes, I think I should share the information. Then, immediately, I don't know why, I change my mind. Then I think that time is passing—what have I got to lose? Why not?

But then Sarkar speaks before I can say anything. "Why don't we go up and visit our celebrity couple and their new baby? Okay? Maybe we'll get our picture on the internet."

The moment passes. I won't tell him. But I will say something else. "Listen, there's something I want to ask you about."

He looks vaguely confused. "Yes?" he asks. Then he smiles.

"Last night I saw another side of you, an angry, impatient, sort of ugly side. Okay, it was only for a second, I know. But when I left your car—or should

I say when I was thrown out of your car? —it was just...I don't know what to call it. Confusing?"

The smile vanishes from his face. He even turns away from me. "I know what to call it," he says. "I would call it disgusting, reprehensible, the uncontrollable anger of a disappointed man, a man who is used to getting what he desires."

"Take it easy, Doc. Even I wouldn't go that far in the evaluation," I say.

"You don't understand, do you, Lucy? I wanted you to be with me. And you did not want to do so. I was angry."

I am, of course, just a little confused. Maybe a bit of romance was in the air but surely not enough to cause disappointment and anger like that. Now I'm not even sure how to discuss the matter with him.

"Uh, okay," I say. "I guess that clarifies it. It was, well, just surprising. I'd never seen you like that before."

"And you will never see me like that again," Sarkar says.

This time as he leans toward me I know that he intends to kiss me. I turn away slightly. I reach and brush my hand against his face.

"Now, don't be angry, Rudi. This is not rejection," I say. "But...I think we should go up and see the new baby right now."

He laughs. "You are, as always, absolutely correct."

Then he opens the door and gestures for me to walk through. We're off to visit the three Waldrens.

CHAPTER 26

THE GENERAL HOSPITAL AREA outside Greta Moss's birthing room is strangely quiet and almost eerily vacant. Where are the NYPD officers, the GUH guards, the nurses, the photographers, the reporters who turned this area into a wacky circus minutes ago? Where's that lady with the cameras? The rent-a-cops in cheap suits?

Rudi Sarkar and I step into the birthing room. The bed has been stripped; the floor is still damp from mopping. The bathroom is empty; it smells of disinfectant. Instinctively Sarkar and I walk quickly to the nurses' station. I am curious, confused, but I am not yet anxious. Dr. Sarkar simply looks concerned.

"Has Greta Moss been moved?" I ask the male nurse at the desk.

"I don't think so," says the nurse. "Let me check." He goes to his computer screen. He looks, he scrolls, he squints. It's taking too long, so I immediately think that something evil is going on. He continues to scroll. I'm about to scream. Then he finally speaks, "No. She's still in birthing room 4."

"Are you sure?" I ask. Yes, he's sure.

Then Sarkar speaks. "Try looking for a patient named G. Leonard."

The nurse scrolls the screen for a moment. "No one listed here with that name," says the nurse.

"Let's check the nursery," I say.

Sarkar and I head toward the magical room at the opposite end of the corridor where the newborns are cared for and displayed.

When we arrive, one of the baby nurses—everyone in maternity knows Rudra Sarkar—immediately opens the security door to the nursery.

"Dr. Sarkar, welcome."

"Is the Moss and Waldren baby in here?" he asks.

"No, but he should be here soon. We received an update only twenty minutes ago. Good delivery. Healthy baby. Scored a nine on the Apgar test."

Nine is as close to the perfect score of ten as most babies achieve.

"We're ready for the kid when he's ready for us," says the baby nurse. Then she adds, "I hear the mother is something of—"

"Never mind. Thank you," Sarkar says. Then he turns to me directly and says, "Let's go."

We rush back out to the corridor. I shout to the desk nurse to call Security immediately. "And call that dumb-ass detective, too. His name is Blumenthal, Leon Blumenthal," I say.

"If this is another missing baby, the Waldren kid..." Sarkar says, "I don't even want to think about it."

We begin opening and closing patients' doors. Babies wail. Weary-eyed dads and beaming grandparents walk the halls. A few bassinets are being wheeled. A few baskets of flowers are being delivered.

"Lucy!" I hear as we open yet another patient's room door. The voice is loud, urgent, and familiar. Of course I recognize the voice. It's Tracy Anne.

I turn toward the sound of the voice.

I thought that Tracy Anne would not be in until much later today, but here she is. She's running toward Sarkar and myself.

"If you're looking for the Moss baby, he's not here," Tracy Anne says. If she is aware of an emergency, she sure doesn't show it. She's as calm and perky as ever.

"Well, obviously we know that," I say. "Where the hell is everybody? The mother? The baby?"

Please have a good answer. Please don't let this be another problem. This one would be an explosion heard *round the world*. A famous couple—a famous model, a football hero—a beautiful new baby…

Then Tracy Anne says, "The Waldren family has been moved to Darlow 12-L. They're up there now. The whole gang of them, the big crazy entourage."

"We should have guessed it. The fancy-ass Darlow floor," I say. Then I ask Tracy Anne, "When did this all happen? Why doesn't anyone know about it? Why don't I know about it? Why doesn't Dr. Sarkar at least know about it?"

Tracy Anne shrugs. She's not being arrogant. It's a shrug that seems to indicate that the entire change of rooms was way out of her control. Then she says, "They did it sort of privately. You know, discreetly. At least that's what I was told."

Sarkar closes his eyes. Then he speaks softly. *"Khuda ka shukr hai,"* he says. Then Dr. Sarkar opens his eyes.

I say, "What's that mean?"

He translates for us: "Thank God."

"Thank God is right," I say, and I feel an enormous amount of anger well up inside me.

Time for another rant.

"This hospital is exploding. Nothing's working. Babies are being kidnapped. A woman is viciously assaulted. Now this, a whole group of people change rooms and there's not even a record of the change. This is insane."

"I understand how you feel, Lucy. But the staff are not miracle workers. And we must trust Detective Blumenthal is doing his best," says Sarkar.

Just before I turn and walk away from the doctor I say, "Yeah? Well, he's going to be doing a lot better once he hears from me."

And for the first time it strikes me: why is Rudi Sarkar such a supporter and defender of Leon Blumenthal?

CHAPTER 27

I RUN DOWN THE back stairs to the second floor, the floor where the temporary NYPD/FBI head-quarters has replaced the residents' cafeteria. As I take the stairs two at a time, I consider what I might say to Blumenthal, my opening salvo. I quickly settle upon *"I am sick and tired of this bullshit."*

I stop at the entrance. I take in the whole chaotic room—lots of empty Starbucks cups, crappy-looking doughnuts (the cheap little minis with confectioner's sugar), and of course lots of officers and agents on lap-tops. It looks like a lot is going on. But my mind says, *You sure as hell wouldn't know it by the lack of progress on the case.*

"Detective Blumenthal," I say loudly as I approach his table. He is, as always, tapping away at his laptop.

He looks up. I'm not sure, but I think he rolls his eyes. It's the standard *Here she is again* offensive, his usual disinterested, condescending approach to me. Well, this time Blumenthal picked the wrong woman to condescend to.

Shouting, I say, "I am outraged."

Yes, I know. That's not what I'd planned on saying. It's a far cry from *"I am sick and tired of this bullshit."* But that is what came out of my mouth.

"Yes, I can see that you're outraged," Blumenthal says with a dry, sarcastic tone.

"When are we going to see some action from you and your people on this horrendous situation?" It seems like everyone else in the room has stopped to look at us. An uncomfortable silence allows our verbal exchange to really ring out.

"When? When? When? What do you think we're working on? Don't try to bully me, Ms. Ryuan."

"I'm not the bullying type," I say loudly but more controlled now.

For the first time he displays a bit of emotion. "Are you crazy?" Then he throws his head back and guffaws.

"Listen," I say. "Since you and your team don't seem to be taking any action, I'm doing something."

This time I'm sure Blumenthal is really rolling his eyes. As curious as his group might be, they're slowly getting back to work.

I reach into the pocket of my slacks and pull out three photographs—screenshots from the surveillance recordings Troy and I had been watching.

Blumenthal takes the pictures and does nothing more than glance at them. He then shuffles them and looks at them briefly again. Then he lays them out side by side on his desktop.

"Okay," he says. "These seem to be an unidentifiable nurse with a fairly large butt walking down a hallway, most likely a hallway in this hospital."

I'd like to slug him in the mouth. I want to say, *"Congratulations, Sherlock,"* but instead I decide to seize the moment and use it. I explain the intrigue of the pictures. "These screenshots were taken from a security video in this hospital on the day Katra Kovac was attacked and mutilated, the day she had her forced C-section. Plus—"

Blumenthal interrupts. "Plus," he says, "the nurse is wearing very high high-heeled shoes, a very unusual choice of shoe for a nurse."

"Go to the head of the class," I say.

Then a tiny bit of a smile from Blumenthal: "I can't believe anybody uses that expression anymore: 'Go to the head of the class.'"

A pause. He gathers up the photos. "Where'd you get these?" he asks.

"I told you: from an internal security surveillance video."

"How'd you get the video?" he asks.

"That's for me to know and you to find out."

"You are certainly an encyclopedia of antique sayings." He tries to hand the three photos back to me.

"Don't you want to keep them?" I ask.

"I've just seen them. Thank you very much," he says.

"But these could be helpful," I say.

"I don't disagree. They *could* be helpful, very helpful. I'll keep them in mind."

Vesuvius explodes again. "Keep them in mind? You're going to *keep them in mind*?" I shout. And I expect that my pale, lightly freckled Irish face is turning red.

"Look. Our team has studied these exact same recordings. Don't you think part of our process was to view the footage from every security camera in the hospital? They took screenshots of appropriate moments in the tapes. So we've been there."

"I believe you, but what I don't believe is that any of *your team* took notice of that woman in the nurse's uniform wearing stiletto heels. Did they?"

"I really can't share information about our progress or process with you," he says, and he is clearly becoming impatient. But certainly no more impatient than myself.

I quickly grab the photos from Blumenthal's hands. He goes back to his laptop.

Then I say what I'd planned to say when I first walked into the inquiry office: "I am so sick and tired of this bullshit."

CHAPTER 28

I'M OUT OF BLUMENTHAL'S makeshift office, quickly heading back to the Midwifery Division. In the giant complex of Gramatan University Hospital, this is where I feel safest and happiest. I don't want to sound like my crazy cousin Margaret Mary, with her shaved head and 1960s love beads, but this is a happy place, a place of simple joy. This is where the midwives and the mothers and the babies all come together. I'm all for women who opt for the kind of hospital birth Dr. Sarkar provides, but I believe there is a difference between the two styles. In the world of the midwife, giving birth is a natural process, not a medical procedure.

I have no appointments listed this afternoon, sort of a minor miracle in itself. Because I have no patients, I'm just a little confused when Troy comes in—without knocking, of course—and tells me, "You've got one agitated young lady sitting in your examination room, Lucy. That's all I'm gonna say." He pauses, then starts talking again. "Well, I will say one other thing. It's someone you may remember from the not-so-distant past."

Curious and, because of the current circumstances in the hospital, a little apprehensive, I walk into the examination room.

Valerina Gomez is seated on the examination table. She is dressed in a torn and dirty gray sweatshirt, cheap-looking jeans, and flip-flops.

Val looks about as awful as a pretty woman can look—or like a woman who just gave birth to twins, and lost one. Her hair is oily, unwashed. Her lovely face is marked with bruises and red blotches, patches of acne, and lots of smudged, caked-on makeup. She is shaking: her arms, her legs, her shoulders. As soon as she sees me enter, she bursts out crying.

I put my arms around her shoulders, and during the thirty or forty seconds that I am holding Val I cannot help but consider the dramatic differences between her and Greta Moss.

Each woman is beautiful, but Greta is tall and hyper-styled. Val is small and sexy and, well, hot. Val has been totally screwed by life—the worst of luck in where she grew up, in her finances, in her future. Greta? Well, her fairy tale is told all over the internet every day.

Finally Val is calm enough to speak. "Lucy, they took my baby!" she yells.

Oh, Christ. I think that yet another baby has been stolen. But I'm understandably being an alarmist. Val quickly clarifies.

"No. She wasn't stolen, if that's what you're thinking. I was supposed to be discharged from the hospital with my baby last night. And that's when they told me. A doctor or a midwife or a nurse or somebody told me that my baby girl and I are all set and ready to leave. Then a nurse comes in, and she is all efficient and mean, and she says that the doctor or whoever is wrong. I cannot have my baby. 'Yes,' I say. And then they said, 'No, that is not possible. You yourself can get out of here, but the baby must stay.'"

She brings her hands to the sides of her head. She stops talking, and she cries loudly. I have a good idea of what happened: Maternity Discharge looked at her records and saw that her blood contained a mixture of cocaine, as well as oxycodone and hydrocodone, both powerful opioids. The discharge desk or Nurse Franklin called Social Services, and they put a stop on allowing Val to leave with her daughter.

Val begins to compose herself. She starts talking again. Between sobs and shakes and coughs she explains some more. "They bring a nurse and a social worker and a cop, like I'm a criminal, to see me in the discharge office, and they say what the social worker already told me. I cannot have my baby. They will keep her like an orphan."

I try to explain to Val that her little girl will not be kept "like an orphan." Instead the infant will stay in the GUH neonatal nursery until the great jumble of the New York City Department of Social Services sorts things out. I tell her that she can visit the baby anytime she wants.

"But I want my baby now," she cries. "She is my baby. I do not need the mayor to tell me when I can visit my own baby."

I have a choice to make now. I make it: I let her have it right between the eyes. I don't shout. But I am way more than stern. "Look. I tried to get you help. You compromised your pregnancy."

Val is now sobbing uncontrollably. I'm trying to practice *tough love,* something I'm not very good at. I'm good at *tough,* and I'm good at *love*. I'm just not good at them when they're together.

"Why are you so mean to me?" she says. "Why is everybody in this city so mean to me?"

"Because you don't listen. Do you love drugs more than your baby?"

That lights up her face with horror. "No. I love my baby. I want my baby," she yells.

"I know you love her. I know you want her. But you have to show and prove that you love her. You do that by cleaning yourself up."

But I can't keep yelling at her. The situation is the usual crazy mess for users: heartbreaking and infuriating.

"Where are you living these days?" I ask.

"I think I can stay with my auntie Sofia," she says. Then she explains that her mother, who I know is a prostitute and a user, won't allow her back in her apartment.

"Where does your auntie live?"

"On St. Ann's Avenue, 149th Street."

Great. Possibly the worst area of the worst neighborhood in the South Bronx. And that's a contest that's got a lot of competition.

I tell her that right now we're going to visit her baby in the nursery. "You'll hold the baby for about ten or fifteen minutes. Then we've got to go someplace else. We need to go to a social service and addiction center in Washington Heights."

She interrupts me. She speaks firmly. "No, I like the center on East 35th Street. Don't boss me around, Lucy. I'm in charge of my life."

I can't take it anymore. "Listen, you are not in charge. We're picking a place where they can help you and help you get your baby back."

I walk out of the room to clear my mind. Under my breath, I say, "Jesus Christ! When will it ever end?"

CHAPTER 29

I WASH VAL'S FACE. "I should have used Easy-Off oven cleaner to remove all this foundation," I tell her as I scrub. Then I dress her in a clean white T-shirt and a clean pair of powder-blue hospital scrub pants.

Now Val is ready to see her daughter and to play Mommy. I have to say that Val does a damn good job of it. She cuddles and feeds and changes her baby in the hospital visitors' nursery.

Meanwhile, I gather copies of any papers the hospital has on file that can help us get through the Manhattan outpost of the Department of Social Services—MSS. Val clearly has the bio-maternal instinct. It takes a lot of cajoling and threatening to get her away from her baby and out of the hospital. Once we're down in the mechanical sewer they call a subway in Manhattan, we take the A train from midtown all the way to the neighborhood that is almost at the northernmost end of the island: Washington Heights.

Now we trade the chaos of GUH—the guards, the cops, the agents, the nurses—for the chaos of MSS. The guards, the social workers, the pregnant women, the abused women, the homeless women and men, the creepy storefront lawyers. Even Val, a very tough street-smart young woman, is frightened by the sheer noise and confusion of the place. There are, at the very least, nine or ten different languages being spoken here.

The lines are long. Most everybody, including Val and myself, has complicated, emotional stories to tell. So many of the people and their caregivers don't have the correct papers, the correct signatures. I've been to this place a hundred times before. Most of the people who work at MSS know me as Lucy the Baby Catcher. Most of them like me a lot. But some of them think I'm just a pushy bitch. You know what? Both opinions are perfectly valid.

I know one of the social workers pretty well. Lateesha Ro is one of the MSS officials in charge of sorting and providing all the *needs approval* applications that Val requires—childcare support funds, infant day care, addiction and alcohol rehabilitation. Without my pushy attitude we could spend the rest of the month in this place. You need application approval before you can do anything else. But since I helped birth three of her kids, Lateesha sneaks me to the front of her line. Needless to say, those folks who've been waiting patiently (and impatiently) in line for a long time are none too pleased. Lateesha Ro is, however, tougher than anyone. She announces loudly to the many others waiting that "Ms. Ryuan is a medical official, and she takes complete precedence. This is a medical emergency."

One of the guys waiting in line sizes up the situation quite accurately. "That's bullshit," he shouts. And for a moment I think he's going to smack Val or me or both of us.

Okay, I'd be angry, too, but I don't let that stop Val

and me from cutting to the window where Lateesha stands. We get there without sustaining an injury.

Val is still shaking, disoriented. I have to remind myself frequently that she is what my mother would often say about some of her teenage mothers: *"She's just a child giving birth to a child."*

Yeah, Val's very frightened. So I do most of the talking. Most of the questions are easy and expected. But there are a few important decisions to be made. I act as Val's *official advocate*. Lateesha is cool with that.

For example, I know that one of the best, and also toughest, rehab spots is located in a repurposed Catholic Church in Bushwick, Brooklyn—Our Lady of the Rosary. It's a live-in program. And I know a few of my mothers have come out of Our Lady of the Rosary pretty clean and ready to go. Of course I also know a few who have not made it work at all. *"The gals with the pin-cushion arms,"* Troy calls these women.

Val is shaking badly. She's crying. She's pulling nervously at her hair. I decide not to tell her that her program will be in a church. We can fight about that when she gets there.

"Now," says Lateesha. "Let's figure out childcare for the kiddies you're leaving behind, and the new little one." God, how I wish everyone in this line could be treated as patiently and respectfully as Teesh is treating Val.

"I don't have any other kiddies that I'm leaving behind. Plus I can take care of my one and only baby. I don't need no one," Val yells. Her voice is loud enough to be heard over the noise and shouting of the packed MSS office. The nearby men and women look at us.

What the hell is she up to? Is she just about to go crazy on me?

"You're gonna be in rehab, honey," Lateesha says. "Don't you understand that?" Lateesha isn't fazed by anything.

"You're going to be living at the place, Val," I say.

"I can't do no rehab without my baby."

Lateesha speaks directly to me. "I can tell you right now that we don't have much to choose from *anyplace* in Brooklyn. If we change the rehab location to someplace like the Bronx, we could get the baby closer to the mother. Of course that depends on who's going to be tending to the newborn. That's something we have to settle first and foremost."

And then...well, an angel must have started whispering in my ear. I suddenly got a minor brainstorm.

I look at Lateesha and say, "I think we may have a good solution for this. Right near me in my neighborhood is a woman who specializes in foster care for infants. Let me see if she's available."

"Is she licensed and on record with us?" Lateesha asks.

"Oh, I'm sure she is," I say.

This is a complete lie. But I also know it's a good idea.

I'm standing a few feet away from a sign that says NO CELL PHONE USE. I ignore it and I text Sabryna, my best friend and downstairs neighbor.

Will u take care of a newborn for 2 months while baby's mother in rehab? Favor for me. Adorable baby. Good karma.

Within thirty seconds Sabryna texts back.

R U crazy? No way. 2 much else 2 do.

Within fifteen seconds I text back.

NYC pays $10.50 per hour.

Within ten seconds my phone pings.

I'M IN!!!

CHAPTER 30

"SO DID YOU FORGET to bring the baby, Lady Lucy?" Sabryna asks me loudly when I arrive later at her crazy little Jamaican store.

For some reason a live parakeet is perched on the plantain barrel. Never saw a parakeet before in the store. I won't even ask.

"I was dealing with the big New York City foster care mess today. I think it's all under control. Tomorrow Social Services will most likely drop off the baby. They've got the paperwork, and they'll have a boatload of questions for you. Be ready. And don't give them funny answers. Social Services is not into comedy."

Sabryna nods. I know she'll come through. "I'm a little scared, Lucy. But I love babies…and the money, that sure doesn't hurt."

"This is going to be great for you, and great for this baby."

I truly believe what I'm saying. Sabryna is simply a superior human being—honest and hardworking and smarter than almost anybody I know, including myself. And she'll know just how to handle the one or two social workers who will show up with Val's baby.

I know because I guided her and Devan through a mountain of paperwork for their citizenship application. I also supplied the help of a friend's daughter, a paralegal, who treated the case as if she were standing in front of the Supreme Court.

Sabryna will be truthful, but she'll be wise enough to phrase her answers with just the necessary amount of truth.

Here's a possibility I could imagine:

> **SOCIAL WORKER:** And what is the status of young Devan's father? Where is he in his son's life?
> **SABRYNA:** Oh, Lawrence left us long ago. Now he is in a better and even more beautiful world.

No doubt Sabryna will cast her eyes heavenward and certainly not expand upon her sentence with the information that Lawrence deserted Sabryna and their son shortly after Devan's birth. He hopped a grain freighter for the "better and even more beautiful world" of Barbados. Hasn't been heard from since.

I check my cell phone and see that the time is six thirty. Immediately Sabryna sees me looking at the time, and she announces: "I will start closing up the store early. The usual seven o'clock will be far too late with a baby coming. And…"

She says the word *And* with great force. Then pauses.

I ask, "And what?"

"*And* if Willie and Devan are not coming through that door in one minute, they'll both be getting a whipping from me."

Then miraculously the door of the store opens quickly, and our two little guys appear.

Devan and Willie greet us and kiss us. Hugs all around.

"What's for supper, Mama?" Devan asks.

"That is *not* a respectful question," says Sabryna. "Your supper is what Lucy and I put on your supper table."

"Uh-oh," says Willie with a quiet sadness in his voice. "I bet they're making Lucky Pot supper."

Every week or so Sabryna and I pool all—that's right, *all*—our leftovers. She makes a big pot of rice, and we toss in the leftovers from both our kitchens. It can turn into something delicious and magical, or it can turn into something mysterious and only barely edible. When it's not so tasty, Devan supplements it later with a plate of rice and beans, and Willie microwaves a Hot Pocket or two.

Sabryna closes the store as she promised, and soon she and I are standing at her stove and creating a gourmet masterpiece: curried oxtail, cubes of meatloaf, frozen peas, four Kraft Singles, half a large can of V8 vegetable juice, and—*ta-da!*—this morning's remains of Willie's Kellogg's cornflakes.

"That's just the crunchiness this dish needs," Sabryna explains.

The results could go either way. Turns out the Lucky Pot supper tonight is neither a wild success nor a nauseating disaster. The curry flavor in the oxtail seems to dominate, and that's good. The cornflakes never had a chance.

But of course much better than a plate of passable, edible-enough food is the fact that four very hungry people are sitting together having a beautiful time. Jokes and scowls and stories from our different days.

Finally, Sabryna and I exchange secret knowing glances. It's time to tell both boys about the arrival of Val's baby tomorrow. As is often the way with kids, it's almost impossible to know how they'll react.

Sabryna is calm and smiling as she tells them. "*We* are going to have a houseguest." One of the many great things about Sabryna is that she can only smile if it's a real smile. And this is a real smile, and it is a big smile.

Willie and Devan look at each other. Then Sabryna tells them the tale of the new baby. We have no sense of what the boys are thinking.

Then Devan speaks: "How long will this baby be living here?"

I don't like the tone of *"this baby."*

So I field the question: "A few weeks, a few months, maybe even longer." No reaction.

Willie asks, "What's the baby's name?"

"I don't think she's absolutely fixed on a name. She's thinking she may name the baby for a relative, like an aunt or a grandma."

"So this baby is a girl?" asks Devan. His reaction sounds neither positive nor negative at the gender news.

"Can *we* give her a name?" Willie asks.

I'm thinking, and I'm sure Sabryna is thinking also, about the list of names we went through—Stupid-head, Antonio Brown, Dirtball, Lucy the Second, Killer Kahn, Spaz—before we settled on The Duke for our dog.

Sabryna has the correct, all-purpose, never-fail parental answer: "We'll see. We'll see." For this magical phrase to work, it must be said four times. So Sabryna adds another round. "We'll see. We'll see."

Willie yells, "Good deal." And this apparently requires a high five between him and Devan.

There are, of course, follow-up questions. But

the questions are practical ones: "Where will the baby sleep?" "Does the baby cry?" They ask nothing exceptionally serious, like, "Whose baby is this?" "Where did she come from?" Apparently in their world of *Guardians of the Galaxy*, babies can just, well, magically show up, like the baby who's showing up tomorrow.

We clear the table. The baby news has made the boys particularly helpful with the cleanup. *What in the world are they thinking?*

Sabryna begins scooping out sensible small portions of chocolate ice cream. Then quite suddenly the downstairs buzzer rings. We've heard it a thousand times before, but just in case we'd forgotten, Devan says, "It's only the night buzzer for the store."

Sabryna sighs. Then she says, "Probably some foolish neighborhood guy needing to pick up a six-pack of Red Stripe."

"Maybe it's the people with the baby," Willie says.

Sabryna goes to the very unreliable intercom and presses a button. "We're closed," she says firmly.

"No. I look for Mrs. Lucy's house," comes a foreign-accented male voice.

"Who do you want?" Sabryna asks.

"The midwife," the man says. "Is this her house?"

I'm instinctively worried that there's an emergency somewhere. I hurry to the intercom. I sure hope I won't be hurrying back to Gramatan University Hospital or making some unscheduled, unplanned neighborhood visit. I take the phone. "This is Lucy Ryuan. How can I help?"

The vaguely familiar voice comes back at me.

"I am Patrik Kovac. I am the father of Katra."

CHAPTER 31

I LEAVE WILLIE DOWNSTAIRS with Sabryna and Devan. A few minutes later Katra's father and I settle into my tiny and very untidy apartment.

Patrik Kovac sits on the one cleared chair in my living room. I sit on the edge of my foldout sofa. The foldout is, as always, open, messy, and covered with papers and books and clothing.

"There is a problem that I cannot keep inside me," Patrik says as I pour him a cup of reheated morning coffee, coffee that wasn't too great tasting when it was fresh.

"I cannot tell police. I cannot tell the neighbors. So I must tell you," he says.

Of course I am both extremely curious and extremely nervous as to what he's about to tell me. I am so accustomed to tales of abuse and poverty and immigration problems that I pretty much assume his story will fall into one of those categories.

"First I will ask, the people who hurt Katra, the people who stole my grandchild, do you catch them yet?" he asks. "Are they in the jail cell?"

"No, not yet." I do not share with him my belief that Blumenthal's investigation team is dragging its ass on the matter.

Then he leans forward in his chair. "Here is what I can tell you. The thief will be Russian, a man, maybe a woman, maybe both, maybe many people," he says. And his hands are shaking so much that he must rest his mug of bad coffee on the pile of magazines near his chair.

"And how do you know that?" I ask.

"Because I know, because I know you will know when I tell you my story."

Inside me is the urge to scream, *For Chrissake, get on with it, buddy. Just tell me the story*. But I don't have to scream. Patrik Kovac begins to explain.

Three years ago, he and his wife and his fourteen-year-old daughter, Katra, entered the United States. Back in Croatia they had bought forged immigration-visitor papers that showed proof of relatives living in Sunnyside, Queens. Of course they actually had no relatives living in Queens or anywhere else in the United States. Their visitor permits were good for only three months. Patrik and his wife, Mariska, lived in fear every day. He tells me that a person "never becomes accustomed to fear. But we move on. Things will work out."

I still am amazed by Patrik's youthful presence. He looks like a Brooklyn hipster.

"Katra works as nanny for a mother in Flushing. Mariska works to clean office building at 34th Street. Me? I try. But no job. Sometimes I sweep barbershop and beauty parlor. But no job. Little money. But we will move on."

I think Patrik may be planting the seeds of a sweet American immigrant success story. But I turn out to be really wrong with that prediction.

"Then last year Katra becomes pregnant." He looks

to the ground as if he's just spilled the saddest story of his life. And it very well may be that among his many problems this one is indeed the saddest.

In my world, pregnancy is not an unusual condition. It's my life's work.

"Katra, she say the father of children she cares for makes her pregnant. Then she says she is fired. And the wife says she will have her thrown out of country. And then..."

A long pause.

"And then?" I ask. I'm bracing for bad stuff. I'm guessing that perhaps Patrik went after the baby's father with a knife. I'm thinking that maybe they planned an abortion and then changed their minds. Turns out what I'm thinking isn't nearly as frightening as what he tells me.

"One morning, early, five o'clock, two visitors, a man and a woman, knock on the door. I think they are Russian. I think they look like Russians, the accents are like the sound of Russian."

Now the story really begins. The two "Russian" visitors have heard from one of the Kovacs' neighbors — they do not tell Patrik who has informed them — that Katra is going to have a baby.

"They say they can give us money for Katra's baby. They will buy the baby. They will give us one thousand dollars now and then they will give us nine thousand dollars more when they take the baby."

I just nod. I've heard of these deals before. Not often. Not many. But I have heard of them. When you're a New York midwife, you hear lots of scary stories.

"So we cry. And we cry. And we cannot stop crying. Mariska and Katra and I stand and cry in front of strangers who want to buy baby. The woman, she is nice. She comforts Katra. 'Oh, the baby will be loved,' the woman says. 'She will be kept warm and in good schools always.' The woman knows the people who want the baby."

Another pause. I say absolutely nothing.

Then, "Katra says okay. 'Ten thousand dollars!' she says. 'So much money.'"

"And you and your wife agree?" I ask.

"No. No, we do not agree. We scream that this cannot happen. We cry more and more. Finally, Mariska say maybe it's for best."

"So then you agreed?" I say.

"Yes. It is bad, but we say okay. Then we cry more and more."

I'm no genius. I'm no psychologist. But I'm smart enough to know that a story that ultimately ends in a brutal forced C-section and the kidnapping of a newborn is not over yet. I want to reach for my iPad and look up my GUH chart on Katra. I have a vague recollection that her arrangements with my midwife group were legit. But there's sometimes chaos and many screwups at a huge hospital, and…and Mr. Kovac has more to tell.

He says the female Russian visitor visited almost every week to see how Katra was doing. The woman brought candy and cookies and always bottles of sweet wine. Katra was growing bigger. She was healthy. She was apparently happy. The woman apparently did some basic prenatal examination: stethoscope on belly, blood pressure. But one day something different happened.

Last month the woman arrived with her sweets and her wine, and Katra made a startling announcement. "I want to keep the baby," she said.

"Don't be a stupid fool," the lady said. "The arrangement has been made."

"We will return the one thousand. We will not take the nine thousand," Katra said.

"The ship has sailed," the woman said.

The disagreement between the woman and the Kovac family was noisy, Patrik says, but brief. The woman was stern and cold and actually spit on the floor.

I take his hand and say, "This is a very bad lady."

Then Patrik says quietly, "But we are also very bad, to make this evil arrangement."

I shake my head no. I ask if anything else happened.

"Only when the bad lady is walking out the door."

"And what was that?" I ask.

"She say, 'Don't try to change things. If you do, no matter what you want or what you try to do, *we will find a way to get Katra's baby.*'"

And so they did.

CHAPTER 32

IT TAKES ABOUT THIRTY minutes for Patrik Kovac to unload his entire story of Katra's pregnancy and the Russian couple. It must be frightening to tell. It is frightening to hear. But once it's ended, I know I have to get in touch with either Leon Blumenthal or Rudra Sarkar or both.

Patrik, tears on his face, still trembling, comes with me to Sabryna's apartment. As always, I walk inside without knocking. Sabryna clicks off the television, and all three of them look at me nervously. Their curiosity is, of course, completely understandable.

"There's no time to explain everything. I promise I will. I'll also say that the news is not good. But we might end up okay," I say. "Right now I have to get back to the hospital. Like I said without saying, this is big stuff."

"Isn't it always?" says Willie, with a touch of child-like sarcasm.

"No. This really is," I say. "Sabryna, can Willie stay here?"

"Doesn't he always?" says Sabryna, with a touch of adultlike sarcasm.

Then Sabryna turns her attention to Patrik. She

says, "And I'm supposing that you're going to be here, too?"

Kovac looks at me for the answer to Sabryna's question.

"He could use a better cup of coffee than mine, probably with a big shot of Jameson in it. And see if he wants a plate of Lucky Pot."

Then I look at Patrik Kovac and say, "You're not really a true American until you see a Yankees game in the Bronx and have a nice big soup bowl full of Lucky Pot."

Understandably, Patrik looks confused. But I don't have time to run with my joke. I need to talk to one of those dozens of law enforcement personnel sitting around at my hospital doing nothing. I take out my cell phone and call the GUH main line.

Eventually someone says, "Gramatan University Hospital. How may I help you?"

"It's Lucy Ryuan, midwife," I say. "Please connect me to the NYPD/FBI setup in the residents' cafeteria."

Finally I hear Blumenthal's voice. I identify myself.

"What's up now, Ms. Ryuan?" I wouldn't call his tone of voice *polite,* but I might call it *civil*.

"I'm at home right now, Detective," I say, "but I've just met with Katra Kovac's father. He gave me a boatload of information on the attack and kidnap situation. I'm going to Uber back into Manhattan right now. You and I need to meet."

"Okay," he says. The tone of voice is now actually *polite*. "I was about to go out for a little supper. But I'll wait right here. Never want to miss one of your lectures."

I ignore the wise-guy crack and say, "Hey, I can bring something from home for you to eat."

"That'd be cool," he says. Maybe he is being sarcastic. I can't tell anymore.

"Yeah," I say. "We've got some delicious leftovers."

"Sounds good. Thank you."

I don't dare ask him the question I'm thinking. *How do you feel about meatloaf and cornflakes?*

CHAPTER 33

Immaculate Conception Hospital
West Chelsea, New York City

IMMACULATE CONCEPTION HOSPITAL sits directly next to the High Line on West 24th Street. All patient rooms have a view of either the majestic Hudson River or the wacky-beautiful High Line itself.

The patients pay dearly for the view. In return they receive the pampered service most of them are used to. A person might go to NewYork-Presbyterian for bypass surgery or Mount Sinai for cancer, but if they need a facelift, an eyebrow lift, or a tummy tuck, that person heads over to Immaculate.

Immaculate is the only hospital in New York City to offer an unusual and frequently sought surgical service: hand rejuvenation. After all, nothing undermines a magnificent facelift more than bumpy, blue-veined, wrinkled old hands.

Immaculate is also the hospital to visit if one is very rich and slated to give birth. The birthing rooms were designed by the late "Prince of Chintz," Mario Buatta, with a lot of flowered fabrics and lamps made from antique Chinese tea containers.

Immaculate Conception may sound like the name

of a Catholic hospital, and when it was founded in 1880, it was run by nursing nuns, but now, facelifts and chintz curtains. Times have changed. So have cafeteria conversations.

"I played tennis yesterday with my friend Kenny Kelleher. He's the gastro guy up at Gramatan. He says the cops and the FBI are guarding the place like it's Fort Knox," says dermatologist-surgeon John Aquilino.

Dr. Aquilino is having a late-afternoon taste of a delicious 2006 Puligny-Montrachet in the Immaculate Conception wine bar with Dr. Jeffrey Schlotman, a surgeon whose specialty is fast-recovery breast re-duction.

"That kidnapping stuff must be driving Barrett Katz crazy," says Aquilino.

"Couldn't happen to a nicer little prick," says Schlotman.

"The crazy location. The welfare patients. The welfare bums. The whole thing. I wouldn't let anyone I know go to Gramatan for a hangnail. You're better off dead."

"You get what you pay for," says Schlotman.

They agree.

CHAPTER 34

I AM IN SUCH a rush to tell Patrik's story that I don't take the time to even spoon up the leftovers I promised. Instead, I end up bringing Leon Blumenthal food that's even worse than meatloaf and cornflakes: six small peanut-butter and cheddar-cheese crackers, barbecue-flavored potato chips, and two Drake's Ring Dings. All are courtesy of the lobby vending machine.

I drop Blumenthal's "dinner" on his desk-table. He glances at the assembled junk food and says, "I'll eat this later. When I can give it my full attention."

That's obviously my signal to start talking.

Blumenthal listens intently as I tell him the extraordinary story that Patrik Kovac just told me. Blumenthal nods occasionally. He types frequently on his laptop. He does *not* eat even a morsel of the crackers or snack cakes.

"Did Kovac say if he or anyone in his family got the names of the Russian duo?" he asks.

"I don't know. I didn't ask."

Shit. I'm not a pro. I'm arrogant, but I'm an amateur. *Damn it.* That's probably exactly what Blumenthal is thinking, too. Well, too bad, because Mr. Kovac came to me.

"Don't worry," Blumenthal says. "We'll ask. But chances are great that they didn't give their names, and if they did, Kovac was so nervous that he probably wouldn't have remembered the names anyway. Did he say if his daughter, Katra, knew he was coming to see you?"

"Uh...no. He didn't say..."

"And you didn't think to ask," Blumenthal adds.

What I'm thinking now, however, is that Blumenthal is ready to heave a sigh of frustration and toss me out, but I also want to believe that he is interested in Patrik's story. And, well, when all is said and done, I'm the person who owns the story.

What Blumenthal says next, however, does not re-assure me of his interest. He flips his laptop closed and says, "Okay, good. What you've found out, this stuff you just told me, it might turn out to be helpful."

I explode. Out loud. Big. Really big.

"'Helpful'? This is a goddamn breakthrough. This is what they call a lead. I don't know you that well at all, Detective, but under normal circumstances, with a normal detective, this would be considered very, very big news. You take this info from Katra's father, and you add this to the high-heeled woman in the video, and then you just sit there."

Now it's Blumenthal's turn to explode. And he does a full Vesuvius. He stands up so quickly that it seems he might actually hit the ceiling.

"You're judging me on *how I react* to what you've told me? I haven't been enthusiastic enough? Is that it? Are you waiting for smoke to come out of my ears? Or would you prefer that I jump on this table and dance a jig? Maybe we should plan a testimonial dinner for you. We'll ask the mayor to—"

I try to interrupt. "Listen. All I'm saying—"

"No. Listen for once to what I'm saying. Could you do that, Ms. Ryuan?"

My teeth are clenched. I'd like to punch this dude. But I shut up. He quickly calms down, runs his hand through his hair. He tries to sound even-tempered, and then he begins to explain.

"My job is to gather *all* the information. Got that? *All* the information. Yes, the catch you made on the video, the nurse in high heels, that's terrific. Absolutely terrific. This news about what Patrik Kovac told you is equally terrific. It's a goddamn lucky break."

Now he looks at the ceiling. Then he looks at the wall. Then he looks at his laptop screen. This is a guy trying to calm down.

The silence that accompanies all this looking is stunning. I, of course, take the opportunity to speak.

"So? What does it all mean? Your little lecture? Your anger?" I ask.

Then he says calmly, "There are some things you don't know."

I rub my burning eyes. I wipe my sweaty palms against my shirt.

"There's some other news," he says. He looks at me, then sits down again in his chair. "This is not good news."

"For Chrissake, tell me. Just tell me," I yell.

"We've had another kidnapping," he says.

Both Blumenthal and I allow quite a few seconds to pass.

"Holy shit," I say. "With all the security? The guards? The alarms? The—"

"Hold it, Ms. Ryuan. Hold it for just a minute. Let me finish."

I hold it. And knowing me, it will probably be *"for just a minute."*

"The baby wasn't taken from *this* hospital. The baby, one hour old, I should add, was kidnapped from Immaculate Conception down in Chelsea."

"Oh, my God," I say. "Didn't they have security? Didn't they have guards? What with everything that's happened up here?"

"Of course they had extra security and guards. They had security all over the place. Every hospital in every borough is on high alert. But it happened. And it'll probably happen again. And I'm going to move heaven and earth and even hell to try to stop it."

I nod…gently. I notice that Blumenthal's hands now have a slight quiver to them. I see the big patches of sweat on his forehead, his upper lip, his shirt.

"Holy shit," I say. "What does this mean?"

"It means, in medical terms, that we've got an epidemic."

CHAPTER 35

BLUMENTHAL AND I NO longer have very much to say to each other. I thought he was passive and uncaring. He thought I was an aggressive bitch. No, of course he never said that, but I'm pretty good at reading attitudes. Right now I've just got to get out of here.

Blumenthal's colleagues—police officers, FBI agents, file clerks, junior detectives, full detectives—watch me turn and walk quickly to the cafeteria door, exit, and close the door firmly, but without slamming it. What they cannot see, however, is the fact that I stop outside the door. I stand and wait. I want to hear if anything is going to be said about my visit.

Sure enough, almost immediately Leon Blumenthal yells, "I need everyone over here. Right now." Then, for good measure, he adds, "Right now means right now."

Here it comes. I know I'll hear something like, *"You all know that crazy midwife. Well, she's crazier than ever."* Or maybe, *"Wait'll I tell you the ridiculous 'tip' I just got from that Ryuan woman."*

Here's what Blumenthal actually says: "Lucy Ryuan, a respected midwife here at GUH, just stopped by. I'm sure you all saw her, and some of you may have even heard parts, if not all, of our conversation. Ms. Ryuan delivered some highly provocative, highly important information. If even half of what she said is true, then we've now got something of a lead, a real lead. I'm going to immediately text some of you with next-step orders. I'd give them out right now, but I'm sure Ms. Ryuan is standing outside listening in."

Son of a bitch. This guy is no fool. But I'm surprised and pleased about what I've just overheard.

And then, "Don't lean too hard against the door, Lucy. Someone might open it suddenly."

It's Rudi Sarkar. He's looking like the autumn cover of *Esquire*. He's wearing dark-gray slacks, a Paul Stuart—I'm guessing—blazer, and his adorable smile. Bright white teeth, good haircut, the whole deal.

"What is it that you are listening for so intently?" he asks.

I know from experience that I will always end up in a better place by telling the truth than a lame lie. And most of my lies do turn out to be lame.

"To be honest—" I begin.

"Please do be honest," Sarkar says.

I begin again. "To be honest, I just came from speaking with Detective Blumenthal, and I was wondering if there would be any follow-up, like if he had an announcement to make to his staff."

"And did he? Something malignant?"

Good God, do doctors just always use medical terminology?

"Indeed he did, but it turned out not to be, as you say, a malignant announcement," I say.

"I am not surprised," says Sarkar. We begin walking toward the elevators.

"I know that you think well of him, Dr. Sarkar—"

"Rudi," he corrects.

"You've already said, Rudi, that you looked into Blumenthal's history and that he's a good guy," I remind him.

"I am not so certain that he is 'a good guy.' But I know that he is a very good detective. And I know this because the police commissioner is a patient of mine."

"Sally Poblete is a patient of yours?" I say.

"Yes, she has been for a number of years."

"Is the commissioner pregnant?"

"No," he says. *There goes that smile again.* "But she is trying to be."

I nod. Sarkar continues. Is he being indiscreet or is this well-known information? I decide not to ask.

"Ms. Poblete already knew that Blumenthal was the senior detective on this baby-thievery case." Only Sarkar would use a word like *thievery*. "And Ms. Poblete told me we should be grateful he is on this. She called Detective Blumenthal 'one of the finest of the finest.' But she did then add that occasionally Blumenthal 'pushes it.' Those are her words. When I asked what she meant, she said that this detective is often quite creative in ignoring the rules. Then she again said that we should be very thankful to have him."

I say nothing, but I'm thinking, *Thankful?* Maybe if he cracks this case. Then I'll be thankful.

"May I escort you up the stairs?" Sarkar asks.

"Yeah, sure," I say, and I walk past the elevators, heading to the door of the internal stairway.

My mind is still churning. Commissioner Poblete said that Blumenthal is *creative* in ignoring the rules?

I come up with an idea. A great idea. A very, very creative idea.

I'm going to find out just how far Blumenthal is ready to *push* it. I'm going to see just how creative he might care to be.

"You go up ahead of me," says Sarkar as we enter the stairwell. "That way I'll be able to catch you if you fall."

"It also means that you'll have a terrific view of my gluteus maximus," I say.

"Lucy, please!" he says with mock surprise. "And anyway, don't worry. Do remember. I *am* a gyne-cologist."

CHAPTER 36

TWO MINUTES LATER DR. Rudra Sarkar and I go our separate ways. He returns to his office, but I return to the stairwell. I'm going back to see Leon Blumenthal.

As I enter the makeshift operations room and approach Blumenthal's table, I swear there's a very slight smile on his face.

"What took you so long to get back to me, Ms. Ryuan?" he asks. Yes, that is definitely a smile on Blumenthal's face.

And he's even better looking now that he's lost the grumpy-dad expression. Funny how a guy's face can turn from meh to handsome just because of the mood he's in and, I guess, the mood I'm in.

"Nothing like a funny detective when there's a multiple kidnapping and a brutal assault to be investigated," I say.

"Haven't you heard the expression 'If you don't laugh, you may end up crying'?"

I roll my eyes a bit.

Then Blumenthal says, "Anyway, how can I help you?"

"I have a great idea."

"I was afraid of that," he says.

"Look," I say. "If you're going to be an asshole, then I—"

"Sorry," he says. "And I mean it." I think he does. There's something almost annoyingly *real* about Leon Blumenthal. He's so real that what he's thinking and what he's feeling always seem to show up at the same time.

"Let's move over to that table near the fruit smoothie machine," Blumenthal says as he stands up. "I think my colleagues may be a little too interested in our conversation."

"That's intriguing. They're going to hear all about it the moment I leave the room," I say.

Blumenthal says nothing.

We walk to the end of the room, and I discover that we are standing in a jungle of "healthy food" vending machines. Who knew that such machines existed when I was buying junk food for Blumenthal an hour earlier? One vending machine supplies fresh-ingredient smoothies; another has a complete selection of Nature Valley bars; a third sends out small packets of sunflower seeds or granola or unsalted raw cashews.

Give me a Wendy's chocolate Frosty and a Milky Way candy bar any day.

Blumenthal and I sit down.

"So what's up?"

"I've got a plan," I say. "Hear me out before you say no."

"Go," he says. And at least he's acting interested.

"It's simple," I say.

"That's always good," Blumenthal says. "Simple works for me."

"It's simple, but it's also dangerous."

"That's not always good."

The moment I am actually about to tell Blumenthal my idea, I realize it does seem incredibly dangerous. But it also seems exciting, and most important, it seems like it could work.

"Begin," he says. "Come on. Let's bring this plane in for a landing."

"Okay. I will pose as a pregnant woman, a poor pregnant woman. I can do an Irish accent. I can do a low-class English accent. I can certainly do a low-class Brooklyn accent."

Blumenthal nods a bit.

I continue. "So we'll get the name of the Russian couple from Patrik Kovac. I'll contact them, or you'll have somebody credible contact them, and then I'll meet with them. I'll make arrangements to sell them my baby, and then—"

Blumenthal begins shaking his head back and forth.

I try to ignore him and keep talking. "We'll start with the first payment. I know that we'll have to get a payment. Depending on where we meet them, we can have surveillance cameras. Then we—"

Blumenthal stands up. "Stop. Stop right there, Ms. Ryuan." And, yes, he is speaking in a fairly loud voice.

"No. I won't stop. This is a good plan. And I know that deep inside you think it's good, too." I stand up to face him.

But he's on a roll. He keeps talking. "No. I absolutely do not think it's a good plan. Deep inside me or just on my surface, I do not think it's a good plan. It's stupid. It's foolish. It's unprofessional. These Russians aren't amateurs. This isn't a TV show. This isn't a movie. Don't you think the Russian couple are part of a larger group? How do you imagine pulling this off? Do you plan on stuffing a pillow in your jeans to fool them? Of course not. Think it through, Lucy. For God's sake, think it through. They'll have gynecologists and pediatricians and thugs with guns and knives. Stick to delivering babies."

That last line—*"Stick to delivering babies"*—is the one that really kicks me hard in the stomach.

I know Blumenthal is being sensible. Maybe he's even absolutely right. But now I'm in that weird position of not being able to back down. I search for a defense. And I come up with a really shitty one.

"I'm trying to be proactive," I say.

"Proactive?" he says, loud enough for a few of the people at the other end of the room to suddenly look toward us. "Proactive? *Proactive* is the dumbest new made-up word in the English language. It's a synonym, a synonym for wasting time, for making a lot of noise for no real reason."

I decide to storm away from the table before he can storm away.

I get to the door of the cafeteria. I turn around and say exactly what I feel like saying.

"Remember this, Detective Blumenthal. Remember that I gave you a golden opportunity. Remember it when another baby goes missing."

"Wait, Ms. Ryuan," he says loudly.

The strength of his voice freezes me in place. The next thing I know, Blumenthal is standing close to me. Closer than he should.

"Look. I really do understand your passion about what's going on. I really do."

"No. I don't think you—"

"Take me at my word."

And suddenly I feel as if I will.

"Take a break. That's my advice. Get away. Take a break. Go to the beach. Go to the country. Go to the movies. Do something. Take ninety-six hours to stop delivering babies, stop thinking about this case."

I look into his hazel eyes. For the first time, I don't have the urge to disagree with him.

"When you get back—after that little break—we can talk again. You have done a lot for this case, and I appreciate the help. You are one smart woman."

CHAPTER 37

I PRACTICALLY RUN BACK to my office. Not in anger. Not in frustration. Not for any reason but that I'm tired, and Blumenthal might be right. And—oh, hell—I don't know what I'm even doing.

Up those same damned back stairs. I'm breathing heavily, and my heart is pounding. I've gone full speed.

It's about midnight, but of course GUH, under siege and security, is as hectic as if it were noon. I fade into the hospital crowd. Guards and NYPD officers patrol the halls. Patients buzz their buzzers. The air is pierced by the cries of "Nurse. Nurse. Please, Nurse." The PA system regularly blasts announcements like "Dr. Somebody, please report to Room Someplace immediately." Orderlies joke with nurses. Babies wail.

I pass through the dark and empty waiting room of the Midwifery offices. I notice the lights are on in Tracy Anne's cubicle. I step inside.

"What's keeping you here?" I say.

"Gina Esposito's husband is driving in from Brooklyn. Gina's having contractions. In fact, I should get over to the birthing room now," Tracy Anne says.

"You want me to hang out? I can help," I say.

"No. Don't you dare try to help. Get home, and get

some sleep. I don't mean to be disrespectful, but Troy and I are both worried about you," she says.

"There's nothing to worry about," I answer, not really believing what I'm saying.

"Well, all I can suggest is this: if you've got a mirror handy, take a good look in it. You look deader than a corpse."

"There is nothing 'deader than a corpse,'" I say.

"Yeah? Well, just look in a mirror."

I chuckle, but I don't need Tracy Anne or a mirror to tell me that I'm exhausted. Pissed off and exhausted. Frustrated and exhausted. Sad and exhausted. But in any case, exhausted.

With a note of eagerness, Tracy Anne says, "When you get a chance, maybe you can fill me in on what's going on. Troy won't let on. He says that it's for you to let me know."

"Honestly, Troy doesn't know the half of it. I'll let you both know real soon. I'd tell you now, but I just don't have the energy," I say.

"It's okay. I've gotta get over to Gina and her baby," Tracy Anne says. She stands and touches my shoulder as she walks past me. "Go home and relax, Lucy. Just a little. Okay?"

I'm standing at the entrance to Tracy Anne's cubicle. Her tiny space is a landslide of papers and medical books, a poster of Beyoncé, a plastic skeleton of the pelvic area, a bad reproduction of an Andy Warhol Marilyn Monroe print.

I reach for my cell phone. A spontaneous gesture, I guess.

I scroll down to R SARKAR (EMERGENCY ONLY). I press the corresponding key for Rudi's home number. After a few rings I hear that voice.

"Lucy, this is a first. You're calling me at my house. I am extremely flattered, to say the least." Sarkar's soothing baritone is in full seduction mode.

"Don't be flattered just yet. I'm calling to ask a favor," I say.

"For you, I would move the world."

"Well, not the world. But how about moving your Lexus?"

"You want me to buy you a Lexus?"

"No, I want you to loan me that big, beautiful blue Lexus of yours. Just for a few days."

"Where are you going?" he asks.

"Look," I say. "If there's going to be an application form, I'll borrow a car from someone else. All I know is that I don't trust my Hyundai to make it beyond five miles from my house. And I'm going a little farther than that."

"Very well. Of course you can take my car on your little trip." He pauses, then he goes in for the big one. "Would you like me to accompany you? As you know from experience, I am a very good driver."

"Absolutely not," I say. "Where I'm going, you wouldn't exactly fit in."

"Ah, someplace like a lady's spa, eh?" he asks.

"Not quite. But I hope I can relax there and come back feeling really refreshed."

"Will you have company on this journey? A man, perhaps?"

"A young man," I say. "And that's it for the questions, please. Any more and I'll just contact Hertz.com."

"My car is now your car."

CHAPTER 38

SOMETIMES A BODY JUST needs to go back to where she came from. So that's what I'm doing. I'm going home, home to Walkers Pasture, West Virginia.

My boy, Willie, and Willie's dog, The Duke, are along with me, and my worries are seat-buckled into Rudi Sarkar's midnight-blue Lexus, playing Catch Me If You Can with the radar machines on the Pennsylvania Turnpike.

Walkers Pasture is just a tiny slice of a town a few miles from the Ohio border, but it's home, and it's the place I visit when my brain needs straightening out. And does my brain ever need straightening out right now. I need a rest from the likes of Leon Blumenthal and Rudra Sarkar, and the army of guards and doctors and cops who have surrounded my life.

Even just on the road to home I can feel my West Virginia twang returning.

The very name of the town, Walkers Pasture, has a story. Here's the short version: In 1895, Mr. Walter Walker dug a coal mine in his hilly, overgrown cow pasture. Among the men who worked that mine were my great-grandfather, my grandfather, one of my uncles, and my own father. Even with all those strong Ryuan men helping out, it took them nearly a century to strip the mine bare. When that happened, the mine was closed, and the state of West Virginia renamed the area The Wholly Incorporated Town of Walkers Pasture. A town? This patch of land? Not really, it was (and pretty much still is) just a few hundred tract houses built during LBJ's War on Poverty. There's a one-woman post office the size of a horse stall, a good diner with decent coffee, a fairly small grammar school, a fairly large opioid problem, and mostly neat front yards, with only an occasional shell of a rusted Chevy Malibu for decoration.

I know it would sound insane to my city-raised friends, but I actually had a good time growing up there. Maybe it was my basic aggressiveness, because I just didn't let people get under my tough skin. Sure, the town has its share of substance abuse issues, but most of us only smoked weed and drank rye whiskey for our highs, my brother and his buddies being the exception to that.

All that aside, the biggest reason for my good memories of Walkers Pasture is my family. My childhood was a happy one because of my mom, a tiny, super-smart woman known to almost everyone in her world as Big Lucy.

I was the only help Big Lucy had in caring for her long-dying husband and her drugged-out son. I worked hard, but Big Lucy worked so much harder. I won't say she was always smiling, but I will say that she rarely cried. She poured herself two snorts of Jim Beam every night, then she and Mr. Beam settled down in front of the CBS news programs. She watched the news so intensely that Daddy used to say she could, at any moment, fill in for the secretary of state. Later on, my mom would say ten Hail Marys in front of her plastic Lady of Fatima statue. She was and *is* one of a kind.

Big Lucy is still a certified midwife, but she doesn't do much birthing anymore. When she started out helping women with their deliveries, most of her births took place in houses—in beds and on couches and tables and floors. When she wasn't catching babies, Big Lucy worked at a nursing home in Parkersburg. Her only fun time seemed to be her alternate Saturday nights with her friend Audrey, the two of them playing the slot machines at the Wheeling Island Casino.

That's my town, and that's my family, and I still keep coming back—especially when I need to shake my blues away and clear my big-city head. Next exit ramp? Walkers Pasture.

CHAPTER 39

WILLIE AND THE DUKE and I make the trip to Walkers Pasture in a little over seven hours, with just one stop: to walk the dog, hit the bathroom for humans, and consume twenty-five Chicken McNuggets.

I do not call ahead. Mom has no idea that we're showing up. That's how we operate with each other. She hears us pull into the driveway. Big Lucy and her cane rush out to greet us with an explosion of "Holy cow!" and "Holy shit!" and "Did you want to give me a heart attack?" She has mastered the craft of smiling and crying at the same time.

Big Lucy shouts at her only grandson, "Who drove? Willie or The Duke?"

Willie, a real little wise guy, answers, "We took turns. And then when we got tired, we let Mom drive."

My mother hugs Willie so tight that even she feels compelled to say, "You just tell me when I'm hugging you too hard, Willie."

"Now!" he shouts.

So she turns to me and hugs me just as hard. As far as I'm concerned, she can never hug me hard enough or long enough. As Mom and I hug, I can see two men over her shoulder. Coming through the screened front door are my dad and my brother, Cabot. To put it bluntly, my dad is a mess, a frightful mess. He can't weigh much more than 110 pounds. A small plastic oxygen tube is attached to his nostril, and the tube itself is attached to a portable oxygen tank on wheels. Daddy hobbles and stumbles along with his walker. Cabot wheels the oxygen tank, looking none too sure of himself.

In fact, Cabot doesn't look a helluva lot better than Daddy. My brother is almost as frail and skinny as our father. Cabot's eyes are red rimmed. His head twitches. His brown hair is greasy and matted. His arms shake terribly as he tries to guide the oxygen tank behind Daddy.

Mom sees her two men on the tiny front porch. She stops hugging and starts yelling. "Harold, you should be staying inside on the couch. Cabot, you should be inside with him. You're in no proper state of mind to be wheeling the oxygen."

Two things are immediately clear to me: one, Daddy simply does not hear his wife talking; two, Cabot is still a serious drug user. I break away from Mom and rush toward my father, who looks up at me. He's confused.

"It's me, Daddy. It's Lucy," I say. I kiss him, but he bends his head back down so quickly that I end up kissing the top of his mostly bald head.

"Where's that little monkey-faced kid of yours?" Cabot asks. He laughs as he speaks, and I know he means it as a joke, but there's a flatness to his voice, a definite lack of humor. It makes me wince slightly, even though I know that Willie and his uncle Cab usually have a really good relationship. It's almost like a friendship between two young boys. Now Willie runs toward me and Daddy and Cabot. The next thing I know, Cabot is rubbing Willie's hair, and I'm trying to hold the oxygen cart steady.

"Hey, bro," Cabot says to Willie. "I got the new Call of Duty game. Come on inside here so I can beat the shit outta you."

"Nice way to talk in front of a child, Cab," I say. But my opinion doesn't count for much down here in Walkers Pasture. Willie has taken hold of Cabot's hand, and they're heading back through the front door. Even The Duke is barking behind them and following. Mom and I are both involved in trying to turn Daddy around to begin the painful journey back to the front door.

"It's amazing," I say to my mother as we baby-step to the door. "Willie's always had a fancy for Cabot. Now even The Duke's taken a shine to him."

"I know. I know. Most grown-ups think Cabot's just a lazy druggie, throwing his life away," Mom says. "And I guess they're right. But you know, Lucy, sometimes children and animals have better instincts than grown-ups."

I disagree completely, but I don't say so.

We are at the front door, helping Daddy get up the step to the inside. I lift his left leg. The leg is in. Mom lifts the right leg. It's in. It feels like the three of us are climbing Mount Everest.

CHAPTER 40

MY MOM HAS A big voice. She never shouts, but if she had been an actress she would've been heard in the last row of the balcony. At the moment she's calling from the kitchen.

"If somebody doesn't come help me shell these butter beans, we'll be eating nothing but pork shoulder and fresh air for dinner."

I'm in my old bedroom. I'm lying on my old bed, the one with the red-and-blue plaid cotton spread. Willie will sleep on the other bed, the one I always called the "guest bed," the one with the matching red-and-blue plaid cotton spread.

Right now everything in our house is looking and sounding like Hallmark cards and Norman Rockwell paintings. Willie and Cabot are playing their video game. Although Cabot is shaking so much that it's a wonder he can even hold the controls.

Daddy's been transferred to his wheelchair, and he's fallen asleep with his earbuds in, listening to some sweet George Jones tunes. And Mom is basting the pork shoulder and apparently shelling the butter beans all by her lonesome. I can guess what else is for dinner: Mom is the only person I've ever known who manages to make Rice-A-Roni from scratch.

"So good that it tastes just as fine as the packaged stuff," she always says. Mom's Rice-A-Roni is deadly rich, with one or two sticks of margarine, and butter beans swimming in more margarine. To top it off, she'll crack open one of her homemade jars of cranberry sauce with pecans.

I jump up quickly from the bed. That sense of teenage déjà vu drifts in and out of my senses: I'm me at fourteen with a basketball game tonight. I'm me right now, and I spot Willie's *Star Wars* backpack on the "guest bed." I'm fourteen, and in a second, I'm a grown-up. And in a minute, I'm standing over a colander with my mom, shelling butter beans.

"I saw that big shiny red Mercedes parked smack across the street, Mom," I say as I begin squeezing beans from their casings. "It's so big that it takes up almost two parking spaces."

"Yeah," she says. "I see it there sometimes." Her voice has a forced sort of nonchalance. But she knows where I'm heading with my question about the fancy Mercedes SUV.

"Balboa Littlefield's car, right? Balboa's always had a red car," I say. "A fancy red car. When I was in high school, Balboa had a red Pontiac Firebird, then a Thunderbird. He must have run out of different kinds of birds, 'cause this one is a Mercedes. A red Mercedes."

Mom doesn't answer. She pretends to be distracted by the arrival in the kitchen of The Duke, who must have grown tired watching Willie and Cabot play Call of Duty.

"How about a nice fresh butter bean, Mr. The Duke?" Mom asks as she tosses one into the dog's mouth. The Duke suddenly has an odd expression on his face. Then he spits it quickly onto the floor.

Mom says to The Duke the same thing she used to say to me and Cabot when we were children: "You just don't know what tastes good."

The Duke, disappointed, curls up at our feet and closes his eyes. I return to the conversation that Big Lucy thought she'd escaped.

"We were talking about the red Mercedes, Mom," I say.

"Were we?" she asks. Suddenly she's quiet and very innocent, two things she never has been.

I say nothing. Then after a few seconds she speaks sternly. "Oh, for God's sake, Lucy, of course you know, I know, we both know that that shiny piece of car belongs to Balboa Littlefield. He's also got a powder-blue Mercedes-Benz just like that one."

Now it's my turn to be perturbed. "That son of a bitch has been making money for twenty years dealing drugs to everyone in this town. Nothing ever changes here," I say. I'm shelling butter beans as fast and angrily as I can.

"Nothing nobody can do about it, Lucy. He's considered to be an upright citizen here in Walkers Pasture. There's even talk that they're going to name that playground with the kiddie pool sprinkler after the wealthy Mr. Littlefield."

"It makes my blood boil," I say. "They'd be better off naming it after the devil himself."

"They just can't stop Balboa. He pays off the cops. He pays off the judges in Wheeling. He gives out packets of marijuana like they were pumpkin seeds."

My turn again. "And Balboa Littlefield is the reason you've got a son inside, age thirty-two, shaking and sweating, unemployed and weighing less than The

Duke, and, I dunno, useless, awful, stinking. I've run out of words."

"That's a first," Mom says.

I'm not amused.

Well, actually I am, but I'm not about to laugh.

Then she adds seriously, "Listen. It's not entirely Balboa Littlefield's fault. It's a problem only because weak folks like Cabot—"

"Oh, please, Mom. Don't. Just don't."

And she stops. At least for a few seconds.

Born and raised here, she has lived on hope and prayer all her life. She has watched the opioid epidemic grow bigger and uglier every month of every year. My brother is just one of so many folks in Walkers Pasture who chew OxyContin like breath mints. Mom knows all this, but she still has nothing but hope and prayer.

My mother kneels on the floor and begins petting The Duke. Then she talks to him. This isn't the first time she's used this dog-and-lady trick.

"Funny how fancy-ass people from New York can be just as dumb and stubborn as folks from a pissant little town like Walkers Pasture. Yep, they find it easier to blame their problems on other people. Now, I'm not saying that Balboa Littlefield is a fine upstanding citizen. Recently I heard him referred to as 'an A-one asshole.' And I sure do agree with that description. I think Balboa is evil incarnate. But the people who buy drugs from him are just as much to blame, especially if they've been helped by other people, like the drug users whose Mom and Daddy paid for treatment center visits over and over again, especially the mom whose knees hurt from praying and never got those prayers answered. We can bitch and carry on about Balboa himself, but because someone asks you to sin, it doesn't mean..." And then she stops. Her words turn to tears.

I kneel down beside her. I hold her shoulders. She stops crying.

"Are those butter beans all shelled, Lucy?"

That's Big Lucy.

CHAPTER 41

"YOU GOT A TAPEWORM inside you, bro?" Cabot asks Willie as my boy shovels in his third helping of honey-baked pork shoulder.

"Maybe I do," Willie says. Willie's voice is sharp and high-pitched. Cabot slurs his words. He's not drunk, but he sounds like he is. I don't think Willie notices his pronunciation, but I'm sure Big Lucy does. Cabot squints his eyes shut and open, then shut again, then open.

"Open your mouth real wide," Mom says to Willie. "I'm gonna check for a tapeworm."

Willie obeys. He stretches his mouth open.

Then Mom becomes a serious detective, looking inside her grandson's mouth. "No!" she declares. "No. No tapeworm in there, just a pile of teeth and a very large tongue."

Willie, laughing, goes back to his pork shoulder, and I wonder if anyone else notices that Cabot's question about the tapeworm is the first time during supper that he has even spoken. Cabot has eaten almost nothing, only a few sweet bites of Mom's ridiculously delicious Strawberry Jell-O and Red Cabbage Salad. (Don't judge it until you've taken a taste.) The only person quieter than Cabot is my father. He sits with his head bowed. He eats nothing.

"You look so tired, Mom," I say.

She shakes her head back and forth. "No. I'm too excited having you and Willie here to be tired. But...soon as Willie finishes eating his pork— assuming he doesn't want a *fourth* helping—I'll start getting Daddy washed and into bed."

"I'll help you," I say.

"No need to," Mom says. "We've got our system, and to be honest, I think Daddy would be embarrassed."

"Would you be angry if I asked him, Mom?"

"Of course not," and I know she is telling the truth. I lean in toward my father.

"Are you sure you wouldn't like me to help Mom when it's time for your sleep, Daddy?" I ask.

But he stares at me blankly. Yes? No? I don't care? Daddy says nothing.

Mom feeds Daddy a tiny forkful of the butter beans and rice. For a moment I think I see a spark of pleasure in his eyes. She holds a Flintstones juice glass to his lips, and he takes a sip of a little red wine mixed with ginger ale.

He still doesn't say a word.

Mom looks away. Her own eyes sparkle. I used to think she had a talent for holding back her tears. Now I see she has a different talent, a talent for making her eyes sparkle when the tears come.

Supper ends with the predictable, adorable, inevitable question from Willie.

"Hey, Grandma, how come Mom never makes a supper that tastes as good as yours?"

Hmmm. Visions of Lucky Pot must be dancing in his head.

"Well, you best ask your mom, but my guess would be that she's working her backside off to earn a living so you can have the finer things in life," says Mom.

Willie smiles. Then he says, "I think you might be right, Grandma."

My mother laughs, then says, "You are a clever little faker, Willie boy."

"It runs in the family," I say.

"Well," says Big Lucy, "I'll take Harold to our room, and I'll leave you all to the cleanup."

"I'll start," says Willie as he pops up from his place. Then he looks over at his uncle Cabot, who has his eyes closed, sleeping like the anonymous passenger next to you on a long airplane trip.

"I see you lost Cabot already," says my mother with a laugh as she wheels Daddy toward the little bedroom right off the kitchen.

I shake my head, and Willie says, "I'll let Uncle Cab sleep. He'll need all his energy for our big video game rematch."

I take the platter of shredded pork shoulder into the kitchen. I know my mother will repurpose it once, if not twice, during the week. Tacos? Noodles, pork, and American cheese casserole? I spoon it into a Tupperware container.

Willie walks in with four glasses. He holds them cautiously with the fingers of his left hand. And he balances four dinner plates waiter-style on the inside of his right arm. Amazingly, he doesn't drop anything.

"Let's not try that again, buddy. Okay?"

"Don't be a-scared, Mom. I'm good at this."

"Did you just say 'a-scared'?" I ask with a touch of mock shock. "You've been in Walkers Pasture less than one day and you're talking like a West Virginian."

Then, from the dining room, we hear a thud, a big loud clump of a noise, the sound of something or someone falling. It is followed within only a second by the sound of china and glass crashing. Both Willie and I rush the few feet into the dining room.

Cabot is on the floor, motionless. The boy is clear out of it.

Willie and I quickly roll Cabot over onto his back. Willie is frightened. I am, too.

"I don't think Uncle Cab's breathing, Mom."

I have a rule with Willie: I never lie to him. Never. Ever. And right now I'm thinking maybe it's time to break that rule. I change my mind.

"No, he's not. Go to the side pocket of my suitcase. Get the med-emergency package," I say. Meanwhile, I begin thumping Cabot's chest. By the time I begin CPR, my mother is standing over me. She's holding a nasal spray.

"Here's his Narcan," Mom says. "He's OD'd. It's happened before." She holds Cabot's head and squeezes the naloxone into his right nostril. It should work. But it doesn't. "Oh, Jesus Christ!" she yells. "Cabot. Don't run out on me. Not now, baby. Not now."

Willie is back. He's barely controlling his tears. He's holding a syringe. And I am now holding the injection version of naloxone.

"Help me get his jeans off." I'm practically yelling. Within seconds the waist of Cabot's jeans is pulled down to his knees. In the next three seconds I notice so many things—his scrawny thighs, his filthy white jockey shorts, the dry brown scabs on his bloody knees.

I quickly push the syringe into his left outer thigh. Silence. Three seconds come across like three hours.

Then Cabot's eyes open. He is trying to focus. He looks at Willie.

"No worry, little bro," he says.

"Why'd you do this to yourself, Uncle Cabot?" says Willie.

Cabot tilts his head in the other direction, slightly away from Willie. Willie storms out of the dining room.

"Mom, call 911," I say.

Big Lucy doesn't budge. "No, Lucy. The EMTs are not going to do anything you haven't already done. You saved him. Your injection. That's what did it. God bless us all."

"He needs rehab, Mom. He needs rehab that's going to stick with him."

My mother nods. Cabot is trying to sit up. He's disoriented. He's rubbing his leg. He's reaching for his jeans.

"Don't move, Cab," I say. "Just stay put for a few minutes. Relax."

Cabot ignores me. He continues to tug at his jeans.

Then Willie yells from the dining room doorway. His voice is loud and angry. "You heard the lady, Uncle Cabot. Don't! Move!"

CHAPTER 42

TWO YEARS AGO, WHEN Willie and I spent Fourth of July weekend in Walkers Pasture, he and Cabot bonded over lots of crazy childish things—video games, cold spareribs smeared with grape jelly, the WeCrash Demolition Derby truck track—but, most passionately, they became best buds over (who would have guessed it?) miniature golf.

Not surprisingly, the two of them did not like the "course" in Wheeling. Not that I ever did a big survey, but all miniature golf courses look the same to me. Not to Cabot and Willie. No, their favorite place in the world was an hour-and-a-half ride away, the Hole in Fun, in Burgettstown, Pennsylvania.

How do my son and brother get to the Hole in Fun? Well, I've got to drive them while Mom stays home to watch Daddy. Fact is, Cabot lost his driver's license about forty times for DUI. So if they're going, I'm driving.

What about Cabot's near-death experience less than twelve hours ago? Well, he still looks like a burlap bag full of loose bones. I take his blood pressure, and it's a very low eighty over fifty-five. The man is still shaking. He's refused anything to eat (except for half a jelly doughnut) since the emergency naloxone injection. But the most alarming thing is that Balboa Littlefield's Mercedes is still parked across the street. Cabot has stood at the living room window and checked out the red car a few times, and I know my brother is just itching to pick up a few dozen Percocets or Vicodins.

"We should get heading to the golf place, Lucy," Cabot says.

I offer him a deal. I tell him that unless I *watch* him consume one fried egg, one slice of buttered toast, and a cup of half tea, half milk, I won't drive to Pennsylvania. I know he'll do it for Willie.

Privately I tell Mom that Cabot should be in bed or in a hospital or in rehab.

Her answer is simple: "You're absolutely right, honey, but the only place he wants to be is at a miniature golf place in Burgettstown, PA."

Egg gets eaten. Toast gets eaten. Mom and I sit together at the tiny kitchen table. We're alone for a few moments.

"You've been through so much, Mom. Daddy, Cabot. It never really stops, does it?" I say.

I'm not really expecting an answer, or at most, nothing more than a simple no or yes.

Instead she decides to open up. "It just looks a lot worse than it really is. Harold will join his Maker soon, and a man as good as your dad is sure to be let into heaven. With Cabot, well, I still think he can make it to getting clean. He's a son of a bitch with the drugs, but he could still pull through. Best of all, I got you and Willie, and even The Duke is being neat and nice this visit."

She pauses. She closes her eyes. Then she opens

them. "You might feel this yourself, you know. It's the birthing life that brought me most of my joy and most of my sorrow. The beautiful new babes for the moms and dads who wanted them so bad…Nothing could have been nicer than that. But…" And she pauses again.

"You're thinking about the babies you lost?" I suggest.

"No, not really. That's God's way. And, if I say so myself, I was a mighty fine midwife."

"You were," I say, and I do mean what I say.

"When I think about it," she says. And she takes a moment to do exactly that. Then she reminisces for both of us. "So many nervous-making things. The Nickelson twins. They had to send one of the two boys to Children's Hospital in Philly to figure out what his gender was. He had a whole hodgepodge of parts down there."

"I remember that. Today they would have waited until the baby was older and let him or her decide."

She talks about the time Larry Staubach, a farm equipment mechanic, was so drunk when Mom arrived for his child's birth that he stood watching the four hours of labor with a bottle of Dewar's in one hand and a pump-action hunting rifle in the other.

"I guess if I did something wrong, he was going to shoot me," Mom says, not joking. "Good thing that little Larry came out as perfect as the Lord intended him. Course little Larry didn't stay perfect. They got him for armed robbery of a hardware store up by Altoona."

Mama's memory battery is turned up real high now. She's enjoying the talking. She remembers piecing together double boilers and goose down pillows to make an incubator until an ambulance arrived. She remembers little children helping out with the delivery when there were no adult hands available. She even remembers an encounter that was so frightening "I thought I was walking through a horror movie."

I vaguely remember her telling me the tale once before.

"Two years ago, this very slick guy came up and sat next to me in Deedee's Diner. Introduced himself very proper. Said his name was Eagleburg or Eaglehead or something like that. He said he supplied newborns for a few rich people who couldn't have children of their own, all up in Harrison, New Jersey, some fancy-ass town outside New York. It sorta sounded creepy. I listened for a minute and then just moved myself to another seat at the counter. I needed money bad, but not that bad."

Mom doesn't even stop to catch her breath. She launches right into her next story. I serve myself a piece of lemon meringue pie.

"Some other time my friend Georgeann Shea— and I know Georgeann was usually an upright honest sort—wanted her and me to go into business together part-time. She knew a place in Maryland where you could get a certificate that legally let you use the title of doctor. She had this plan where she'd do massage therapy and I'd do prenatal and postnatal counseling. Once again, I could've used the cash, but I could never do something that evil. Midwives have to be honest."

Mom is on a roll. She can whitewash her memory of the bad old days to come back now as the very best of times. And why not? Anyway, I love her stories. But I've got to say that four of them is just about my limit.

"Another time there was this woman showed up, same age as me, claimed to be a midwife from Maryland. Hazel was her name, a good old-fashioned name. Hazel says she's a friend of an ob-gyn doc at Mercy Hospital in Charleston. Well, I had my doubts. After all…"

But Mom doesn't have the chance to finish her story. Suddenly Willie's voice comes shouting out from the living room.

"Mom, Grandma. Get in here fast!"

"Oh, shit," mother and daughter say at the exact same time. It has to be something bad for Cabot.

But then we hear Cabot say, "This little bugger beat me in four straight Call of Duty games."

"Are you crazy?" my mother says.

"No, really, Grandma," Willie says. "I really beat him four times."

"But your screaming out at me damn near killed me with fright," she says. This is the first time since we arrived that I hear Cabot laugh.

Two hours later, I'm paying ten dollars—five each—so Willie and Cabot can hit the miniature golf course.

CHAPTER 43

I'VE GOT TO BE honest. Is there a sweeter sight than watching Willie lining up his putt as if he were on the eighteenth hole down in Augusta? Yes, there is. That's the sight of my crazy messed-up brother trying to help Willie with his grip.

I'm sitting on a bench outside the enclosed "course." There's not much of a crowd here at the Hole in Fun: five annoying teenage boys who spend more time hitting one another with their dinky little clubs than they do hitting the ball. I see one mom and her two daughters playing. The mom yells a few times, "Oh, Tiffany, just kick the ball through the windmill door, for Chrissake. It's almost time for lunch."

I take out my phone and check my texts and emails. Tracy Anne tells me that Gina Esposito had a baby girl. The last line of the message is: She's going 2 name her Stephanie Tracy Anne Esposito.

I text back, Nice. Very nice. And I mean it.

Then there's an update from Troy: charts and statistics, mother weights and baby weights and appointment times, test results and problem assessments. Then a question from Troy: "Katz's office called.

Wants to know when you'll be back." Another email from Troy: "Detective B called four x yesterday. Should I give him your number?"

I respond, only a bit confused, only a bit curious. "Yes, give Blumenthal phone number. Thought I'd already given it to him."

I look up and see that my son and my brother are fueling up on Coca-Cola and Fritos at the refreshment stand. I know they're going to want to play again and again. I decide to call my mother and tell her that everything is fine, so very fine. I call her. When she answers, I say, "They're having a good time. They're doing well. Best friends," and then, to my complete surprise, I start to cry.

"What's wrong, Lucy?" Her voice is understandably nervous.

"Nothing," I say. "No, nothing really." I pause. Then I say, "I just wish that…I just wish it could stay like this all the time. Cabot and Willie and you and Daddy. Cabot being calm and Willie being happy. Daddy being…well, alive. You being…you. Busy and bustling around. And…I don't know. That's sort of all I want."

"That's what all of us want, honey. We want so little. And it's so hard to get even that."

I hear the call-waiting hiccup. The caller ID reads L BLUMEN NYPD.

Then I say the irritating words I hate saying or hearing: "Mom, I've got to take this call."

When I switch over, I say, "Hello, Detective. Didn't you tell me to take a vacation, stop delivering babies, stop butting into your case?"

"It doesn't sound like me, but I might have suggested something like that."

"Then why are you calling me, Detective?"

Then he says the magic words. "Because I need you here."

"When?"

Inevitably he answers, "Right this very minute."

CHAPTER 44

THERE'S QUITE A BIT of negotiating to do with my family in West Virginia before I can return to New York.

First hurdle: persuading Willie and Cabot to cancel another round of miniature golf so we can drive the hour-plus back to my parents' house and then begin the trip back to New York. I'm successful getting them off the "course" only because I promise that the next time we visit Walkers Pasture they can play at least *three* rounds of golf.

Yes, I know this basic bribery is not the correct way to raise good children. But I don't think it's going to ruin Willie's future.

Second hurdle: Mom suggests I can go back to New York whenever I want, but Willie should stay down in Walkers Pasture, West Virginia, with her and Daddy and Cabot for another day, as originally planned. I am utterly opposed. Adamantly opposed. So we have an impromptu family meeting in the living room. *Family meeting* has always been a euphemism in our house for *group argument*. We make believe we are the kind of family that always has family meetings; we most certainly are not.

We take our places on the sectional sofa. Mom

serves red Kool-Aid in plastic cups. Even Daddy seems attentive to the goings-on.

My first gambit falls flat on its face: "We were planning to leave tomorrow anyway, Willie."

Willie says, "Yeah, I know, but now I can stay longer and then take the train back to New York. Grandma said so."

So much for that, Lucy. Nice try.

"What about your friend Devan, Willie? He'll be lost without you."

"No way. He doesn't care. Devan has plenty of bigger kids to hang with. He actually prefers all those big dudes. Devan will not be lost without me," says Willie. I'm afraid Willie's right about that.

"What about Sabryna's new baby? Don't you want to see her?" It dawns on me that I do not know Val's baby's name. When we filled out the million forms, we used the phrase "Baby Girl Gomez."

Willie says, "Oh, c'mon, Mom. The baby?" He shrugs and looks up at his uncle.

Cabot looks at me and says, "Oh, c'mon, Mom. The baby?"

And speaking of moms, mine says, "Well, it seems to me that this meeting has hit a little bit of a snag. Come into the kitchen, Lucy honey. You can help me make some sandwiches for your road trip."

Of course I know what she's about to say. But of course I follow her into the kitchen.

"I know why you're fretting, and I don't blame you," she says. "You don't want Willie spending so much time with Cabot."

"Bingo!" I say.

"You know they won't ever go three feet out of my eyesight," she says.

"That's good to know, because Balboa Littlefield's car is parked only a hundred feet away."

"Oh, don't be such a Little Miss Worry Wart," she says. "Tomorrow we'll all drive to Pittsburgh and send Willie home."

"You know I love Cab," I say. "But I'm just afraid he'll be a bad influence on Willie."

"And you know I love Willie. And what I'm hoping is this: that Willie will be a *good* influence on Cabot."

"Bingo!" I say. "You win."

CHAPTER 45

I TELEPHONE RUDI SARKAR—from his own car—as The Duke lounges along the full length of the back seat, eyeing me. Hands-free dialing. All the caller does is speak into the air and say, "Dr. Sarkar's office." I tell Sarkar that I'll be back in Manhattan around nine, maybe earlier. I want him to know that his car will be ready and available for him. For some reason, I don't tell him that Leon Blumenthal has virtually ordered me back to New York.

"How were things in Walker Pasture?" he asks. There's a very significant playful smirk in his voice.

"How'd you know that I...?" I begin, and then I stop.

Of course. I should have thought of it: Rudi Sarkar's got a tracking system on his car.

"By the way, it's not Walker Pasture. It's Walker*s*, with an *s*, Pasture. It's possessive case but without the apostrophe. I wouldn't want you to get lost if you ever decide to visit." As if the proper spelling and pronunciation of my little town's name makes any difference.

"Sorry about that," he says. Then he sarcastically adds, "You know that English is for me a second language."

This little verbal tennis match has gone far enough.

"Hey, listen, Rudi, I really do appreciate the loan of the car," I say. And I mean it. I've never driven anything this fancy. "Again, I really appreciate it."

"No problem, Lucy. In fact, it has been a pleasure."

A few hours later, after a much needed dog-business break out in front of our building, I drop The Duke in our apartment with a bowl of Big Lucy's tasty pork shoulder. Then I take the Manhattan Bridge into the city and park Dr. Sarkar's fancy car in his personal parking space at the hospital. As I exit the elevator and arrive at the residents' cafeteria, I immediately notice that a little redecorating has taken place. Much of the space has been divided up with portable partitions. They're not exactly floor-to-ceiling, but they do afford a little bit of privacy for some members of the law enforcement group. The remainder of the new setup is basically a bunch of modular cubicles with a few folding card tables on the periphery. These flimsy tables seem to be for assistants and secretaries.

One of the NYPD detectives smiles at me and nods toward a cubicle that has four walls and an actual door. "That's Detective Blumenthal's office," the detective says.

"Fancy digs," I say.

"It's good to be the king," the detective says.

I smile, but I'm thinking, *How good can it be?* Shiny suits from Men's Wearhouse, Trader Joe's wraps for lunch, an office made out of rented partitions, and, most of all, kidnappings and an attempted murder case that seems to be nearly impossible to solve.

Blumenthal's office door is wide open. It's a relatively small space with a ridiculously large cluttered desk, a filing cabinet stuffed to overflowing with paper, and the world's largest collection of used disposable coffee cups.

"I love what you've done with the place," I say.

"It's better than what we had before," he says. Then without waiting a moment he says, "Look, you wanted to help out, and now we've got a really smart plan for you to help with."

There goes my blood pressure. Simmering to boiling.

"Do you mean that this is a really *smart* plan, as opposed to *my* plan, the *dumb* plan?" I ask.

"That's exactly what I mean." A pause. "Now, may I go on?"

Leon Blumenthal is shameless. Yeah, he may look sort of handsome in that shiny suit, but nonetheless, he remains a shameless, sarcastic bully. And already I'm predicting that within three minutes we'll be screaming at each other.

Some other woman would have stormed out of the crappy little office already. But that's not me. I won't give Blumenthal the satisfaction. Plus I really want to be a part of this.

"Yeah, go on," I say, and I hope he doesn't notice the smoke coming out of my ears.

"But first, here's what went down before we came up with this. Myself and another detective went out to Queens to see your informant, Patrik Kovac."

"Who was the detective you brought?"

"Bobby Cilia, he's a good guy. You don't know him."

"Isn't he the detective who followed up with Sarkar and Dr. Whall about who told who to leave the operating room?"

"Yeah, but how about for now I finish briefing you."

I nod. I like the word *briefing*. It sounds so official. Blumenthal continues.

"Anyway, Patrik Kovac totally cold-shoulders us. Bobby and I ask questions. Patrik just keeps saying, 'You are confusing me perhaps with another man.' I tell him what you told me. I tell him that I was the first-responding detective when his daughter was attacked and her baby stolen, and I can tell by the way Patrik looks away from us and the way he stutters and stammers all over the place, well, I can tell he's either bullshitting us or just totally afraid to cooperate."

I nod. I say nothing. Sure enough, Blumenthal starts to say what I've been thinking.

"It's possible that…" he begins. He hesitates and begins again, "It's possible that…" He is reluctant to admit that he did something wrong.

I just can't help myself. I help him finish his sentence. "You mean that it's just possible the Russian mob got to Patrik Kovac and scared the shit out of him before you got it together to reach out to him."

Blumenthal snaps his index finger at me and nods. "Exactly," he says. "But hold on, Sherlock. On the surface of it, it seems that our interview with Patrik Kovac didn't come to anything. *But* Cilia and I did get something good, something we could use."

Again, I can't help but interrupt. "I bet I know. You got some helpful info from the woman at Immaculate Conception, the mother over there who had her baby stolen."

"Son of a bitch, Lucy Ryuan, you are smarter than a person needs to be."

I don't tell Blumenthal that this is the exact phrase my mother often used when I was a precocious kid. Only when my mom said it, she would smile and say, *"You are smarter than a person needs to be, you annoying little pug-nose brat."*

Blumenthal is sounding like a coach at half-time. He's enthused, intense, and angry, all at the same time.

"The mother of the kidnapped baby is named Hannah Neal. You can imagine what a mess she was. Eighteen years old. Heartbroken, just heartbroken. The tears, the screaming. It was grim. Sad. Really unbelievably sad."

"Yes, I can imagine that," I say.

"But we did get some good stuff from Ms. Neal. It turns out that she dealt with a guy who had a stupid name. At least the name was straight from Central Casting. Fyodor Orlov. Sorta like the names on *The Rocky and Bullwinkle Show*. You know, the villains, Boris and Natasha."

"Jesus, Detective. What year were you born?" I say. "Rocky and Bullwinkle?"

He ignores me and keeps going. "Anyway, Hannah is in the exact same situ as Katra. Hannah Neal is just eighteen. Pregnant. The baby's father disappears. A friend tells her about Orlov. Just like with the Kovac girl. Orlov and Hannah meet…Oh, and by the way, the first time Hannah meets with Orlov, he's with a woman, and before they even talk, the woman gives Hannah Neal a pregnancy test, the kind you do yourself."

"The kind you do yourself?" I say. "I didn't think the woman showed up with an ultrasound machine."

I know that Blumenthal is telling me this to remind me that a pregnancy test would be the first thing I would've had to do if I'd shown up posing as a pregnant woman.

Blumenthal ignores my sarcasm and starts talking again. "At first we thought Hannah Neal had a pretty decent description of the man and woman. So we had her sit with a department sketch guy, but nothing came of it. The more changes she told the artist to make, the more Hannah said it didn't look like the guy. Finally, we gave up on that.

"But here's what we do have: not just Orlov's name and description...This is the best...Hannah Neal talked with Fyodor Orlov by cell phone. So now we have his cell phone number."

"And that helps how exactly? Are you going to arrest him with a text message?"

Blumenthal once again ignores my witty line. He says, "Maybe you're *not* as smart as a person needs to be."

"Leave the insult humor to the professional comics, Detective."

Blumenthal smiles slightly, then he picks up his cell, punches a button, and says, "Bobby, get over here. I've got Lucy Ryuan with me."

Thirty seconds later a skinny young guy practically runs into Blumenthal's office. He's going to be someone else capable of making my blood boil. I can tell. This kid is just too damned enthusiastic for my taste. Cilia and Blumenthal together may just cause me to explode.

"Lucy, Bobby. Bobby, Lucy," says Blumenthal. Then Blumenthal adds, "Brief Ms. Ryuan on what we want her to do."

Okay. I'm ready to hear this.

CHAPTER 46

ASSISTANT DETECTIVE BOBBY CILIA sits on the edge of Blumenthal's desk. He twists his skinny body so that he is able to face both his boss and myself.

Bobby isn't just skinny, blond, and young. He's skinny, blond, young, and good-looking. And he seems pretty happy about it all. I don't know why I should find this annoying. But of course I do.

"So here's the deal," Bobby says, tossing that longish blond hair back as if he were in a shampoo commercial. "Have you ever done any acting, Ms. Ryuan?"

Before I can come up with a wiseass answer, Blumenthal says, "Never start a presentation with a question, Cilia. Get right into it."

"We want to set up a phone call between Orlov and you," Cilia says. "You're going to tell him who you are...*who you really are*...a senior midwife at Gramatan University Hospital."

"Yeah," I say in an I-sort-of-understand-it tone. "Go on."

"NYPD people, of course, will also be on the line. We'll be trying to track the location."

Cilia is building up enthusiasm big-time. Somebody

should hose this guy down. Cilia stands up, but Blumenthal, clearly having trouble allowing someone else to be in charge, takes over. Ball to Blumenthal.

"So here's what you do…and we have a script worked out for you. Not a strict script, you know, sort of a guideline. You tell Orlov who you are. You tell him what you do. Then you tell him that you've got a terrific deal for him. Instead of his having to chase down women who are willing to hand over their newborn babies, well, you, because you're a midwife, because you're in the midst of all the baby action, you tell him that you always know lots of women with unplanned pregnancies. You're also deep in these gals' confidence. So you can sniff around. You have perfect access to these women. So you can see if they'd be interested in a deal like Orlov's. What's more, you'll be so helpful, *you'll even supply him* occasionally with a newborn. And if—and this is an important *if*—if a woman reneges on her promise, you can facilitate having her baby stolen or find him another one."

When Blumenthal finishes presenting the plan, he seems pleased with himself, pleased with his plan. This is either the CIA or *I Love Lucy*.

"So I'll be offering up myself as the Russian mafia's dream come true," I say.

Blumenthal says, "I wouldn't say that, Lucy. I'd say you'll be the NYPD's dream come true."

"Thanks," I say. And then I decide to share with Leon Blumenthal and Bobby Cilia exactly how I feel.

"Look, guys, I know I sound like I fit neatly into the *tough broad* category. But since I heard this little scenario, I gotta tell you: I'm scared as shit." As if to prove my point I extend my arm. My hand is shaking.

"I'm not good at this sort of thing. I'm no actor. I'm no good at lying. I'm…I don't know…"

Bobby Cilia says, "Hold on, Ms. Ryuan. This is *not* acting. This is *not* lying. This is police work."

Ordinarily I would have simply classified this little go-getter as an asshole. But his passion is so real that I wish I could steal some of it and inject it into my veins.

Then Blumenthal hits me with a sharp left hook. "Lucy, now I've got something to say: You wanted to help us. You bitched and moaned. You said NYPD was lousy."

Cilia adds his thoughts to the issue. "It's going to be beautiful. We have phony files for you to bring to Orlov, files about pregnant women you're working with, their due dates. Pics of other babies you've helped deliver. All of it is fictional. The files were concocted by the FBI's CARD team, experts in child abduction cases. It's going to be perfect. *You're* going to be perfect."

Nobody speaks for about thirty seconds.

Then I speak. Very quietly. "Okay. When does this happen?"

"We're set up to do it now, if you're ready," says Bobby.

"I guess I'm ready. Or ready as I ever will be."

Shit. This is exactly the kind of thing I wanted to be involved with. Why the hell am I so frightened?

Blumenthal seems pleased. He's even got a trace of Bobby's enthusiasm.

"No point in waiting," says Blumenthal. "Strike while…" He and Cilia high-five each other. Blumenthal doesn't even finish the cliché. And nobody offers me a high five.

Bobby hands me his cell phone and says, "Okay, take a look at the outline we wrote for you. We've put together a kind of a rough script for you. I think that'll help you with Orlov...Just press 5-2-2-3."

I press the buttons. A script appears. I read from it out loud. "Hello, may I please speak to Fyodor Orlov? This is Lucy Ryuan calling."

Then I look up at my two new police partners.

"I love your opening line," I say. My voice drips with sarcasm. "Sharp. Original. Insightful. We're off to a really good start."

CHAPTER 47

THE SCRIPT IS IN my estimation a fairly foolish masterpiece of wishful thinking. Sentences like:

Don't be impatient, Mr. Orlov.

Yes, it is a good idea—no, great idea.

It's been a real pleasure talking to you.

Finally, I say, "Let's go do this quasi-entrapment thing before this script makes me change my mind. It sounds like it was written for Barney the dinosaur."

"Who?" says Blumenthal. I assume the man is not a father.

Bobby Cilia says, "Okay, let's get started." Then he adds that we're going to make the phone call from Blumenthal's office. But apparently not before three more people are added to the audience. Cilia and Blumenthal invite an annoyingly pretty FBI agent named Oriana; a plainclothes detective whose name is Chub-o for reasons that are fairly obvious; and a middle-aged black guy whose facial expression says, *Done it all, seen it all, nothing can surprise me*. His name is Fred, and he wears bright green clip-on suspenders. I think the suspenders are meant to be a fashion statement.

And of course there's me. And I'm still nervous as shit.

I ask Bobby Cilia for a Diet Coke. He brings me a regular Coke. "The sugar will be better for you."

Why the hell does every man in New York know what's better for me?

The phone makes a noise.

"You're getting a text message," I say to Bobby. After all, it's his phone.

"Just answer it," Blumenthal says.

I read it quickly. Fortunately, I read it silently.

LUCY, IT'S GOING 2 GO GREAT. LB

Huh? Oh. It takes me a second to realize who the text is from. *LB* is Leon Blumenthal. I look at Blumenthal. He winks at me. He freaking winks at me. *Who winks at anybody anymore?* But there's something nice about it. He's telling me, in his own awkward way, that he knows I'm nervous as shit, that I should stay calm, that this will be fine. *Okay.* Who knew that one wink could communicate so much?

"Let's get moving, people. We got to get moving on this. It's late. Even the Russian mob goes to sleep sometime," Bobby yells. This kid can't wait to be in charge of the place.

Goddamn, I'm nervous. How the hell did I end up here? This is just what I wanted, but come to think of it, maybe it isn't.

"Lucy," Blumenthal says, "remember, the script is just a rough map. Use your instincts. You're smart. Trust your instincts. Just keep it all very *small* and very natural."

"Ready, Lucy?" Bobby asks.

"Uh-huh."

"I'm calling."

A woman's voice. "Yes?"

"Hello. This is Lucy Ryuan. May I please speak to Fyodor Orlov?"

"Just a moment."

That was a lot easier than I expected. I hear no voice, no speaking, no noise as I wait on the phone. Blumenthal gives me a few nods, a few gentle hand gestures. *Stay calm. It's going to go all right.*

Now a man's voice on the phone. "You are Lucy Ryuan?"

"How do you know?" I ask.

He simply says, "Please respond to my question."

I detect a very slight Slavic accent—Russian, as Patrik said, or perhaps somewhere else in Eastern Europe.

"Yes, I am. Is this Fyodor Orlov?"

"It is. How may I help you?"

"Well, I'm a supervisory midwife at Gramatan University Hospital."

"I know who you are. You were supposed to deliver the Kovac baby."

I'm thrown. I hesitate. Blumenthal nods gently. He holds out the palms of both hands in his own *stay calm* gesture.

"Yes, I was supposed to deliver it," I say. "The baby's mother was attacked, and the baby was stolen."

"Mmm, sounds familiar. Precisely how may I help you? Or even more precisely, what the hell do you want?"

The accent is almost buried, and his English is perfect. He's done a lot of work to mask his origins.

"I've had a thought, something you might be interested in."

"I doubt that very much. In fact, I am virtually certain that you are participating in a scheme to trap me. You see, I know how incredibly stupid the police of New York City can be. With that in mind, I know that if I cannot bribe the police, then I just wait. They will screw themselves over."

Blumenthal is motioning me to *keep going,* and suddenly, like an actress feeling her stage fright evaporate, I speak with strength.

And I'm as surprised as anyone.

"Mr. Orlov, listen to me. Here's the deal. Please listen."

There's silence from Orlov's end, so I keep talking.

"I can guarantee you a supply of healthy babies from my hospital, Gramatan University. I can do it all very discreetly. I can do it neatly. Frankly, I can make it a lot easier for you to even obtain babies. The pregnant women trust me. I'm sure you have some connections at hospitals already. But I can assure you, none of those connections will be as helpful to you as I can be."

There is a pause, a long pause. I am determined to wait Orlov out. I will not speak again until he speaks.

Finally. "I would be a fool to trust you, Ms. Ryuan, but I have had people watching you, and I know a few things about you—a single mother, a poor family, a drug-addicted sibling with a criminal record. So I am not certain. Perhaps we can work out something. I have the phone number of your assistant. I will—"

I am shocked. "Troy? Troy is working with you?"

Orlov laughs. "Of course not. All I said was that I had his contact information. I have much information on you and your colleagues…and your son, young William."

I am suddenly too sick to speak. My eyes feel hot and salty.

Orlov continues. "So here is how we will proceed. I will text this Troy person, and I will give him the address of where you and I might meet. A place. A time. Intimate. Secret. And please keep in mind that I know so very, very much. It would be silly for you to have a group of stupid New York cops hiding in the bushes."

Orlov hangs up. The room fills with words like "Great job," "Good setup," "Very nice, very nice."

But Leon Blumenthal knows that I am very scared—mostly for my boy, but also for my mom, my brother, for myself.

When the room empties, leaving only Blumenthal, Bobby Cilia, and me, Blumenthal says, "So what do you think, Lucy? Are you still willing to go through with the meeting, on your own?"

I simply nod my head in fear and confusion.

Blumenthal speaks quietly. "Depending on where Orlov wants to meet, we'll have NYPD strategically placed…Not quite 'hiding in the bushes,' but hiding somewhere nearby. And of course we'll work with a decoy or two, but you're basically going to be on your own."

I nod my head. It means two things at once: *I understand* and *I'll do it*.

"Are you sure? We can always scrap this," Blumenthal says.

My own cell phone rings. I answer. It's Troy.

"Where are you, honey?" he asks.

"I'm back in New York," I say softly.

"Well, you must be having one hot romance cooking, *and* it looks like I'm going to be your secret little helper. I just got a text, which I'll read to you: Urgent. Tell Lucy. Meet me 3 AM Crane Hill Cemetery Sunnyside Equipment House 3. Thx 4 yr help. Boy Sam."

"Thanks, Troy," I say.

"This stuff makes sense to you, Lucy girl?" he asks. "Your man's name is Sam?"

I don't answer.

Troy speaks again. "I'm only asking, Lucy. Do you understand all this? Does this message make sense to you?"

"Yes," I say. "It makes complete sense."

CHAPTER 48

AT TWO THIRTY IN the morning an Uber drops me off at 48th Avenue in Sunnyside, Queens. I've been followed at a safe distance by two detectives in a dark-blue Toyota Camry. They're followed—or so I'm told—by Leon Blumenthal, Bobby Cilia, and two FBI agents. God only knows what Russian is following them.

I've been fitted out with a wire. The *wire* is different from anything you or I have ever seen in a movie or TV show. It is just a piece of flat round metal with Velcro on the back. A minuscule bit of plastic protrudes from the rim. The whole deal is barely the size of a dime.

It is attached by the Velcro inside a pocket of my black jeans. The whole fastening procedure took about five seconds.

I walk the two long blocks to Crane Hill Cemetery. The streets are empty except for a truck unloading cases of laundry detergent in front of a Met Foodmarket. Closer to the cemetery gate are three young men. They look threatening, but I'm not afraid. I know that both the guy unloading the truck and the three gangland-looking guys are police decoys.

Bobby Cilia initially suggested the decoys be two cemetery groundskeepers and an elderly widow visiting her husband's grave.

"Are you nuts?" was Blumenthal's reaction. "At three in the morning only psychos are visiting graves." The eager Cilia kid has a lot to learn.

I feel curiously…free? Like an actress on a big movie set. I wear a loose shirt and carry a very large purse. It holds nothing but dozens of make-believe files about make-believe babies.

I've thoroughly studied a detailed map of the cemetery, so when I pass through the entrance gate, I know exactly where to find Equipment House 3. I pretend to be confused. I look left and right and left and right and then I nod to myself, as if I've newly discovered the small, flat brick building where I've agreed to meet Orlov.

The big black painted wooden door is unlatched, and I walk into a very dark room.

Strangely enough, I'm not particularly frightened. I'm nauseated by the sickly smell of lawn chemicals and fresh-mown grass clippings and fertilizer, but it's as if I'm walking through my dramatic acting class role, a woman in a cemetery. I'm just another actress in another movie. This room is just another movie set. The gaffers are about to move the lights. I'm rehearsing my lines. *"Can I get you anything, Ms. Ryuan? A bottle of water?"* says an imaginary assistant. My agent is betting on this one. Maybe…I'd better stop this craziness. *Shit!* I'm scared.

Back to reality. Should I look for a light switch? I run my hand over the wall near the door. All I get is a small but nasty splinter from the molding.

Then I am startled by a woman's voice. I think it's nearby.

"Please, Lucy Ryuan, you can go back where you came from," comes the voice, which has a Slavic accent.

Now I'm scared. And confused. *"Go back where you came from."* Does she mean West Virginia or Brooklyn or Gramatan Hospital?

"Where?" I say. My voice is urgent. Or I think it is urgent.

"Go to the outside. Go to the pathway and walk left. You will meet someone. You will hear a voice call to you," she says.

"Orlov?" I ask.

No answer.

"Who is it?"

No answer.

"Is it Orlov? Tell me."

I hear what sounds like a Russian word of exasperation, then, "Just do what you're told, Lucy Ryuan."

So I do what I'm told. At least I'm trying to do what I'm told. I leave the shed, and I follow the pathway. When I come to a barely discernible fork in the path, I hesitate. That's when I realize the woman who gave me my initial instructions is still walking close behind me.

I hear her voice. "I told you to turn left. Don't you listen?"

I follow the pathway to the left. I am walking among a field of gravestones—elaborate mausoleums, simple concrete crosses, even simpler ground markers.

Suddenly a man's voice calls. "Here, over here." He then says, "2499 to 3500." What the hell kind of secret code is this?

"Stop, Lucy Ryuan," comes the woman's voice. I still hear her walking behind me. Then she stands next to me.

"Follow me," she says. Now she steps in front of me.

I notice two things. First, a brass sign with an arrow. It simply says MEMORIAL STONES 2499–3500. As I follow the woman, I look down. The second thing I notice are her feet. I realize she is wearing precisely the same shoes Troy and I saw on the hospital security video. I am pleased, I guess, but I am not surprised.

"Is the woman with you?" I hear the man's voice. We are much closer to him.

"She's with me," the woman says.

"Good. Bring her over here, Nina. I'm right where you left me. I'm just over here."

CHAPTER 49

THIS IS THE BLIND date from hell.

Orlov is not at all what I was expecting. I assumed he'd be broad, heavy, brunette. A middle-aged thug. Instead he is slim and fit, almost young. But his hair is white. The shade of Anderson Cooper's. His suit is light in color, too, either very expensive and chic or very cheap and chic.

We face each other; perhaps a few feet separate us. We stand in a sort of hazy spotlight. Then I realize it is the woman, Nina, who is holding a simple household flashlight on both of us. Orlov's face betrays nothing, communicates nothing. He has no smile, no sneer, no grin, no wrinkle. I want to take my cues from him, but the man offers no expression. I strike a kind of random pose, hands at my sides, one hip slightly extended. I'm trying to look solemn but accessible, whatever that means.

"You are here with a proposition that in no way interests me, Lucy Ryuan," he says with the same very faint accent I remember from our phone conversation.

"Then why am I here at all?" I snap back at him. I have no idea where my courage is coming from. But I'm certainly happy that it showed up.

"I very much wanted to meet you, Lucy Ryuan," he says. "I wanted to see the woman who is brave enough to bring babies into this world but cruel enough to be willing to give them away."

I am ready to give him the planned explanation—I need money, my son is terribly ill, the hospital is about to fire me—but Orlov is clearly in charge of the conversation. Before I can say anything, he speaks again.

"And on the subject of this meeting, you have been fortunate enough to meet my colleague, the indispensable Nina."

He does not offer a last name. I am struck by the use of the word *indispensable*.

My courage continues. "We have met already, before tonight, although she doesn't know it."

The beam from Nina's flashlight quivers.

"No. We have never met, Lucy Ryuan," she says.

"Oh, but we have. I've seen you. Seeing you was as good as meeting you."

Nina looks alarmed. Orlov's face betrays nothing.

I continue. "I saw you on film, a security video. I saw you fleeing from the crime scene, the day that you—or some butcher who was with you—slashed Katra Kovac's belly."

Nina looks quickly at Orlov. Then she steadies the flashlight.

Orlov looks at me and speaks. "Quite frankly, no one gives a good fucking goddamn about what you've seen, what you know."

I am looking straight at Orlov. So I cannot tell whether Nina shows relief at Orlov's words.

Sooooo…if they don't give a good fucking goddamn, does it mean I'll be safe? Or does it mean that, unlike Nina, I am easily dispensable? *What in hell am I doing here? Where precisely are Blumenthal and Cilia? Why did I agree to—*

"Let us return to the subject at hand, Lucy Ryuan. Tell me why and how you can be of service to me."

"But you just said that you have no interest in my offer," I say. "I don't feel like wasting breath."

He ignores what I've just said. He forges ahead. He's in charge.

"Let us play a game. Let us pretend that I know nothing about you. Let's say I'm a businessman and you have come to sell me your goods and services. Let's call your service The Baby Snatchers. There. That's a name. A good name. You can use it. Free of charge. I'm a little pussycat when it comes to business. You could eat me for lunch. So there, let's get going. We're in the boardroom."

Now he doesn't stop smiling. The grim and sleazy smile is practically pasted on his handsome face. The forced pleasantness in his voice makes him sound like the sickest bully in the classroom.

Then Nina steps right into the sick drama. She is as obedient as a ventriloquist's dummy. She speaks with a phony American business-professional accent: "This is our last presentation, Mr. Orlov. Please yourself to meet Lucy Ryuan. She represents The Baby Snatchers, Inc. You have five minutes, Lucy Ryuan."

This is insane. No, wait. This is beyond insane.

"Please begin," says Orlov. "You have only five minutes."

The plan with Blumenthal was that they would jump in only if the meeting turned dangerous. So we had a plan for *dangerous*. We had no plan for *crazy*.

Nina suddenly screams out in anger. "Mr. Orlov has told you to begin. So begin. Begin. Begin."

In an unexpectedly calm voice—colorless but conversational—I begin. "Myself and my carefully chosen colleagues will be able to help you in a variety of ways. Those of us who work daily in the Gramatan Hospital midwifery unit have access to probable and predictable delivery dates of many pregnant women. Many of those newborns are going to be placed in foster care or put up for adoption. I can facilitate for you and your organization—"

Orlov lets out the kind of laugh—a cackle really—that I associate with childhood nightmares of witches and warlocks. He seethes with a diabolical anger. And he has no problem showing that anger. "This idea is stupid, stupid beyond my comprehension, clearly stupid beyond your comprehension."

I stick my hand quickly into my leather bag and randomly pull out a bunch of infant files. I thrust the files toward Orlov. "Here," I say. "Here's the proof. Here are actual midwife reports of real mothers with real babies, babies on the way, babies just born."

I watch as Orlov turns his head toward Nina. She gives a small *Maybe this is for real* shrug. Orlov apparently thinks otherwise. He grabs the files from my hand and scatters them on the ground. He then steps forward and puts his face only a few inches from my own.

"I want you to report to the NYPD that I will *never* do business with them. Do you understand me?"

Astonishingly—or not—I find that I am not frozen in fear, and I decide that my one bit of revenge will be to ignore him. He expects me to buckle under his orders. I am determined that I will not.

"I asked if you understand me," he says.

I continue to say nothing.

"Do you understand?"

On the nearby pathway a parked car, a car that I never noticed in the darkness, turns on its headlights.

It must be Blumenthal and Bobby Cilia. With any luck, it just might be the whole goddamn cavalry.

Orlov glances in the direction of the car. He says to Nina, "The driver is ready. Let's go."

Orlov and Nina walk quickly to what is instead their own waiting car. Orlov turns and looks at me. He yells, "The question. Again. Do you understand?"

I don't remember answering. I don't remember movement or noise or voices.

What I remember next is Leon Blumenthal hugging me, my head against his chest. Blumenthal says, "We wouldn't have let them hurt you. You know that, Lucy. You got some great stuff out of them. You were absolutely terrific."

I say, "But they said nothing...they..."

"We're going to get them," Blumenthal says. "You'll see."

"We're going to get them"? "Terrific"? What the hell?

I guess I'll never understand police work.

CHAPTER 50

AFTER A FEW HOURS of rough sleep, I'm tired as hell the rest of the day. And I'm not in the mood for big decisions. The only significant choice I make is to wear my eyeglasses instead of my contacts. On the subway into Manhattan, I miraculously get a seat, and I miraculously make it to Gramatan University Hospital without falling asleep in that seat.

I notice six NYPD officers instead of the usual three standing outside the main entrance. I also can't help but notice a small crowd of spectators and a larger crowd of TV cameras.

I head for the employees' entrance. Only two officers are there. Inside I have to show my hospital ID to two different check-in detectives. I also get to be frisked (first time that's ever happened here) by a woman with a security wand. The rear entrance lobby is crowded with the usual mix of nurses and orderlies and doctors.

"Over here," I hear, Tracy Anne's voice.

I quickly find her face in the group. She's standing with Dr. Sarkar. He's wearing his white coat with his official badge: R SARKAR, CHIEF OB-GYN.

"What the hell's happened now?" I ask. I'm ashamed to admit that I wish I had worn my contacts.

Tracy Anne looks bad—bad under any conditions but particularly bad for her. Her hair, which is always, always, always perfect, is a total grease-bag of loose ends and frizz. Tracy Anne and Sarkar look at each other. Then Tracy Anne looks at me.

"You haven't heard?" she half asks, half states.

"Two more infants have gone missing," adds Sarkar.

Anger erupts in me. "'Gone missing' sounds like the newborns got up and walked out on their own. Don't use those words. Call it what the media calls it. Say they've been kidnapped or stolen."

"Lucy, you're exhausted. From last night at the cemetery," Sarkar says.

Before he can continue, I say, "Last night? How the hell do you know about last night?"

"Leon Blumenthal told me," he says.

Tracy looks away from the two of us, as if she's heard something she should not have heard. I'll have this confidentiality argument in a moment, but for now I have a more important question.

"Does Blumenthal know about this latest kidnapping yet?" I ask.

"Yes, we called him immediately, around three thirty this morning, when the incident was reported to Security," says Sarkar.

So Blumenthal knew about this while he was watching me with Orlov and Nina. He knew this when he was hugging me and congratulating me, when he told me I had been *absolutely terrific.* And then Bobby Cilia drove me home while Blumenthal rushed back to GUH to jump into the new kidnapping investigation. And I was snoozing alongside The Duke in my apartment? Son of a bitch!

"Who are the babies? Who are the mothers? What's the situation?" I say as fiercely as I can.

"They're twins," says Tracy Anne. "Twin boys. They came in at good weights. They were a planned C-section because they were a multiple. You know the mother, Dolly Korest. She and the husband are…like…like…your perfect Upper East Side couple. They're—"

Sarkar jumps in. "The Korests are apoplectic, as you might expect."

"Yeah, as I might expect," I say.

The lobby suddenly seems much more crowded than when I first walked in. It's also far noisier. All these people seem to be walking faster than normal. I'm used to the pace and the crowd of GUH. When you work at GUH—or any big hospital complex, for that matter—you get used to big crowds. It is a place with hundreds of doctors and med students and nurses, thousands of patients, visitors, technicians, custodians, cooks, ER people, paramedics, ambulance drivers, physiotherapists.

But this? This looks almost like a crowd surging out of a stadium after a football game. I feel as if the crowd is pressing in on Sarkar and Tracy Anne and me. Then, another surprise from the crowd. They all begin parting into two groups, forming a sort of cleared passage in the middle. I look at the central point of the passage and see Leon Blumenthal walking quickly. Next to Blumenthal, trying to keep up with him, is Dr. Barrett Katz. Katz is in his usual blue Brooks Brothers button-down shirt, but his tie is askew, his collar unbuttoned. His suit jacket is missing. I realize I've never seen our CEO without a suit jacket before. On the other side of Katz is a uniformed police officer, a woman. Behind this officer is another officer, a man. It seems as if everyone but this group of four is holding a cell phone in the air. It looks like all the phone cameras are aimed at Dr. Katz.

I break through my area of the crowd, and I rush toward Blumenthal and Katz. I push myself into Blumenthal's face. Katz and the officers look at the two of us, but they keep on moving.

"Not now, Lucy," Blumenthal says. He tries to move past me, but I stand firmly in front of him. He bumps into me. But I'm going to hold my ground.

"What's happening, Detective?" I ask.

"I've got to go," he says. He looks over my head. I assume he's looking for Katz and his escorts. Then I realize that Blumenthal and I have attracted attention, a small group of men and women with cell phone cameras and other recorders are aiming them at us.

I say as quietly as I can, "You lied to me last night. There were two other babies taken…kidnapped. You knew that. And you sent me home like a little kid."

He grabs me by the shoulders. "I sent you home because you were exhausted and confused and in a state of shock. I did it for you," he says.

"That's bullshit," I say. I know he's lying. But I'm exploding with questions.

"Whatever's happening with Katz, does this have to do with the missing babies?" I ask.

Blumenthal says nothing. Then comes a barrage of questions from the small group of reporters who have not followed Katz but instead stayed to watch Blumenthal and me.

"Can you tell us what this is all about, miss?"

"What's your role in the unfolding story here?"

"I understand you're the supervising midwife."

My own cell phone is suddenly alive with texts. One from Blumenthal.

Will xplain all Trust me LB

One from Troy.

Teen girl w preemie need u or TracyA NOW T

And one from my mother. Mom's text is, of course, written like a letter.

Hi, Lucy. Willie boarded the Pittsburgh train at 7:30. It arrives at Penn Station at 4:56 this evening. All is well. I think Willie has a bit of a cold. He says he doesn't. Kids! He's as stubborn as you were when you were his age. OOXX, Mom.

CHAPTER 51

I'VE ONLY BEEN TO Penn Station about two million times, and every time I'm there it looks uglier than the time before. Trash cans overflow. Fluorescent lights flicker on and off. I read a newspaper article that they don't fix the broken chairs in the waiting room because they think they're going to rebuild the entire station soon. Great idea, but I'm pretty sure I read that article about fifteen years ago.

I'm early to meet Willie's train. It's scheduled to arrive at 4:56, and I'm there at 4:54. For me, that's early. I look at the ARRIVALS board and see that it's listed at TRACK 12 ON TIME. On time? This must be my lucky day. And it is, until I arrive at track 12 and see a large handwritten sign by the ARRIVALS board.

TRACK CHANGE.
PITTSBURGH 4:56 ARRIVAL
NOW 5:10
TRACK 17

Story of my life. Too good to be true. Eventually, after a search that sent me from one staircase to another, I am standing outside track 17, which bears another handwritten sign: PITTSBURGH ARRIVAL. That's it. Four other people seem to be waiting—an old man in a heavy black woolen coat, a young black woman in what appears to be native African dress, and two teenage boys smoking some very unpleasant-smelling weed.

A few minutes later track 17 begins discharging passengers. Estimated count? Fifty people. I push my way into the crowd and scan for Willie. The crowd thins down, and I don't see him. I do what any normal mother would do: I panic and picture myself sobbing to Big Lucy that *"I should never have listened to you! I should never have let him take the train alone!"*

So maybe this is not my lucky day at all. I walk toward the train. I'm about to panic, but I know that in thirty seconds, if there's no Willie, I'll start yelling at everyone in sight. Then…

"Hey, Mom," comes the familiar shout.

Thank you, God. I'll be a good person from now on.

I turn to my left, the direction of Willie's voice. He is standing in the doorway of one of the train cars.

Behind him is a very pretty girl of about seventeen. Her black hair is tied in a ponytail. She wears a white T-shirt with the logo of the Pittsburgh Pirates, and her smile is beautiful and broad. She is holding Willie's hand. With her free hand she pulls a wheelie suitcase.

Willie breaks away from the girl when he sees me. We hug and kiss and exchange the usual: "How was the trip?" "Good. I had a tuna sandwich." "How was the time with Grandma?" "Great. Uncle Cab and I played more Call of Duty. I always won."

And then Willie says, "This is my friend Diane. I was in the bathroom, and she helped me."

"Were you sick?" I ask.

"No, I was stuck," says Willie.

Diane, whose voice is as sweet as her face, explains, "I was leaving the train just now, and I heard this little voice coming from somewhere I couldn't quite place."

"It was me," offers Willie.

"It was coming from the bathroom. I guess Willie might have done something with the lock," she says.

"You always tell me to lock the door, Mom, in a public place," Willie says.

Diane says, "Your mom is absolutely right. Anyway, we found a conductor, and he had this little doodad that unlocked it, and here we are. A little late but present and accounted for."

"Diane is the only person I talked to on the train except for the man who sold me the sandwich and a Kiwi Strawberry Snapple."

"Willie's a good boy, Ms. Ryuan," Diane says. "You've got him well trained."

I ask Diane if she lives in New York.

"Bed-Stuy, in Brooklyn," she says. "Right near you."

"I told her we live in Crown Heights," says Willie.

"I'll treat us all to a cab," I say.

Diane goes through the proper "Oh, no, I couldn't."

Willie goes through the predictable "Oh, come on, of course you can."

And I say the obvious "I insist." Then I order an Uber.

I look at the screen on my phone, and the price is so high that I can't help but say, "My God. They want ninety dollars!"

"Surge pricing," the ever-smart Willie says.

"Why don't we just take the number 3 train to the Kingston stop?" says Diane. "We can get it just downstairs."

"Awesome," says Willie.

I tell our new friend Diane that Willie is the only kid in New York who prefers the subway to a taxi.

"I sort of agree," she says. "The subway's the fastest…if it's on time."

"And that's a big if," I say. Then I add, "I suppose we have to go back upstairs to the big station area for the subway entrance."

Immediately Willie says, "No. Look. There's the number 2 train." He points to a sign that indicates where the 2 and 3 trains stop.

"Go left at the short passageway next to the Auntie Anne's Pretzels," Diane says. "It's faster. As long as we don't stop for a pretzel."

"I can't make any promises," says Willie.

The tunnel bears right. It seems to become a little darker. Two teenage guys pass us, obviously in a hurry. The tunnel has very few people in it, and ahead of us is a sign that says DOWNTOWN, WALL STREET, BROOKLYN. We head toward that sign. On our left is an open metal door. I wouldn't notice that door except for the loud groaning coming from inside.

Diane speaks, her voice full of urgency, "Oh, my God. It looks like somebody's hurt." She stops. All three of us walk through the door into what appears to be a small storage room. A man, possibly a homeless person, is lying on the ground. To my surprise Diane yells, "Fuck, man. This guy is bleeding."

Did she just say *fuck*?

The door slams. The lights flicker. Then Willie yells, "Mom. No lights." And immediately a deep hard pain spins across the front of my head.

"Mom!" I hear. I fall on top of the homeless man, who squirms out from beneath me.

"Somebody got the kid?" the man shouts.

I hear Diane's voice. "I got the boy." The front of my head is throbbing. Blood drips into my right eye and nose. My eye burns. I taste the blood. Then the room is flooded with light.

The homeless man doesn't look very homeless anymore. He is standing. He's a big guy—football-lineman-size. He wears a crisp white shirt and black pants.

Then I see Diane. She has an intense hammerlock on Willie.

"Let go of him," I shout.

Willie struggles. He's a tough, wiry little guy, but he is, after all, just a little guy.

"Let go," I yell, but then the big asshole grabs me tight around my waist with one arm. With his other hand he turns my purse upside down and empties its contents onto the floor.

"Pick up the wallet and give it to me," the man says, and now I see that he is holding a very small pistol against my ribs. For all I know it's really a toy, but I'm not about to test that theory.

He loosens his grip on me and I bend down but with the gun still jammed against me. I lift my fake-alligator wallet—stuffed with credit cards and coupons and photos and notes and, of course, two hundred dollars fresh from the ATM machine—and I hand it to him.

"Give me those pills," the guy says. He's pointing to two CVS prescription bottles. One is a bottle of Lexapro, an antidepressant that every other person in New York City takes. The other is Lipitor, an anticholesterol medication.

"These won't do any good for you," I say about the Lipitor.

"Give me the goddamn pills. We're not a team, you and me." He pulls the necklace from my neck—

a cheap yellow Murano glass bauble on a five-dollar chain. Then he shouts, "Go."

Diane lets Willie out of her grip. The door opens and closes within seconds. The room is plunged into almost complete darkness.

Willie and I hug each other. I cry a little. Willie doesn't. I say, "Are you okay?"

Then he says, "Are you okay?"

How can we possibly be okay, but of course we both tell each other that we're fine.

I yank out my cell phone from my jeans pocket. I call Blumenthal.

"I think these people may have something to do with Orlov," I tell him.

Of course he thinks I'm wrong. "Listen, Lucy. I'm not trying to play down the fact that you were in danger, and your son was in danger, and…but anyway, what happened to you has been going on for a few weeks at Penn and Grand Central and Port Authority. These muggings. They get a kid, and then they hijack the kid, and if the kid is traveling with a woman, they…you get it."

Willie opens the door to the unlighted room, the room where he and I were just mugged. Three officers immediately crowd their way in. Two of them have their guns drawn.

I speak into the phone. "The cavalry is here," I say.

"Yeah," says Blumenthal. "I notified them about a minute ago."

"Can I ask what you all are doing about these 'Welcome to New York' muggings?"

"All I can say is that we're doing our best, Lucy," Blumenthal says.

"Yeah," I say. "And we all know how great that is."

CHAPTER 52

I REALIZE AS WE enter Midtown Precinct South of the NYPD, I've never been in a real New York City police station before. Oh, I've been in a few jail-houses back in West Virginia, always to bail out my brother, Cabot. But those places looked like the little marshal's offices you see on old television westerns. This precinct looks like a smallish office building, and it is dull and ugly inside. Gray painted walls, cheap aluminum desks, dirty linoleum.

In a small room, we go over the recent events with the officers. One officer tells me that "yes, occasion-ally they use old storage rooms along the passageways to the subway." She seems unconcerned.

I try not to seem concerned. But for me, the whole world is fast becoming a crime scene.

After Willie and I spend almost two hours flipping through about five hundred photos and sketches on a computer screen, men and women who've previously been involved in crimes, a very bored detective says we can leave. When I suggest that the NYPD might want to put up the cost of an Uber trip, they agree to take us home to Crown Heights in a police car.

I tell Willie that the impact of the awful event

might not hit him right away. "You know," I say. "Sometimes reactions to traumatic events sneak up on us, like someone dying or a car accident." I'm waiting for him to react to what I've said. He does.

"Don't worry, Mom. I'll keep an eye on you." Only Willie.

The police car pulls up in front of our little building.

"Hey, look," Willie says. "The lights are still on in the store. They're open late."

Sure enough, even though it's close to nine o'clock, Sabryna's crazy little Jamaican jumble of a store looks like it's open for business.

Willie says, "Cool. I hope Devan is around."

I, of course, am imagining some criminal nastiness in the store. *Why are the lights on? Why is there no one behind the counter? What the hell's happening here?*

The store door is locked. Willie knocks on the glass.

No answer. The police car has already driven away.

"Keep knocking," I say. "Sabryna could be in the back room, cooking."

Suddenly Devan appears. He has a big grin on his face, and he actually runs to the door, unlocking it from the inside. As soon as we step through, Willie and Devan greet each other as if they had been apart for twenty years, not a few days. Hugs and arm punching and up-in-the-air hand slaps.

"How you been doing down there in East Virginia, man?" Devan asks.

"I did great. I am great. And it's *West* Virginia," Willie says.

"Damn, you're still an asshole. 'East Virginia' was a joke, dude," says Devan, and the arm punching begins again.

Then Sabryna yells from the rear of the store, "Well,

lullaby and good night yourselves, Young William has returned." She comes out carrying her new charge: Valerina's baby. The baby wears nothing but Huggies on this hot night. Sabryna has tied the tiniest red-and-yellow striped scarf—a ribbon really—around the baby's adorable head.

"Are you open or closed?" Willie asks.

"I'm not quite sure," says Sabryna. "I figure if I'm up with little Tyonna anyways, I might as well sell something."

"Tyonna? Where'd you get that name from, Sabryna? Valerina said she was naming the baby Anna for her great-grandmother."

"Valerina can call her baby anything she wants. She's the mama," says Sabryna. "But as long as the baby's with me, I'm calling her Tyonna. In Jamaican, Tyonna means *princess*. And that's zactly what this little one is, a princess. The yellow-red headscarf 'round her head will be just a practice crown for the little princess later in life."

There will be no arguing with Sabryna. And actually, I think both names—Tyonna and Anna—are beautiful in their own different ways. Perhaps the name Anna Tyonna Gomez will happen.

I say to Sabryna what she always says to me when I've come home tired and rattled and baggy-eyed from a tough birthing or long day at the hospital.

"You are looking sure enough spent, lady," I say.

"You don't zactly look like a festival queen yourself," says Sabryna. Then she touches the baby's cheek and says, "She's finally nodded off. This baby fights sleep."

"That'll come in handy when she gets a little older and she's studying for exams up at Harvard," I say.

"No, Lucy. We all need our sleep time. Every one of us. I sure wish I had more of it."

"Yes, ma'am. Like I said, you look sure enough spent."

"I know I do, but I'm lovin' it. Th' only thing I miss is my time with you know who," and she nods in the direction of Devan, who's busy challenging Willie to a contest of who can eat a bag of potato chips the fastest.

Sabryna rocks Tyonna Anna in her arms. For a moment the two of them look like a couple slow dancing.

Sabryna lowers her voice. "Devan comes home sometimes, and I know he's been smoking ganja. His eyes are bugging out, and he's angry that he's got to help out in the store."

"Okay," I say. "I've got an idea. I'm not going in to work tomorrow."

"I wish I could steal your day off," Sabryna says.

"I tell you what. I can't give you the day off, but I can help you out. I'll take the baby for most of the day tomorrow. That way you don't have to be watching her *and* watching the cash register. I'll take her. *And* I'll leave Willie to help you and Devan. Maybe you can even get a few hours of sleep time."

"I can't say no," says Sabryna. "It sounds too much like paradise."

I begin humming, then singing. It's one of the Bob Marley tunes Sabryna loves:

Sun is shining, the weather is sweet
Make you want to move your dancing feet.

Sabryna begins dancing gently, holding the baby against her cheek. Willie and Devan look up at us.

They seem if not genuinely delighted at least a little amused.

As she dances, Sabryna smiles and speaks. "There are two things I need to say to you, Lucy girl."

"Okay, say what you need to say."

"Number one. Thank you. I so appreciate it."

"You're welcome. And what's the second thing?"

"Promise me this is the last time you ever try singing a Bob Marley song in public."

CHAPTER 53

IT WAS AT THE top of the closet in Willie's room.

No. It was behind the pressure cooker that I was always too afraid to use. No. It was hidden under the Scrabble Junior box. Damn. It must be packed not so neatly between a rolled-up yoga mat and a large papier-mâché Easter bunny that had missed the last five Easters. Finally, I found it. It was the little yellow Snugli.

Not so many years ago I carried Willie all over New York City in that little yellow Snugli. My baby boy and I would walk to Brower Park, where it was shady and cozy, and the Brooklyn Children's Museum was right nearby if we needed a bathroom. Best of all, the park had a gentle spray sprinkler for kids. On the hottest days, I'd carry Willie under the sprinkler, and even though he was only a few weeks old, I could swear that he laughed when I splashed a tiny bit of water on his beautiful little face.

"You're a peanut! You're a delicious little peanut." That's what I'd say to Willie, and that is exactly what I say today to Tyonna. I open my mouth wide and pretend that I am going to eat her up. In case she doesn't know what's happening, I tell her, "I'm going to eat you up. Grrrrrrrr." This new baby almost looks up at me. I imagine she's already thinking, just as Willie once did, *Who the hell is this crazy lady?*

Tyonna smiles. No one else would be able to know that she's smiling, but I can see it. And I tell her.

"I see that smile. Yes, I see that smile. I do."

It's early afternoon, and soon Tyonna and I are sitting in that same Brower Park on a metal bench, a foolish modern design with no back to lean against. I take a bottle of baby formula out of the insulated bag. It's been resting against an ice pack, and I worry that now the bottle may be too cold. I rub the bottle against my arm.

I can almost hear my mother say, *"Stop worrying about it. Just go ahead. She'll take the bottle. The baby knows what's best for her. Don't wait till she starts fussing."*

My mother, even absent, is right. Tyonna happily takes the bottle. She's hungry.

I hold the baby close to me. I tap her back gently. The burp. Oh, the wonderful sound of the baby's burp.

I see if she wants some more. No. I try for another burp, but she's done.

On this summer day, even here in the shade, the heat is oppressive. I look around and see people surrendering to the heat—women fanning themselves, men with bandanas around their foreheads, people pouring cold beers down their throats. But I also see children defying the heat—shirtless boys playing soccer, girls and boys jumping, splashing, screaming under the spray sprinkler.

"You want to go swimming, Peanut?" I say. I touch her nose again. "How about we go for a quick dip in the sprinkler to cool off, and then we'll go into the museum and get changed, and then we'll head home to see Auntie Sabryna." The *auntie* title is my idea. Sabryna will go for it. I think.

CHAPTER 54

TYONNA AND I HEAD on over to the spray sprinkler area. I put the diaper bag in easy reach and easy view of where we'll be standing. We stand only a foot away from the edge of the small drainage outlet.

"Let's get wet!" I say to Tyonna.

I hold Tyonna precisely the way I held Willie when he was a baby, so the water doesn't sprinkle on her directly. The spray hits my face and hair, and I shake my head so a few drops fall on the baby. I swear that I see Tyonna smile. I swear I hear her chuckle over the noise of children squealing and steel drums clanking.

Then it happens.

Sometimes people say, *"It happened so fast that I don't really remember how it happened."*

How can that be? I know everything that goes on around me. I do. I really do. But I am wrong. It erupts so quickly, so horribly, that I don't precisely remember how it even started.

I see the two of them—a blond man in a light-gray suit, a woman in a tight black skirt and high-heeled shoes. They stand at the edge of the sprinkler area. They are initially right next to our diaper bag. Then the man in the suit walks toward me. The sprinkler water cascades on the man in the suit. A few people from the crowd watch the pair getting wet.

I know them. The vaguely handsome man—yes, it's Orlov. Then I recognize the woman's shoes before I actually recognize the woman. I hold the baby closer. I eye the diaper bag at the water's edge.

Orlov is near me. Orlov is now next to me. I hold Tyonna even closer. She is crying.

"Hold that baby, tightly, Miss Ryuan. Try to quiet her down, if you will. And please remain quiet yourself."

In this split second I am certain that I see sympathy in Nina's eyes.

So make a scene. What difference will it make if I scream? And then I see the difference.

Orlov holds and hides a knife in the palm of his hand. I know almost nothing about knives, but I happen to know that this one is a Laguiole en Aubrac Shepherd's Knife. It is a favorite glamorous Christmas gift for dads and big brothers back in Walkers Pasture. The knife is both sharp and beautiful. It is especially grotesque when held near Tyonna's beautiful little face. My mind flashes to Tyonna's neck sliced almost through, her tiny head dangling from her tiny shoulders.

I look at the woman. "How can you, Nina? Are you a mother? Don't do this." For a second, she locks her eyes with mine. I think I see understanding.

Nina says something in Russian to Orlov. I, of course, have no idea what her words mean, but as Orlov answers her I find the courage that only real fear can bring on: my voice memo app is, as almost always, open and easily accessed, since I use it frequently to take notes about patients. So I slip my hand into the pocket of my shorts and press the Record button.

At least I think I do. I hope I do.

Orlov and Nina exchange a few angry sentences in Russian. And then—

And then suddenly I wake up on the concrete ground. My face is swollen. My right knee aches. Tyonna is gone.

A young woman helps me sit up. Then I struggle to my feet. My knee feels as if it's on fire.

I can see Orlov and Nina in the distance. They are not running, but they are walking fast, disappearing fast. I should scream for help. But the knife…

I have no chance of catching up to them, but I stand and hobble in their direction. I watch Nina and Orlov slip into the back seat of a big black car.

I stand where I am and cry. I am trembling. I am cold and wet and hot and dry, all at once. Strangers have gathered around me. A few of them have already called 911. In the mumble-grumble of the crowd, I hear, "The baby. The woman had a baby." And "They took the baby. They took this woman's baby." I am crying.

For the first time I am in a total panic. I am alone. I screwed up so badly.

A young black man is speaking to me. "I got just the beginning, the beginning of the license plate is 'W7.' That's all I got. I'm sorry."

Me too. W7. That's all I got.

CHAPTER 55

OFFICER DIAS RESTROPO AND Officer Matias Moreno are partners. No, not in the marriage sense of the word *partners*. They are just two ordinary guys, two ordinary cops. If asked, they would tell you so. They would say simply: "We're just cops. Not good cops. Not bad cops. Just cops." If asked how good the Restropo-Moreno team is, their sergeant would give them the most common Yelp review: "Good but not great."

Restropo and Moreno patrol the area between Roosevelt Avenue to the south and Grand Central Parkway to the north. An occasional free Colombian lunch at Leños Bar Restaurant is as close to a kickback as they ever take.

They both come from South American families, both are Colombian, and they think today would be a fine time to tap Dias Diego, the owner of Leños, for a nice meal of *chuleta valluna,* the deep-fried pork dish that is perfect when paired with a cold Coke and a large order of red beans and rice.

Before the fried pork arrives, Dias Diego visits the police officers' table.

"I don't know whether this is of interest to you, *mis amigos,* but there's been an automobile accident across the street. Nothing serious. You can take a look at it from the window near the bar."

Both Restropo and Moreno have a similar thought: in the time it will take them to walk to the window, evaluate the situation, and, God forbid, go out and get involved, the crispy breaded crust of the *chuleta* will be soggy, and crispness is the whole delicious deal. So they do what they often do: they shoot Rock, Paper, Scissors—best two out of three. Moreno loses. And moments later he is standing next to the neon Schlitz sign at the front window, watching a small crowd gather around a black Mercedes S500. From Moreno's deduction, it looks like the Mercedes side-swiped a light-green gypsy cab, a nondescript Toyota. The Toyota driver is arguing with the people from the Mercedes: two men, along with a woman who is holding an infant.

Meanwhile, lunch is getting cold. Moreno returns to the table, breaks open a can of Coke, and tells Restropo, "Just some stupid fender bender."

No sooner has Moreno taken a gulp of his Coke than they hear the clear, clean whizz of a bullet and the sound of the crowd yelling. Both cops jump up and run to the window.

The Toyota driver is on the ground, bleeding from his right thigh—not a great location to take a bullet. As the two cop partners rush out the restaurant door, Re-stropo notices the woman quickly place the infant into the arms of one of her companions. The woman then begins to run east on Northern Boulevard. The two NYPD officers are more concerned with the wounded man on the ground and the crowd around him.

The expected "Stand back! Stand back, everybody!" Then the expected call for "Significant backup. Urgent. 8015 Northern Boulevard, Jackson Heights. Urgent. Shooting. No fatalities."

God bless 911. Paramedics show up in five minutes. The female paramedic cuts the wounded man's pants leg at midthigh while her partner begins tight-suturing near the wound. Another paramedic fixes an oxygen mask on the wounded guy, then secures his head in a neck brace.

Moreno and Restropo try to sort out the scene. The cast of characters: two men—a good-looking blond and a heavyset guy in a dirty white shirt and a pair of baggy black pants. The blond guy is holding the baby.

"The woman shot the driver," says a teenage boy, pointing to the victim on the ground. "She shot him and ran like hell, over that way." He points in a general easterly direction.

"That's bullshit," says the blond man. "Someone in this crowd shot him."

Restropo and Moreno work fast. The hell with lunch. By now the Coke will be warm and the fried cutlet will be soggy. Restropo calls in an APB and gives the description of the runaway woman to the police desk: "short black skirt, white shirt, red shoes. A little on the fat side, I guess."

"Fuck that!" yells the blond guy. "Check the crowd right here for weapons."

Yes, the blond guy, the guy holding the baby, the guy yelling, he has a slight accent.

Moreno kneels next to the female paramedic. She gives him an update on the wounded man's condition. "He's gonna be okay. Whoever shot him missed the femoral."

Sirens. More sirens. Another ambulance. Two more patrol cars. A social worker takes the infant.

"We're taking the baby to the hospital for tests." The social worker gets into the second ambulance.

One of the newly arrived officers moves to the rear of the big Mercedes, then throws a thumb signal to Restropo. "Come here," he says. Then he shows Restropo the screen of his cell phone: FRAGMENT PLATE W7 at child abduction? Check.

Restropo looks down at the actual license plate. W7656445.

"Holy shit," says the new cop on the scene. "Looks like you and Moreno landed a big one."

And they have. Fyodor Orlov is under arrest. The driver, the big guy in white shirt and black pants, is also booked. Best of all, Valerina Gomez's baby is safe.

Only Nina, the female accomplice, is still on the loose.

CHAPTER 56

I GET A TWO-CAR police escort from the Brooklyn Children's Museum to Gramatan University Hospital in midtown. I am beyond nervous: I am numb with fear.

Halfway over the Brooklyn Bridge the PD radio blasts the news: they've got Orlov in custody. We also learn that Valerina's baby will be getting a total medical examination. They're bringing the baby over to GUH. Very thorough, very top-level. Top-flight pediatricians. Blood pressure, cardiogram, blood tests. The works. I'm still numb, but *happy* numb, almost like being stoned.

As soon as the car arrives at GUH, we jump out and rush like mad to one of the pediatric examination rooms. This is a big deal, real big. Along with three pediatricians, they've got a hematologist, two cardiologists, even a dermatologist, for God's sake, for my sake, for Tyonna's sake. Also in the examination room are a social worker, two NYPD officers, and—whaddya know—Leon Blumenthal.

"This baby made it through like a star," one of the pediatricians tells me.

I'd still like to slap Blumenthal's face, but I figure

one of us has to speak first. And it looks like it's going to be me.

"I've got to call Sabryna," I say.

Blumenthal nods. It's quite the conversation.

Then I tap Sabryna's number on my cell phone. She's somewhere between frantic and furious.

"Whaddya do with the baby, Lucy, take her on a boat to China?" she says. "Tyonna is my responsibility. Where is she?"

"I should have called. I'm sorry. Tyonna's at the hospital, my hospital, GUH, with me. Everything's fine," I say.

"Well, why wouldn't everything be fine?" asks Sabryna. "How come you brought her into the city?" she asks, the word *city* being every Brooklynite's name for Manhattan.

"No special reason. I wanted to look in on a few things, and I thought Tyonna might want to see where she was born."

Where'd that come from? I'm just not good at the task of lying.

"I think you're a crazy lady, Lucy. You better get her back here right now," says Sabryna. "You hear me, crazy lady? Right now." Oh, Sabryna's angry, but I can tell that she may be calming down a bit. She's most likely pleased that Tyonna is good.

"I'll be back there in Crown Heights in less than an hour. I'm sorry. I lost track of time." Then we say good-bye. Well, I say good-bye. Sabryna hangs up the phone.

I watch a nurse give the baby a sponge bath, put a clean diaper on her, and rub cream on the baby's pudgy little legs. Then finally Blumenthal speaks.

"Lucky Lucy," he says.

"What?" I say.

"Lucky Lucy. If you were a boat, that's what we'd name the boat." For good measure he repeats the name of the make-believe boat: *"Lucky Lucy."*

"Lucky?" I say angrily. "Two goddamn days in a row I've been mugged!"

"And two goddamn days in a row you beat the odds. You got away with a little scratch in Penn Station, and this second time around you still got only a scratch, and—thank you very much—we ended up getting one of the kidnappers."

If I needed further proof that there is a world of difference between Lucy Ryuan and Leon Blumenthal, this is it. To me my experiences were near-death deals; to him they were *business as usual*.

I am about to call him a *stupid son of a bitch* when Assistant Detective Bobby Cilia walks into the room. Cilia looks back and forth between Blumenthal and me. Then he starts talking. "The driver's a wash. Seems to know absolutely nothing, but we'll see. We can't get shit out of Orlov. I was with him a half hour in the car and he just kept his mouth shut and stared straight out into space."

Blumenthal says, "I'll be at the precinct in fifteen minutes. We'll work on Orlov there."

"You'll *work on him*?" I ask.

"Yes," says Blumenthal. "You think I'm talking waterboarding here? No, Lucy. Certainly not that extreme. But we need to find out everything he knows." He pauses, then says, "Are you ever going to trust me?"

"I'd like my answer to be yes," I say.

Then Blumenthal turns to look directly at me. "Okay, enough. Is there anything else you and I need to talk about?" Blumenthal doesn't really wait for my answer. He simply answers his own question: "No. I don't think so. The two cops who handled the Queens accident from the get-go are talking to my people. And we've got Queens and Long Island covered for a sign of this Nina woman."

A pediatrician approaches. She's carrying Tyonna. The doctor looks first at Blumenthal, then at me. Blumenthal holds up both his hands in the *not me* position.

"The baby goes to Ms. Ryuan," he says. Then he speaks directly to me, "Get her back to Sabryna as fast as you can. I'll get someone to drive you. And take another day of R and R."

I want to say, *"Don't you dare tell me what to do, asshole. You're not my boss,"* but instead I take the sweet-looking, sweet-smelling baby and brush her face gently.

Then I reach into my pocket and remove my cell phone, the phone that has the recording of Orlov and Nina. I'm now holding the baby against me with one arm and holding the phone in the hand of the other arm.

"Will you take the baby, Detective?" I say.

You'd think I'd asked Blumenthal to hold a grenade.

"Babies don't like me. In fact, they hate me."

I don't even bother saying *"I'm not surprised."* I'm sure Blumenthal knows that I'm thinking it.

I manage to press some buttons on my phone.

"What's up, Lucy?" he says.

"What's up is the recording I sent you just this second. When I'm out of here, give it a listen."

"Give me a preview," he says.

"No," I say. "I've got a baby who needs a nap." Then, as the baby and I head toward the door, I say, "Oh, and, by the way, when you listen to the recording, be sure to have a Russian language translator standing by."

CHAPTER 57

"YOU TAKE MY BABY out for a walk and where'd you walk her? Africa? Canada? Nicaragua?"

"Are all your guesses going to be places that end with the letter *a*?" I say.

Understandably, Sabryna does not appreciate my humor.

Loudly she says, "Where you been, lady?"

Here we go. Sabryna is pissed. So much for my thinking that she calmed down. I can't say that I blame her. I move to hand her the baby. Sabryna reaches out to me and quickly pulls Tyonna into her own arms.

"Come on, Lucy. Start your confession. You owe me a fine explanation."

I am just no good at lying. When I tell someone a lie, he or she always knows I'm lying. My voice becomes sing-song. My eyes look everywhere except into the other person's eyes.

"It's like I told you. I got a call from the hospital. They were backed up. I thought it wouldn't do any harm to go there and take the baby with me."

"Well, you thought stupid," says Sabryna. "All's you have to do is call me on your phone and tell me what's happening. I worried so's my head was bursting until I heard from you. And I'm not too sure that I'm believing your story even now."

Oh, shit. I knew this wasn't going to work.

"Tyonna had a great time at the hospital. You know, with all the other babies."

Sabryna tilts her head. Her forehead wrinkles with a quizzical expression. "What in hell's wrong with you, Lucy? They're stealing babies like they were candy bars in my store, and you go bringing Tyonna to a hospital, the place where they're doing the stealing."

Okay, my mother was right. Once you tell a lie you end up drowning in it. And, sweet Lord, I am twenty feet underwater.

"Okay, okay. I was wrong."

No response from Sabryna. But I'm coming up for air.

"In any case, I'm sorry. But tell me. How did Willie and Devan do?" I ask.

"They did just fine. Willie is up in your place sleeping. Don't worry. I checked up on him thirty minutes ago. He's fine. Unlike some people, *I'm* a very reliable caregiver."

Sabryna could not have said that last sentence any more emphatically.

"And where's Devan?" I ask.

"He's out with his friends, Warren and Kwame. They're older boys. I wouldn't let Willie go with them. Because I'm—"

I cut her off and say the line for her. "I know…because you're a very reliable caregiver."

She ignores that. No laughing. No smiling. No comment.

"When did this baby eat last?" Sabryna asks.

"I fed her just before I left GUH. Her belly's full."

"Yeah," says Sabryna. "She fell asleep the second she was in my arms. She must be real tired...after her day with all that traveling."

I'm not going for the bait. Then suddenly Sabryna speaks fairly loudly, a note of alarm in her voice. "Sweet Jesus! What's this red mark on her poor little foot?"

I look. I know exactly what Sabryna has seen. It's a minuscule dot where the GUH nurse took a drop of blood for testing.

"I don't see anything," I say.

I've got to get out of here. I cannot keep up this lying any longer. This is not my talent. I'm going to crack.

I suddenly remember that there's a small bandage on the back of my neck from the bad fall I took at the playground sprinkler. I check with my hand to make sure my hair is covering it.

"Anyway," I say, "I'm going to go upstairs, see how Willie's doing. Then I need to get some sleep. I'm exhausted."

"And I'll put this little one down," says Sabryna.

"Listen," I say. "I'm sorry I caused you so much worry."

"And I'm sorry that I went off at you," she says.

"Thanks," I say, and I give Sabryna and Tyonna each a gentle kiss.

"But just so you know," Sabryna says, "I know there's more to today's story than what you're telling me. I'll get it out of you."

"I'm sure you will." And I really am sure she will.

CHAPTER 58

I CLIMB THE STAIRS to my apartment, where The Duke barely opens his eyes to greet me. Of course the first thing I do is check on Willie.

All is well. He has fallen asleep with his Nintendo Switch console. I once told him that he should just have that damned thing surgically attached to his hand. He actually said that was a *"great idea."* I think he was joking.

I take a shower and wash my hair. I think about putting moisturizer on my face. I think about emptying the dishwasher. I think about...Who the hell am I kidding? I'm just too damned exhausted to do anything but go to bed.

I glance at the open sleeper sofa. All I've got to do is clear away a few piles of clothing, a half-empty container of chicken lo mein, a laptop, one television remote control, one Roku control, and assorted snail mail. Instead of trying to find the energy to clear an actual space for myself on the bed I fall onto a small pile of sweatshirts (clean sweatshirts, by the way).

And of course all of a sudden, precisely when I close my eyes, I feel wide-awake. And of course I can think of nothing but the kidnapping and mugging at the park. I see Orlov, his white-blond hair, his firm grip on Tyonna. I see Nina's fashionably unfashionable shoes. I can almost feel the sprinkler water on my face. I see Tyonna's happy little face. Then the knife, I see Orlov's knife.

I've got to stop. I've got to sleep.

Instead I see the black Mercedes pulling away. I watch Blumenthal's cold, unmoving face as he icily orders me around. I worry about Sabryna and our friendship. I haven't had a friend as close as Sabryna since grammar school.

I consider popping an Ambien. I consider popping a Xanax. I consider pouring myself a small glass of special-occasion Chivas. Then a brainstorm, what the shrinks call *a breakthrough*.

I realize what might really put me at peace: knowing what Orlov and Nina said to each other in that recorded conversation.

I grab my cell phone and call Leon Blumenthal.

"Lucy, what are you calling for?"

No hello. Just that.

"This is important," I say. "Did you get that Russian conversation between Orlov and Nina translated?"

"Of course I did."

"So what were they saying?"

There is a pause.

"What were they saying?" I repeat.

There is a shorter pause. Then Blumenthal speaks. His voice is quick and quiet. "I can't tell you. It's classified."

"I can't believe you said that. You've got to be kidding!"

"No, I'm not kidding."

"Well, just give me a general idea of the conversation."

"I'm sorry. I can't," he says.

"You're not sorry," I say. "You're just an asshole."

"Lucy, listen…this is official NYPD info. This—"

"'Official NYPD info'…Bullshit. And even if it is 'official,' it's NYPD info that I supplied," I shout.

I'm furious. I call him an asshole once more. I stammer a bit and say, "This was *my* information."

My voice is so loud that I've woken Willie. He and his game console are standing at the bedroom door. I click off my phone and take Willie into my arms. We hug.

"I'm sorry, sweetie," I say. "Mom was having an argument."

"Yeah, I sorta thought so."

"I'm sorry I woke you."

"I'm not," he says.

Then I walk him back to his room.

As I tuck Willie under the sheet, I get an idea, a very smart idea.

CHAPTER 59

AFTER I FINALLY MANAGE some sleep, at 5 a.m. I text Sabryna.

Please keep an eye on Willie. I've got something really important I must do.

Of course Sabryna's already awake, down in the shop. She texts back.

No problem. Go solve your problems, lady.

At 7 a.m., I'm getting off the Q train. The air is warm, misty, yet strangely refreshing. I'm only a few blocks from the Atlantic Ocean.

Even at this early hour a few hundred people are sitting or running on the boardwalk at Brighton Beach, Brooklyn. This area of Coney Island is called Little Odessa because Odessa is where many of the first immigrants hailed from—at least that's what I was once told. Now the immigrants come from all parts of Russia. It is crowded and busy and very foreign, very, well, Russian.

I walk along the boardwalk. On my left is the beach, where later in the day the older heavy women will be wearing one-piece black bathing suits with little black skirts attached. Some of these old girls will even wear old-fashioned rubber bathing caps. The shapely younger women will be wearing barely-there bikinis. To my right are the shops and restaurants, most of them now shuttered.

No, I am not here to look for Nina, and I'm certainly not looking for anyone who might be her hidden accomplices. I am also not looking for men in cheap suits, men who might be members of the Russian mafia.

I am looking for a fish store, called Seafood King. When I find that fish store, I should also find Irina and Nik, the owners. Irina is a mother whose baby I helped deliver about two years ago. It was a tough birth, almost fifteen hours of labor. When it was time for Troy to relieve me, Irina and Nik pleaded with me to stay. Irina said I was her good-luck charm. I agreed to stay. The result? A midwife almost as exhausted as the mother. And a terrific baby boy, Pavel, nine pounds, two ounces. Ouch.

According to Google Maps, Seafood King is near the water and not far from the New York Aquarium. I see the aquarium ahead. Seafood King should be just off the boardwalk on the right.

Yes!

Irina is at the wooden display cases in front of the store. She shovels heaping loads of chopped ice on top of the flounder and bluefish and shrimp. I call to her, and she freezes in place. It's how I imagine the saints reacted when the Blessed Virgin appeared to them. Her eyes are wide open. Her hands cover her mouth.

I rush toward her. "Yes, it's me. It's Lucy!" I shout.

"Gospodi pomilui," she shouts back at me. It means "God have mercy." Irina taught me this Russian saying when I was yelling *"One more big push"* during Pavel's birth.

We hug each other. Nik joins us. Pavel joins us. We hug. We kiss. And of course there is an immediate offer of food. I hold Pavel.

"I'll get us some good smoked belly salmon," says Nik.

"No," I say. "It's too early for me to eat a thing. Some of that nice strong tea you used to bring in the thermos. Do you have any of that?"

"We always have that ready," says Nik. "And I will bring some smoked salmon and black bread in case you change your mind."

When he returns with the tea and salmon, we talk. We all agree that, one, Pavel is handsome and strong, two, Pavel looks exactly like Irina's grandmother (whose photograph Irina wears in a locket on a chain around her neck), and, three, I must have come all the way to Brighton Beach for a specific reason.

"Yes," I say. "There is a reason. I have a favor to ask of you."

"Of course, anything," Nik says. "I will move the sun and the stars for you."

"Well," I say, "it won't be quite that challenging."

"Let her talk, Nik. Let her talk," says Irina.

"It's a small favor, but it's important to me," I say.

"Like Nik says, anything, anything," says Irina.

I take my cell phone from my bag. I explain that they will be hearing a brief conversation on my phone. It's spoken in Russian.

"What I need is for you to translate it for me," I say.

"For a translation you needed to come all the way out to Brighton Beach?" Nik asks.

"As a matter of fact, I did. First, you are the only Russian speakers I know, and, second, I want it done, shall we say, discreetly."

"We are Russians. We know how to be, like you say, discreet," says Irina.

I'm not quite sure what she means, and for a split second I worry that she could somehow be caught in the web of Orlov and Nina and…Ridiculous! I'm here. Nik and Irina are the best people in the world.

"Ready to listen?" I ask.

When they nod yes, I press the button, and in a few moments we are all listening to the angry conversation between Nina and Orlov.

"Play it again," says Nik. And I play it again. And again. And again.

"You know," says Irina, "they are not speaking Russian."

My heart drops. I never thought of that possibility.

"What is it? Polish? Hungarian?" I ask.

"No," says Irina. "It is Ukrainian. But not to worry. They are very similar languages."

"Don't scare me like that," I say. They listen to the conversation one more time.

Irina explains: "The woman is saying, 'This is stupid and crazy. If we get caught we will be dead, finished.' Then the man says, 'I am in charge here. You will do as I say.' Then there is a moaning sound. I do not think it is the moaning of the woman."

"No, it's not," I tell her. It is at this point that Orlov or Nina must have pushed me to the ground.

Irina continues: "The woman is saying now, 'I cannot be a part of this. The baby belongs to this woman.'"

Nik says, "Then the man says for her to 'shut the hell up so we can get this baby and get out of here. Our customers need a baby right away. Now!'"

There is background noise. Children shouting. I

think I hear the two kidnappers walking off. But who can tell in all the chaos, with all the people.

But what does it all mean? Not much, I think. We already know Orlov is the boss. I always suspected Nina has some maternal sympathy for the mothers she's stealing from. And finally, the only interesting thing to emerge from this translation is this, the use of the word *customers.* *"Our customers need a baby right away. Now!"*

CHAPTER 60

IT'S AN EASY GUESS and a good guess that Blumenthal is still at the precinct where Orlov is being held. Needless to say, that's precisely where I *want* to be. But, as is usually the case, where I absolutely *need* to be is at Gramatan University Hospital to be available to my pregnant mothers.

GUH is a mess: Tracy Anne has not shown up as yet that morning, and no one knows where she is. Troy has worked for thirteen straight hours, through the night. So he's having a catch-up nap in the sleep room. Two quite dependable trainees are working with two very young mothers who have gone into early labor. I look in on both. So far, so good. I'll check in with them every fifteen minutes.

What about me? Well, my list shows that I have three women who could be delivering at any moment or, at the very least, in the next few hours.

Meanwhile, my waiting room is full, very full, eleven women full. Four are there for the prenatal diet and exercise class. We do it. There's a lot of moaning and quite a few bathroom breaks, but eventually the one-hour class ends.

Damn it, there's still no word from Tracy Anne. I've

called her. HR has called her. So I email my favorite backup midwife over at NYU Langone. Her name is Lizzie Witten, and she's the best in the business. Great news: Lizzie Witten's available, and she'll be at GUH in twenty minutes. The moment Witten arrives, I run down to the temporary NYPD/FBI investigation room on the second floor, where I'm told Blumenthal is right now back at the NYPD Major Case Squad offices downtown.

I am, as I have often been, pissed off at Blumenthal. His long silences come across as smugness. His voice usually has a bored or impatient tone to it, as if it's nothing but a painful chore to speak to me, to answer my questions. And his lack of gratitude for my help in this case so far makes me want to punch him in the face every time I see him.

The more I think about Blumenthal, the angrier I become. After my encounter in the cemetery, after my mugging in the park, after my trip out to Brighton, the volcano inside me feels like it's about to explode.

So I take the subway down to One Police Plaza. Hell. I just can't control myself.

"Welcome, Ms. Ryuan," Blumenthal says when, without knocking, I walk into the office I've been led to by another detective in the squad. "Always a pleasure."

"I'm warning you, Detective. Don't start up with me," I say.

"Why are you here?"

"I wanted to tell you in person that I had my cell phone recording translated."

"I'm not at all surprised. I suspected you would do that."

My hands are practically vibrating with anger. My mouth is going dry. Then it happens. I explode.

"You self-satisfied son of a bitch. I've done more to move this case forward than you or anyone else in this department. *And I'm not even part of this goddamn department.*"

"Lucy, listen—" he begins.

"'Listen'? 'Lucy, listen'? Don't you dare start with that 'Lucy, listen' phrase," I shout. "Don't fucking condescend to me. *I'm* the one who spotted the shoes on Nina. *I'm* the one who played decoy in the cemetery and met with two criminals, two killers. *I'm* the one who got my head smashed open in the park."

"Stop it," he says. Loudly. Very loudly. Then he says, "And I'm the one who appreciates it all. You're the one who needs to be petted and kissed and thanked a thousand times. I *absolutely* appreciate all you've done…and all you can still do to help."

I have to interrupt. "Then why did I have to schlep out to the bowels of Brooklyn because you wouldn't give me the translation?"

"That's because it was classified, and we can't transmit classified information over the phone or by email. If you had just waited, if you had just trusted me. And anyway, now that we both know what Orlov and Nina were saying to each other, let me ask you: does it make any difference?"

The conversation goes silent. Finally, I break that silence.

"No," I say. "It doesn't make a damn bit of difference."

Silence once again. Blumenthal looks down at the floor. Then we both look through a glass panel of his office wall. We look out at the men and women in the office who are pretending not to look at us.

Now I speak quietly. I almost want to hold him

by the shoulders so that he'll listen. "Detective, please, please pay attention to what I say. If you do, then you'll understand why I am the way I am." Then I say, "This is all about *babies*. This isn't a jewel theft on Fifth Avenue. This isn't a druggie who cuts his skeevy dealer in the belly. This isn't a robbery in a bodega or a husband who skipped out on his wife with the savings account money. *This is babies!* I'm not a very good Catholic. There's a lot I don't believe in. But I do believe that babies are miracles. They're gifts from God. This is the biggest tragedy I've ever been close to. This means everything to me."

There is no pause. Blumenthal looks straight at me and says, "Lucy, I feel exactly the same way."

And suddenly I believe that he does.

When he speaks next, he is all business, but it's important business. "I want to tell you that I think I'm onto something—actually, someone—who can help us," he says.

"Did Orlov start talking?" I ask.

"No. He's still closed tight. But like I said, I've got something else—*someone* else."

"Okay," I say. "What is it? Who is it?"

Blumenthal picks up his cell phone and drops it into his shirt pocket. He walks to the office door.

"Just follow me."

CHAPTER 61

I WALK WITH LEON Blumenthal down some flights of stairs to a parking garage, then we take a sweaty drive in an unmarked police car north to West 35th Street and the Midtown Precinct South. It dawns on me that I was quite recently here. After the mugging at Penn Station.

When we enter, I immediately get the impression that Blumenthal is a pretty respected guy here. He walks the wide, gray corridors while handing out a lot of friendly nods. He takes me well past the room Willie and I sat in that evening, and deeper into the building.

"Go left here," Blumenthal says. A stenciled plastic sign on a glass door is meant to spell out the words INTERROGATION ROOMS. Instead some clever asshole has blacked out the first seven letters of the sign and inked in SEGRA. So now it says SEGRAGATION ROOMS.

"Very classy signage," I say. Then I add, "Ignore the fact that the word's misspelled. What the hell does that mean?"

Blumenthal shrugs. "Who the hell knows?" he says. "A lot of angry, crazy people pass through every precinct in this city."

We arrive at a door marked ROOM 1. Next to that door is another door. This second door is marked OBSERVATION ROOM 1.

"You wait out here for a minute, Lucy. I'm going in to clear you with the interviewer and, even more important, with the guy we're interviewing."

So it's a guy.

Blumenthal knocks and enters. I immediately recognize Bobby Cilia's voice coming from inside the room.

"Detective Leon Blumenthal enters the room at ten seventeen. Good morning—"

The door closes, and I'm left standing alone in the hall. Not many people are walking this hallway. One officer with one weeping woman in cuffs. Two officers walking together while both are looking at the screen of a cell phone.

I'm about to check my phone, but before I can punch in my code, a young and quite pretty woman appears next to me. The woman is blond and un-necessarily skinny. She is wearing a sundress—light, cotton, sleeveless, big red floral print on a white background—and carrying a chic brown Birkin bag. She speaks to me.

"Forget it." She points to a sign: NO CELL PHONES IN INTERROGATION ROOMS.

"Wow," I say. "I should read more. That sign is bigger than my car."

Then she says, "Have you by any chance seen Leon Blumenthal slithering around here?"

"Yeah, he slithered into this room right here," I say, pointing to the interrogation room.

"I'd better not interrupt. Leon hates that," she says. At first it seems as if the woman is going to walk away with her sunny little sundress, in her heels with red soles, but then she stops.

"Hey," she says. "I have to ask you something: are you Lucy Ryuan?"

"How'd you know that?" I ask.

"I only figured it out because you're here, and he's there, and whenever I see Leon, he talks about you. By the way, I'm Barbara Holt."

I should introduce myself, of course, but what I end up saying is this: "Blumenthal talks about me?"

"Yeah, he refers to you as his 'unofficial special assistant.'"

It takes me a few moments to process this info. I wonder if he says it sarcastically or respectfully. Probably both ways, depending on his mood and our relationship of the moment.

But before I can respond, my new friend suddenly says, "Damn. I was supposed to be in a meeting downtown at my office ten minutes ago. I should quit my job and spend all my time keeping track of Leon. I hope I see you again, Ms. Ryuan."

"Yes, me too," I say.

And Barbara Holt's fancy red-soled shoes take her quickly down the corridor toward the EXIT sign. One thing I know is this: I'm really not hoping to see her again.

I am, however, considering the information that Blumenthal has told people, even just one person, even as a joke, that I'm his special assistant. I'm also wondering, of course, who exactly is Barbara Holt, and what exactly is her role in Blumenthal's life?

Then the door opens. Blumenthal comes out, and I hear Bobby's voice begin: "Detective Leon Blumenthal is leaving the—" Blumenthal closes the door behind himself. I'm suddenly looking at Blumenthal in a whole new way.

"We're going into the viewing room. Two-way mirror."

We enter a small, dark, stale-smelling room. High-school-student-type desks.

A light-brown curtain covers what I assume is one side of the two-way mirror. I sit down, and Blumenthal says, "Okay. I'm going to pull the curtain open and turn on the speaker."

Opposite Cilia, facing the mirror, facing us, is...I stand up to get a better look. My hand flies to my mouth. I yell.

"Holy shit. It's Troy!"

CHAPTER 62

I RUSH TO THE door of the viewing room.

Blumenthal shouts, "Lucy, wait. You cannot go in there."

"The hell I can't."

Blumenthal has joined me and blocks the door. "We're just questioning him," he says.

"Is he under arrest? Is he a person of interest?" I ask, wondering if I need to punch Blumenthal in the stomach (or somewhere close to the stomach).

"No, he's not under arrest. He's not under suspicion. He's not anything. He's here to help."

"Great news. Then I'm going in," I say.

Turns out I do not have to punch Blumenthal anywhere. He moves away from the door, and as I enter the interrogation room, Troy rises from his seat and hugs me.

"What the hell's the story? Why are you here?" I yell. I have about a thousand more questions, but Blumenthal jumps in.

Blumenthal says that *he'll* explain. Bobby Cilia says that *he* should explain. And seizing one of the rare moments when I have a bit of control over the situation, I suggest that Troy can do his own explaining. So Troy starts.

"First of all, I'm sorry, Lucy. I'm sorry as hell. You finding out this way. I shoulda come to you right away. I shoulda—"

"Yeah, yeah, yeah," I say. "Just tell me what happened. How'd you end up here?"

"I'm gonna tell you. But first you gotta promise you'll forgive me for not going to see you sooner. It's just that things were getting crazy rough, and I couldn't get hold of you. So I went to the detective. I'm so sorry. I'm—"

"Jesus Christ, Troy! Just tell me what happened. Tell me the goddamn story!"

And he does.

"Last week Tracy Anne comes in to see me all teary and shaky and nervous. She sits me down and closes the doors, and she makes me promise not to tell anyone anything about what she's going to tell me. So I swear on a stack of make-believe Bibles, and she tells me that she's been…that she's been freelancing."

Freelancing, when you're a midwife, means that you're helping with deliveries but not in connection with a hospital. It's, well, a totally unconnected *freelance* job. It's usually dangerous. It means you have no real support system—no other midwives, no prenatal care, no postnatal care. It's pretty much like the frontier days when a midwife showed up when the pain began and did her best to help the delivery. Freelancing is usually used by illegal immigrants and drug addicts and very often by women who don't want anyone else to know they're giving birth—that would be women like teenage prostitutes and homeless women. Most of the freelance midwives aren't trained with the depth and knowledge professionals are. At least Tracy Anne has impeccable training and an excellent education. But it's still a bad thing to do, and because of Tracy Anne's association with GUH, it's also totally forbidden by the hospital for her to do it.

Back to Troy. He's calmed down a little, but he's still doing some serious shaking.

"So Tracy Anne tells me that she's done six free-lance births in the last two weeks, and she did a few more before that. Well, more than 'a few.' So many other births that she's even lost track. It seems the last six were all teenagers and they were all drug addicts. One of them surely had AIDS, Tracy Anne said, and another one was bleeding out so much they had to bring her to a really sketchy off-the-street clinic in Bed-Stuy."

Bobby Cilia shakes his head in wonder at the horror of this tale. Blumenthal stands in stony silence.

"Anyway, Tracy Anne tells me that she's getting all her freelance jobs from this Russian couple. I know, I know. Just like the ones you're closing in on—that's when I knew I couldn't let the story rest without telling someone. And poor Tracy Anne was ready to kill herself. I mean truly, literally, she was talking about how she was in such deep shit already that there was no way out but to kill herself."

I say nothing, but I am incredibly angry and incredibly sad that one of my most trusted midwives has stooped to such a dangerous and unethical level. And I'm thinking, *Why? Why do this, Tracy Anne?* Okay, I'm sad, but I'm also shocked. No one is better at her job than Tracy Anne. And if you're thinking that in her I saw the younger me, well, you're absolutely correct.

It's also pretty clear that Troy knows everything about this. He keeps talking, and I keep being amazed.

Now Troy tells us that Tracy Anne was paid a thousand dollars per delivery. They were all "at home" deliveries, although the home might've been a filthy basement room where dealers were cooking crack, or an outdoor alley in a Bronx housing project.

"The thing is, Tracy Anne said these Russian people said they were selling the babies to give to rich people. At least that's what they told Tracy Anne. And of course she believed them. Why not? It made her feel better."

"Yep. She wanted to believe them," says Bobby. And I think he's right about that.

I jump in. "Where is Tracy Anne now?"

"That's just it," says Bobby. "She disappeared two days ago. We're looking for her."

I look at Troy. "You don't know where she is, Troy?"

"No. I don't," he says.

"Are you sure?" I ask. Big mistake.

Troy goes from being nervous and contrite to being angry and belligerent. "No, damn it! I absolutely do not know where that girl is hiding out. She's scared. She's in trouble with the police, with the hospital, with the Russian crazy people. So of course she's gone and made herself disappear. She could be dead for all I know."

Bobby says, "This girl is deep in the shitter."

Troy starts talking again. "Look here, Lucy. I broke a confidence by coming in here. I know that. But I had to…"

Blumenthal finally says something, and it's not sympathetic to the situation. "Yeah, you broke a confidence about somebody who broke the law. They don't give out medals for that."

I look at Troy and speak. I'm taking a safety risk

with my question. "You're positive that you don't know where Tracy Anne is?"

This time Troy answers calmly. "Positive as a man can be. But please don't ask me again. My heart hurts every time you ask that question."

My mind is rushing with other questions, not just for Troy but for everybody in the room:

What took Troy so long to tell anyone about this?

Is Tracy Anne telling the truth? And where the hell is she?

How can the NYPD get Orlov to talk?

Where's Nina?

And there's one other question. It's small and dumb, but I just can't shake this one out of my head:

Detective Blumenthal, what's the deal with you and this Barbara Holt woman?

CHAPTER 63

THIRTY MINUTES LATER, FYODOR Orlov is sitting at the table in the same interrogation room where Troy had been questioned. Leon Blumenthal sits on the opposite side of the table, facing Orlov. An armed police officer stands watching both men. Orlov has declined his right to have an attorney present.

Bobby Cilia and I are on the other side of the mirror in the viewing room. Will Blumenthal be able to get information from Orlov? Both Blumenthal and Orlov look remarkably calm and determined, given the situation.

"We now know a great deal more about you and your accomplice, Mr. Orlov," says Blumenthal.

Bobby looks at me and whispers, "That's a mistake. Detective B shouldn't call him mister. He shouldn't be showing any respect for the guy."

My response to Bobby is a very clever: "Yeah, I'm sure you're absolutely right." That's my personal shorthand for *If you knew more than your boss, you'd be sitting where he is right now.*

Orlov's response to Blumenthal is complete silence.

Blumenthal begins talking again. This time he talks faster. As he talks, he builds up even more speed.

"We know, for example, that you've been assisted by one of the midwives at GUH, Tracy Anne Cavanaugh," says Blumenthal.

Orlov's reaction? A smirk, a sickly smile with twinkling eyes.

I fantasize about crashing through the two-way mirror and choking the bastard. When that thought passes, I'm not very surprised to find that I'm thinking about Barbara Holt and her Louboutin shoes.

"Your partner, your lady friend—we have her," says Blumenthal. This is, of course, a complete lie. "We" do not have Nina. "We" do not even have a clue as to where Nina is.

"Yeah," continues Blumenthal. "Your buddy, or girlfriend, or mistress, or whatever the hell you want to call her, is sitting about a hundred feet away from you, down the hall, in a room just like this one. She's being asked the same questions. She's just—"

Orlov stands quickly. The guarding officer steps in toward him and pushes him back down onto the chair.

"Cuffs, Detective?" the officer asks.

"No, not yet," says Blumenthal. "But maybe soon."

"You are all so fucking stupid!" Orlov shouts. "You know nothing. You know that there are babies going to rich people who so long for what they cannot make themselves, but knowing even that, you still know nothing."

Blumenthal does not react. He lets an icy silence hang in the air, and it is that one minute or so of silence that seems to agitate Orlov.

The Russian speaks. "You have Nina Kozlova, but you still have nothing."

I turn and speak to Bobby Cilia. "Well, we now do have one thing. We just got Nina's last name."

"It's funny," Bobby says. "Funny how these Russians are sort of programmed to say people's full names. The guy doesn't call her just Nina. He calls her Nina Kozlova."

I had never thought of that, but it feels like it could be true. Nina Kozlova.

The dialogue between Blumenthal and Orlov has fizzled, and I decide it's eating up time that could be better spent looking for both Tracy Anne and Nina. When I mention this to Bobby, he says, "You're right. But Detective Blumenthal has his own way of doing things. And his own way of doing things has been proven mostly successful in the past."

"So you think he'll spend the rest of the day sitting here and allowing Orlov to laugh at him."

"No, I don't, not at all," Bobby says. "I think he'll move Orlov into a private interview room."

"I'm new to all this. This room here looks pretty private," I say.

"*Pretty* private. The other room, the private room, is *very* private."

"And that means?"

"That means there's no video recorder, no two-way mirror, no observers. It'll be just Detective Blumenthal, maybe myself, maybe another detective, probably an emergency medic. Absolutely no one else."

I say nothing. I'm an enthusiastic amateur, but I'm an amateur. Yet I absolutely get what Bobby is saying.

The liberal in me abhors the concept. The midwife in me says, *Why the hell not try it? The babies! How can I forget the babies?*

As if on cue, I look back through the two-way mirror and watch Blumenthal stand up. He looks at

Orlov. There's a slight smile—not quite a pleasant smile—on Blumenthal's face.

"I want to thank you for your help and cooperation, Fyodor. In fact, you've been so helpful that I'd like to continue this conversation."

Blumenthal looks at the cop standing by the door. "Officer, would you please escort Mr. Orlov to room 301B. And after you've secured the interviewee, please make the usual arrangements."

All Bobby Cilia says is "Told ya, ma'am."

CHAPTER 64

SECONDS LATER LEON BLUMENTHAL enters the observation room.

"Where will you be taking Orlov?" I ask Blumenthal.

He ignores my question. Instead he thrusts an iPad into my hands.

I assume that whatever is on the iPad has something to do with the baby-napping cases.

"Read it," Blumenthal says. Then he looks at Bobby Cilia and says, "It's the official release from the AG's office."

Bobby nods. Obviously Cilia and Blumenthal know something I don't know. I look down at the screen and read:

New York State Assistant Attorney General Roseanne Fiore announced today the indictment of Dr. Barrett Katz, chief executive officer, of Gramatan University Hospital, the world-renowned medical complex in midtown Manhattan. Dr. Katz, who has taken a leave of absence, is accused of committing Medicaid fraud by falsifying hospital reimbursement records for guardians of handicapped or otherwise challenged patients.

Ms. Fiore said, "Dr. Katz's behavior and methodology were illegal in fact and shocking in scope." Dr. Katz established bogus deposit accounts for patients, usually senior citizens, with significant dementia challenges. Their guardians were promised special "extra care" treatment for their charges when they agreed that certain Medicare payments be sent to Dr. Katz's private bank accounts, many of which were set up in Caribbean countries and two cities in southern France, Marseilles and Nice.

Bail was set at two million dollars for Dr. Katz, and he was released on his own recognizance. No trial date has been set.

In Dr. Katz's absence, Dr. Rudra Sarkar, GUH chair of obstetrics and gynecology, will assume the role of CEO. In a statement released by the hospital, Dr. Sarkar said, "We are astonished by these accusations, and we fully stand by Dr. Katz at this time."

Dr. Katz was not available for comment. He is said to be at his summer estate in Peconic, Long Island.

I look at Blumenthal, who shrugs and opens both his eyes in a *What can I tell you?* expression.

"How long has this been going on?" I ask.

"About three years," he says.

Then Bobby jumps in: "But the investigation from the AG's office has only been going for ten months. Even so, the evidence is there."

"And how long have you personally, privately, *secretly* known about this?" I ask Blumenthal.

"Exactly four days," he says. Anticipating my anger, he adds, "And that's the absolute truth. This Katz guy is best buds with half the big shots in New York, and those big shots include the mayor and the commissioner, plus some of Gramatan's biggest and most important donors."

"I believe you," I say. I do believe Blumenthal, but what pisses me off is that Sarkar never mentioned any of this to me, not even when I saw Katz leave the hospital with what I now realize was a police escort. I should have insisted that Sarkar tell me what was happening. But—a big *but*—he should have offered up the info without my asking.

I nod my head slowly, and with an appropriately small smile, I say to Blumenthal, "Maybe NYPD should have set up a whole special unit just to deal with crime at Gramatan University Hospital."

"Could be a job in it for you," Blumenthal says with an equally small smile.

Before I can invent a wiseass response, my cell phone begins ringing. It's Troy.

"What's up?"

"I'm back at the hospital," he says. "I thought you'd want to know."

"I told you to go home and rest," I say.

"I was going to, and I was just about to leave from here, to go home, but then that Bella Morabito woman showed up. She's in labor, and the other backup midwife hasn't shown up yet. The Witten woman showed up, but she's up to her neck in mothers-to-be."

Shit. Bella Morabito is a forty-three-year-old immigrant from Sicily. She has a fifteen-year-old daughter and a history of three miscarriages. She is also just about the nicest woman on earth—warm, funny, friendly. But I'm not looking forward to this delivery. This one could turn out to be very difficult. Like some of Bella's previous birthing experiences, it may not turn out at all.

"Stay with Bella, Troy. I'll be there in ten minutes."

CHAPTER 65

I WALK INTO BELLA'S birthing room and see so many people that it actually takes me a moment to find Bella on her bed. Her teenage daughter, her husband, her mother, Troy, two trainees in the midwife program, plus three other women, who are presumably Bella's friends or more relatives.

Bella is groaning significantly, but I recognize it as the healthy groaning of a healthy woman in healthy labor. A small speaker sits on the side table next to a laptop. From the speaker comes a song accompanied only by a guitar. The tune is easily recognizable. The Beatles. "Let It Be," sung in Italian.

Quando mi trovo in momenti difficili
Madre Maria viene da me

"How are we doing here?" I ask.

Bella grabs both my hands and says, "Signora Lucy, please make it all good."

"We'll do our best," I say.

"No," she says. "You must do better than that. You must make this happen right."

Troy gives me an update: all is well, blood pressure

normal, temperature normal, baby in good position, fetal monitor is happy-happy, dilation has grown to nine centimeters.

"I think we're ready," I say.

"I think we're *very* ready," says Troy.

Then I say, "I didn't notice, Troy, are there guards and officers on the floor?"

"You sure didn't notice," says Troy. "We got one NYPD woman and one rent-a-cop right outside this door."

Things move quickly, and I advise Bella to steady her breathing. She does. She's with the plan.

Then I ask that we clear the room of unnecessary personnel. Apparently nobody in the room believes himself or herself to be unnecessary. So nobody leaves. I'm not going to argue. All I can do is tell Bella's husband, Marco, to move closer to the bed.

Only occasionally does Bella let out an "Ooh" or an "Oof" of pain. It all happens quickly.

"Whoa, mama," says Troy. "This is happening faster than they do it on TV."

Troy's referring to a GUH midwives joke that every birth on the British television show *Call the Midwife* requires about two minutes of labor before the baby arrives.

Back to work.

Here it comes. The baby's head crowns, a perfect little yarmulke of jet-black hair. We're ready to go. Troy gives the "Little breath, little breath, big push" order, and Bella does her best. A pause, and when Troy says so, Bella pushes again. Almost all of the head is out. Good, very good.

Troy asks for "One more big push." Bella gives it. Then again. Then a pause. Then again. Then a push.

Nothing. Bella is crying out now. Then she yells, *"Spegni quella maladetta musica!"*

"What's she screaming?" asks Troy.

Bella's husband translates. "She says 'Turn off that damn music.'" Marco slaps the laptop closed. The Beatles are gone, but the baby is simply not moving out of Bella.

I put my fingers inside. As I feel around, I realize exactly what's happening. I tell the assembled that "the baby's shoulders are just too big for delivery."

I ask for everyone except the husband and midwife team to leave the room. I urge Bella to extend her legs out from her body, which Marco and Troy help her with. Then we move her onto all fours. But after these less intrusive methods, the baby still won't budge. I've got to perform a "significant" episiotomy. Just like before, nobody moves to leave, but I have more important things to do than police a crowd dispersal.

"Get them out, Troy," I say. He opens the door. Friends and some family leave. The door closes. An unpleasant nervous silence falls over the room.

After Troy and Marco help Bella onto her back again, I begin cutting, carefully but quickly. Nothing's moving except the scalpel. The baby's shoulders are really wide. "Who have you got inside there? A Green Bay Packers linebacker?"

I cut as far as I can sensibly go. There's some bleeding. I'm not worried, but we can't cut any more.

"Call obstetrics *and* pediatrics," I say, just short of yelling. "We've got shoulder dystocia."

"What is dystocia?" Marco asks.

Troy has an answer for him. "The baby's shoulders are stuck in your wife's pelvis."

Two minutes later Dr. Sarkar appears.

CHAPTER 66

THE FIRST THING SARKAR says to me when he enters the room is this: "You're in charge. I'm just here to help. That will be our understanding and the manner in which we will proceed."

Somehow I believe him, I trust him. He is, after all, first and foremost a doctor, a doctor involved in one of doctoring's most precious events. Of course he's also a colleague and friend who failed to give me an honest update on Dr. Katz.

"I can't incise the episiotomy any larger, and it's bleeding pretty significantly as it is," I say, as if he couldn't see this already.

"Let me take a closer look," he says as he reaches down and pushes his way through the layers of bloody gauze. He turns to one of the midwife trainees and says, "I need a huge amount of pressure right where my hand is."

He sees the frightened look on the young intern's face and reacts. "For God's sake, if you're too nervous to do what you're told, you'd better become a ballerina or a waitress." I have never seen or heard Sarkar so angry or sarcastic before.

I say, "Let me do it."

Then the intern says, "No, I'll do it. Really. I can do it."

"Very good," says Sarkar. Then he turns to me and says, "What do you think? Should we get her in for a C-section?"

I have a strong opinion, and I don't mind sharing it. "No. I'd rather try to get the baby out right now. How do you feel about a clavicular fracture?"

"I'll do whatever you want. There are pluses and minuses for each approach."

"Fracture, then," I say.

In spite of the trainee's intense pushing, the bleeding has not stopped much. Troy removes saturated gauze and replaces it with new gauze.

Sarkar scrubs and puts on gloves. Then he turns to Marco, Bella's husband, and says, "Okay, here's what we're going to do. Since your baby's shoulders are not coming out, and we cannot open your wife any farther, what we're going to do is this: I will go in and gently break the baby's collarbone."

Sarkar correctly anticipates Marco's shock at this information.

"Gently break the shoulder?" Marco says.

Sarkar responds calmly. "It sounds far worse than it actually is. I've done it before. The infant's bones are very, very flexible. They're not rigid and brittle like our bones. They're rubbery. The collarbone may not even break. It may actually just bend."

Now it's my turn to act. I have three pages of consent forms that Marco must sign. The very fact that I have them and that they must be signed seems to contradict Sarkar's reassurances. Marco signs them. As soon as Marco dots the *i* in *Morabito,* Sarkar turns and leans into Bella.

He places his hands just below the baby's chin and then inserts his thumbs inside Bella. Sarkar pushes for a few seconds. Then he yells, "Push hard, madam. Big push. Big push." Then he yells, "Done!"

The baby, a wrinkled, screaming boy with a full head of black hair, is delivered. Immediately Sarkar begins suturing Bella, who is crying and laughing and asking that the music be turned back on.

Sarkar looks at me and says, "Lucy, you'll please finish the stitching."

"Doctor, you know that a midwife isn't allowed to sew. It's against the rules."

"You made the cut, which is not against the rules. You can sew the cut, which is not against *my* rules."

I take over. I've actually done it before—whatever the rules. Sarkar removes his gloves. Troy tends to the newborn, cutting the cord, binding the cord, wiping away meconium from the baby's eyes, nose, and mouth.

"I've got to say it, Doctor—" I begin.

But Sarkar interrupts and says, "Rudi, please, Lucy. You must call me Rudi."

"Okay," I say. "I've got to say it, Rudi. It was a complete joy having you here."

He smiles and takes the swaddled baby from Troy. He hands the boy to Marco, who places him on Bella's chest.

I say, "I'm thinking Bella may just have given birth to the first *Rudra Morabito* in history."

I also cannot help but think what I always think: *It's the only miracle that God lets us in on.*

Sarkar seems as happy as the parents. He reaches in and takes the baby. "I'll take him over to Pediatrics. Neonatal ICU is the best place for me to tape those giant shoulders. Come down and see him whenever you feel strong enough. Tomorrow he'll be staying in this room with you."

A big beautiful chorus of *grazie*s fills the room.

CHAPTER 67

"ONLY ONCE BEFORE IN my lifetime have I seen somebody use that clavicle-cracking method," Troy says.

"I've actually never seen it," I say. "But like Dr. Sarkar said, sometimes they don't even have to break it. That's how elastic a baby's bones can be."

Troy and I are standing outside the birthing room. It's only been about forty-five minutes since the delivery. We sip some pretty awful coffee from the electric coffee pot at the nurses' station.

"This stuff tastes like piss," says Troy.

"I can't agree or disagree," I say. "I don't have the faintest idea of what piss tastes like. But I assume this coffee is lousy enough to beat piss at its own game."

"No word from Tracy Anne?" Troy asks.

"Nothing yet," I say. "Let's head down to the nursery."

"Yeah, good idea," Troy says.

Then I say, "And by the way, don't think for a minute we're not going to have a real long conversation about you and Tracy Anne and why you kept that information from me. I may not have looked angry, but—"

"Yes, ma'am," Troy says. Then he takes both our cups of coffee and pours the contents of them into a huge potted plant in the corridor.

"What the hell are you feeding that plant?"

"Don't worry, Lucy. These plants are designed to withstand everything—arsenic, motor oil, rat poison—"

"Yeah, but you just gave it something more lethal than any of those. You just fed it some GUH coffee."

We arrive at the nursery, and I am really pleased to see that three NYPD officers have been posted outside the nursery near the viewing window.

"See that woman over there, the one in the burgundy pantsuit?" Troy asks.

"I can't miss her," I say.

"I know her. She's a plainclothes cop. Her brother Peter is a good friend of mine."

"That is music to my ears. An undercover cop in the nursery itself."

I say hello to the nurses at the desk outside the nursery.

"Has the Morabito baby been put into his brace yet?" I ask one of them, a very sharp nurse by the name of Keesha.

"Yes, ma'am. Dr. Sarkar brought the baby down here just a little while ago. He had some other doctor with him. That woman just snapped the brace on the baby in two seconds. Baby Morabito is sleeping happily."

"We're going to go take a look at him," I say.

"Go right ahead. He's in crib number four, second row on the aisle," says Keesha.

I'm frightened—for a second or two—that we're about to find an empty crib.

"I know what you're thinking," says Troy.

"Yeah, well, then you're thinking the same thing as me," I say.

We follow the aisle to crib number four. It's clearly marked BABY MORABITO. I bend over the sleeping baby, adorable, pudgy, serene, everything you want your baby to be. I reach in and lift his tiny arm and read his tiny wristband: MORABITO, 5 LBS, 4 OZ.

"I've never even seen one of those braces that they got on him," says Troy.

"Me neither," I say. "But it can't hurt very much. He's sleeping soundly."

"Do you think they gave him like a teeny-tiny drop of Xanax or something?" Troy asks.

"Are you crazy?"

"I was only joshing with you, Lucy," Troy says as he laughs.

"One never knows with…" Then I pause. I dip into the crib once more and read the wristband. Yes, it does say MORABITO, 5 LBS, 4 OZ.

Then I yell. "Jesus Christ, Troy. This is not the same baby we delivered."

"Are you joking, too, Lucy?"

I walk a few feet to the emergency buzzer and press it fiercely, over and over and over. The NYPD officers enter. The nurse at the far end of the nursery, who's been bottle feeding one of the newborns, rushes toward us. Keesha enters.

"What's going on?" Keesha says.

"This is not the Morabito baby," I shout at Keesha.

"Of course it is," she says, almost more amused than angry at the accusation. "Just read the electronic wristband."

"It may be electronic. And it may say 'Morabito.'

But somebody's fucked with it. The alarm didn't go off. And this sure as hell isn't the Morabito baby."

"No, she's right," says Troy. He realizes the hideous deception. "Our baby had lots of black hair. This here baby has lots of hair, but not nearly as much as our baby. And this baby's hair is definitely brown, dark *brown,* but brown isn't black."

Alarms sound throughout the floor, throughout the hospital.

CHAPTER 68

KEESHA CHECKS HER COMPUTER screen while two other nurses quickly check the wristbands on the other babies in the nursery, all of whom are awake and screeching.

Why is crying contagious?

"You're right, Lucy. The alarm system is down," Keesha says.

I look through the viewing window and see that the hallway outside is quickly filling up with security guards, patients, pregnant women, smiling visitors, NYPD officers, nurses, doctors. It's Macy's on Christmas Eve. It's hell on earth.

In a few minutes Dr. Sarkar is pushing his way through the crowd. He's wearing sneakers, navy-blue nylon shorts that go down to his knees, and a sweat-stained white T-shirt. It's obvious to me that he's just come from the hospital gym. Funny when you see someone out of uniform—in this case, no rep tie, no Paul Stuart blazer—he can seem so different, so like a stranger.

I tell Sarkar what's just happened, and his face flushes with horror and fear. Then he immediately examines the baby's wristband.

I, of course, am becoming very panicky and a little angry. Nothing ever happens fast enough for my liking.

"For Chrissake, Rudi. Don't you think we've already looked at the wristbands? We assume the wristband ID monitor is down."

"Yes, yes, of course," he says. Then he begins unfastening the baby's shoulder brace. "So this is not the Morabito infant," Sarkar says. "Then who is it?"

Jesus Christ! That's a good question.

Fortunately, Keesha has a good answer. "We're pretty certain it's the Fontaine baby. We're going to do a blood test and match footprints and fingerprints in a minute."

"This brace wasn't even put on properly," Sarkar declares as he hastily pulls it off. "And it's too big. Not that it matters here."

"The nurse on duty said that you were the one who brought the doctor to apply the brace," I say.

"I did," he says. "I brought one of the residents. Veronica somebody or other. I don't recall her last name."

I am about to say the obvious, that we can immediately find out Veronica's last name. But Sarkar is clearly concerned about the crisis in front of us right now.

"Lucy, make yourself useful and call Detective Blumenthal," he says.

A police officer standing right next to Sarkar hears Sarkar's request and says, "Don't bother. Detective Blumenthal already knows. He's on his way."

So much for making myself useful.

Then I notice a familiar face in the crowd. Bobby Cilia has shown up. He's organizing a dragnet throughout the hospital. We've been here before: janitor closets, pharmacies, bathrooms, ORs, ERs, supply closets.

Maybe it'll work this time. Who knows? Maybe Bobby Cilia knows more about the whole situation than…*Shit!* In my brain everyone looks anywhere from shifty to evil to guilty, except, of course, me.

"Make sure we have enough men both in the basement and on the roof," Cilia says. He talks into his cell phone. He seems to be saying "Okay" and "Got it" a lot.

Organizational decisions of who will do what and who will tell who are made. Officers get their instructions and disperse, but they're soon replaced by new and different people. Officers, G-men, emergency medical techs.

From the far end of the nursery a nurse who is holding a clipboard yells, "People, people, we're missing a baby. We're missing Harman, six pounds, five ounces." The nurse stops talking, pauses for a few seconds. Then she shouts, "We're short one baby."

The phrase *"We're short"* feels as sharp as poison in my ear. The words. The word choice. It sounds so foolish, so much like *We're short of cash, We're short of coffee, We're short of paper*. So simple. So stupid. I've got to hold it together. Now is definitely not the time to be a crazy person. My mind isn't quite working right.

Maybe the baby who Keesha thinks is the Fontaine baby is actually the Harman baby. But with the Morabito baby missing…*Why the hell is this sounding like a hideously unfunny riddle? Why is my head throbbing? Why are my eyes burning?*

My confused thoughts are interrupted by one of the police officers. He thrusts a cell phone toward me and says, "It's Detective Blumenthal. He wants you."

I say, "Yes," and Blumenthal starts jabbering.

"Listen, I'm going to loop you in on everything I know. I feel that I owe it to you."

"No argument about that," I say.

Damn it. I didn't mean to be pouty or petulant. I meant to sound grateful. Wait, I meant to sound professional. No time to stop and explain.

"Listen," he says.

Why does he always begin something he's going to say to me with the word listen? *And why the hell should I care?* "I'm listening," I say.

"Tracy Anne's former boyfriend showed up here a half hour ago. He was busting to talk. He knows a lot more shit than even Troy knows. According to the boyfriend, Tracy Anne kicked him out of her life last month, so he's in a big get-even mood."

"What'd you find out from him?" I ask, even as I'm wondering if Blumenthal can hear my voice over the siren of his car.

"Ask Cilia. He knows everything I know. Cilia was there for the whole interview. He'll fill you in. Stay calm, Lucy. We can close in on this thing if we just trust each other."

Click.

So much for long good-byes. And I'm suspicious about *"trust each other."*

I immediately look around the room and spot Bobby Cilia. He's talking to Dr. Sarkar. They're close in, very face-to-face. I immediately join them.

"I just spoke to Blumenthal," I say. "He says you can fill me in, Bobby."

"He sure can, Lucy," says Sarkar. "That's what Assistant Detective Cilia just did for me. This story is incredible."

"I'm ready," I say.

But before Cilia can start talking, Sarkar looks at his watch. Then he says, "I'm going back to my office to change clothes. Then I'll try calling our leader in hiding, Dr. Katz. Thanks for taking the time to report to me, Detective." Then Sarkar is gone.

I look at Bobby and say, "Now would you repeat for me the same astonishing info you just shared with Sarkar?"

Bobby begins plowing through his material quickly, passionately, yet methodically.

"Here's the deal. We had a very sweet conversation with Tracy Anne's boyfriend. Tracy Anne recently dumped the guy, and he was more than happy to give up some pretty dramatic info on his former lady friend. He was one pissed-off former boyfriend. He even brought himself into the precinct. Once the guy started to talk, it looked like he might never shut up. The guy's an out-of-work actor, but I don't think he was acting with us. He was angry, angry as hell. Anyway, he knew everything that she was up to. Everything."

"Does this guy have a name?" I ask.

"I think his name was Eric. Yeah, Eric, Eric Storm, a real actorlike name. Anyway, this Storm guy tells us that Tracy Anne and two 'Russian assholes'— his words, not mine—had a racket going, supplying babies to rich couples up in Southern Westchester. It's sort of what you and Detective Blumenthal suspected.

"Eric Storm says the town Tracy Anne always mentioned was Harrison. I named a few other rich-people towns up in Westchester, like Rye and Scarsdale. Eric said they sounded familiar but that Tracy used to say—more than once, mind you—

Harrison was the 'real gold mine.' That's the quote. A 'real gold mine.'"

My turn to talk. "So I'll bet your boss, the great Detective Blumenthal, is heading up to Harrison now."

"You got it, lady," says Cilia. "He's already connected with the Harrison PD. Plus he's taking along three guys from the FBI. They've connected with their counterparts in White Plains, the Westchester County seat. This thing is on fire, Lucy."

Suddenly I feel calm, simple, tough. Lucy is Lucy again. I have one of those hunches that's actually a lot more than a hunch. And that kind of hunch is either a breakthrough or a disaster.

I pull out my phone and press the speed dial for Blumenthal.

"I've got to talk to you before you head to Westchester," I say.

"Too late and too bad," says Blumenthal.

I hate the guy. And for once I say so out loud. "You know, you're a real son of a bitch. I've got an idea that could really help, and you say 'too bad.'"

Blumenthal speaks. "Listen, Lucy. I don't have time. I literally do not have the time."

"I'm telling you, Detective. I've got an idea that could really help us."

"Yeah? I've got an idea, too. Here's my idea. You stay put. You do your job and…you'll see. It's all going to work out."

CHAPTER 69

I AM WILLING TO bet my New York City ass that this whole thing is all going to work out just fine. Here's why: because I'm jumping fast and deep into the situation. Blumenthal won't be happy. Bobby Cilia won't be happy. Hell, it's even possible that I won't be happy. But I can't run the risk of *not* getting involved and then end up hating myself for the rest of my life.

Or even worse—and this is wishful thinking—let the case absolutely fail and then hear Blumenthal say something infuriating like, *"Why the hell didn't you just ignore me? You always do. For Chrissake, Lucy, this time you could have been a hero…er, heroine."*

Okay. Back to reality. Game on.

I grab Troy and say, "Get your car. We have to move fast. Go get your car right now."

Uh-oh. Glitch one in my plan. Troy says, "Lady boss, I'm a subway guy. I don't even own a car."

This inspires my decision to act like a maniac CEO type. Ignore reality. Just give orders. *"Get a goddamn car, Troy! Just get a car!"*

He looks at me like the true crazy lady I've become. "You are a woman possessed," he says. "I'll just assume that the Lord himself is talking to all of us through your screams."

Troy runs to the exit stairs. "I'll call you as soon as I know what I'm driving, and where you should wait for a pickup."

"Great!" I say. "Now just move. Move…your… ass."

"I always wanted to be somebody's sidekick," he shouts, and he disappears down the stairs.

As for me, I don't ever remember being so freakin' worried. I'm getting ready to follow a long-shot hunch—a good hunch, a smart hunch, but, like I say, a long shot.

I need to focus on my hunch. So of course I call my mom. This time, however, it's for info related to this case. "Mom, I don't have time to waste. Remember that story you told me the other day about the man a few years ago who wanted you to help him get a few babies?"

"Well, yes. I do remember. He was a handsome fellow. He had a very nice suit jacket with—"

"Mom, I'm in a real hurry here. Did he say that he needed the babies for people in Harrison, New Jersey, or Harrison, New York?"

I don't get a sense of true certainty when she answers. "Well, I'm pretty sure he said it was New Jersey. But those states are all one big blur to me."

Okay. I've got to go with a *"pretty sure."* I say good-bye and disconnect.

I drop two phone chargers and an iPad charger into my purse. I fill my water bottle and then grab two Diet Cokes for Troy. I check the face of my cell phone every ten seconds—as if I might possibly miss the call from Troy telling me where to meet him.

A nervous mind is a crazy mind. At least it is in my mind. I envy the likes of Blumenthal and Sarkar—people who can sort and file their thoughts. Compartmentalize? Move on with one project at a time? That's just not me. My brain works on the crashing roller-coaster blueprint—fast-moving, out-of-control cars that almost collide but, with a little bit of luck, never fall off the track. The problem is this: I really believe that life assigns you only a limited amount of luck—your fair amount. And you don't want to use it up too fast and too soon.

The images of the important cast members of the case—Nina, Orlov, Blumenthal, the cemetery, Tracy Anne—are exploding in my brain. My mind is flipping through the possible rats who are aiding and abetting Orlov and Nina. And then it hits me. I know exactly who the guilty party is. It's everyone. Of course it's the Constitution according to Lucy Ryuan: everyone's guilty until proven innocent. Everyone, that is, because the loony old Irish skeptic in me is totally unable to eliminate anyone.

Tracy Anne has already been identified as Judas. Bobby Cilia seems to have shown up out of nowhere. Troy seems to be our informant, but he was also Tracy Anne's confidant. Our scum-bucket CEO, Dr. Katz, is certainly not above crime. Then there's this Barbara Holt woman. Sarkar weaves way too smoothly in and out of everything. And why does Blumenthal make me keep my distance from the center of the investigation? Could Blumenthal actually be…? *Nah. Well…why not? Of course not. Of course. Yes. No. Maybe. Yes.*

While I'm shuffling these ideas—ideas with no answers, no substance—around in my brain, my cell phone rings.

"I'll be at the Third Avenue Medical Waste Pick-up entrance in two minutes," Troy says, his voice breathless, intimate, maybe even a little frightened.

"What kind of car are you driving?" I ask as I rush down the corridor to the side stairwell.

"I got me a McCoy Miller heavy-duty Type III," he says.

I'm completely baffled by Troy's answer. "What the hell is a McCoy Miller heavy whatever?" I ask.

"It's what the Office of Transportation Requisitions calls an *ambulance*."

CHAPTER 70

TROY DRIVES. I RIDE shotgun. I'm focused on my cell phone's GPS program like I'm playing Mozart on the piano.

"Not FDR Drive," I yell. "I don't want to go to the East Side. Get over to the West Side."

"Calm down, for the good Lord's sake," Troy says. His voice is understandably impatient at my barking orders.

Just about the only thing Troy is enjoying is sitting behind the wheel of an ambu—er, excuse me, a McCoy Miller. The red lights on the ambulance roof are blinking. The siren is screeching. Suddenly Troy throws the vehicle into a sharp U-turn on 57th Street. Well, at least he listened to me. Now we're heading to the West Side.

"I don't know what you do for driving directions, Lucy, but when I'm driving to towns in Westchester, near Long Island Sound, I always go FDR Drive," Troy says.

"There's been a minor adjustment to our plans," I say. "But first of all, I want to apologize for yelling. To say that I'm tightly wound is putting it mildly."

He ignores the apology. He's tense now also.

"What's the minor adjustment?" he asks.

"Detective Blumenthal is heading toward Harrison, *New York*. You and me are going to Harrison, *New Jersey*."

We drive for a minute or so. Finally, Troy breaks the silence.

"What in Satan's hell is the matter with you, woman?" he says.

I don't answer his question. The GPS tells Troy to make a left on Ninth Avenue. "We're going through the Lincoln Tunnel," I say.

As Troy speeds left onto Ninth Avenue, he says, "And maybe you'll tell me why we're headed to a whole other state than the one Blumenthal and the NYPD and the FBI and the Westchester County police are all going to."

I say nothing as we maneuver past the other traffic, which barely pulls out of our way, and Troy eventually turns into the loop that enters the tunnel. Now I'm busy again on my phone, trying to get info from the internet on anything even vaguely connected to medicine or medical research or infant care or adoption services in Harrison, New Jersey.

I tell Troy, "By the time we come out on the Jersey side, you're going to know the whole story of why we're going to Harrison, New Jersey."

Troy dials down the siren, but he doesn't turn off the blinking lights. He roars around the other traffic in the tunnel. The moment we're on the Jersey side, he says, "Okay, Detective Lucy. Lay it on me."

As we approach the interchange to 95 south, I tell him what I've just learned. "There's a pharma company in Harrison, New Jersey. It's called General Infant Health. The initials of which are—"

Troy jumps in. "GIH."

"Yeah, Mr. Genius," I say. "Stunningly similar to GUH. Let's assume it's a coincidence. Anyway, GIH isn't totally unknown, but they're pretty much under the radar. Privately traded stock. Small group of personnel. No real board of directors. Next to places like Novartis and Pfizer, GIH is really small potatoes. This place we're going to in Harrison, New Jersey, is their only office. It houses both GIH corporate and GIH R and D. When's the last time you heard of a pharma operation so streamlined it had both those disciplines under the same roof?"

Troy shrugs his shoulders.

It occurs to me that Troy has never thought about the size of pharmaceutical companies. It occurs to me that until today I had never thought of them, either.

"Anyway, according to what I'm finding online, they're working on a product for multiple types of infant CHD."

Turns out, as a trained midwife, Troy knows about CHD. He defines it for me, as if to prove what I already know: this man is smart.

"Congenital heart defects," he says. "Hard to find a more miserable, awful problem for babies than some of these heart abnormalities." Then he adds, "How do you know so much about this place, Lucy?"

I don't answer him right away. First, I tell him, "We've got to move a lot faster, buddy. Put your siren on again."

The noise and the lights let us accelerate, but it'll still take a while to get there. I'm ready to tell him about GIH and my mother, but even with time enough to say more, I go for the really short version.

"Listen, it involves my mom and me and West Virginia and midwife work and…Please, you've got to do what Blumenthal and Sarkar and Cilia never can do: trust me."

Troy glances at me and we continue on in silence

for a time. When the GPS finally announces, "Exit next right onto Essex Street, continue to Harrison Avenue," I say, "Got that?"

Troy nods toward the exit sign ahead as he again douses the siren.

"Blumenthal has got it wrong. Maybe Tracy Anne's boyfriend has got it wrong. My gut tells me that the people we want are in Harrison, New Jersey, the place that shares a name with the green lawns and country clubs of Harrison, New York. This GIH place, I'm gonna bet, is harvesting our newborns for something other than selling them to rich parents."

"What the hell do you mean?" Troy asks.

"It's probably what you can guess." I pause, to let Troy try to guess. Then I tell him what I think this operation may entail. "I think they're getting healthy newborns into a lab to do experiments on them. They call it 'human research.'"

Troy actually looks away from me in shock and horror.

"As my mom would say, it's the devil's work. They start with white mice. They move on to rabbits. Then they need to get into the real world."

Troy looks at me with a combination of amazement and sadness.

I glance down at my phone's screen and begin reading aloud a travel blurb about the town:

Harrison is experiencing a residential renewal, particularly along the Passaic River. The new Red Bull Arena is New Jersey's premier soccer stadium. Hotels and restaurants are being built to rival Manhattan's...

I stop reading when Troy says, "Look at this place. It's pretty much a dead old mess."

Troy is correct. We are driving through downtown Harrison, New Jersey, just across the river from Newark. Its main street is composed of a few abandoned stores, along with a small hardware store, a Popeye's chicken place, and three deli-type bodegas.

"Turn right on Passaic Avenue," the GPS announces. As soon as we make the turn, the voice says, "In five hundred yards you will arrive at your destination."

"I've got a suggestion," says Troy as he flicks off the ambulance's lights and slows to the speed limit. "And you've got to listen to me."

"Hmm," I say. "I love you like a brother, Troy. But maybe your best move would be to keep your suggestion to yourself."

He ignores my advice, as I knew he would. He simply says what he wants to say. "I think we should call Blumenthal right now, tell him where we are and what we're doing." There's a touch of anger and fear in Troy's voice.

He's right, and he's serious, and I'm not going to do it. "I don't think so. Blumenthal and his pals are way up in the hills of Westchester County. They've got their lead. And we've got ours."

"You're wrong, Lucy. Very, very wrong," Troy says. "This is no time for battling teams."

"Yes, it is, if one of the teams is dead wrong and being stupid," I say.

There is a short pause. Then Troy speaks again. "Maybe. We'll see. You are one stubborn lady."

Troy is now interrupted by the sickly sweet GPS voice from the cell phone: "You have reached your destination."

CHAPTER 71

THE BUILDING THAT HOUSES General Infant Health looks like a dreary suburban high school circa 1955. A low-slung two-story building, a rectangular box of fading yellow brick. I usually don't notice fancy things or even a lack of fancy things, but I can't help but notice that there is absolutely no landscaping—not a shrub, not a bush, no flowers, no trees. Large neon initials—GIH—hang over the front entrance door. Somehow I don't associate neon signs with medical research.

A red-and-white metal signpost points us to the parking lot, only a few hundred yards from the Passaic River. In keeping with the bleak architecture of the building, the parking lot is muddy and unpaved, sparsely sprinkled with gravel. I do notice that most of the fifty or so cars parked in this lot are BMWs and Mercedes, high-end models of each type. Two red Ferraris, one gray Rolls-Royce.

Troy and I formulate a rough plan. We decide that I'll go into the reception area and try to bluff my way back into the offices and labs. Meanwhile, Troy will walk around and survey the campus.

"Yeah, good idea," he says. "No one'll notice a

three-hundred-pound black man strolling around the grounds in the middle of the day."

"You fight the war with the soldiers you've got," I say as he parks the ambulance.

Troy looks at me skeptically. "I don't quite think what you just said makes any sense."

Then we move on to discussing our plan. He'll start at the river, which even at a few hundred yards away is letting off a nauseating scent.

"Something tells me the river is not going to be sparkling clean for swimming," Troy says.

"Yeah, well, if you change your mind and you do decide to dive in, watch out for human bodies and human waste," I say.

"You always give your people really good advice, Lucy."

We are now at a point when Troy needs to walk toward the slope leading down to the river and I need to walk straight ahead to the steps going up to the building entrance.

"Lucy, look, before we split—" Troy says.

"Troy, I'm nervous as hell. Don't bug me. I know what you're going to say. You're going to tell me I should call Leon Blumenthal. And I'm not going to. And I'm telling you, Jesus, I am really nervous, and I'm not sure what to do about it."

"Lucy, okay, okay. Just calm down. Just *try* to calm down," he says.

I always hate it when people say things like *"Don't worry." Oh really? I shouldn't worry? Thanks. I hadn't thought of that.* But when Troy tells me to calm down, well, for some reason I actually do calm down a little. Don't misunderstand me; I'm still scared, but not as scared as I could be, maybe not even as scared as I should be.

CHAPTER 72

TROY STARTS HIS WALK down toward the river, and I push through the big, and unwashed, glass doors of the main GIH entrance.

Okay, I've got it. They purposely designed this place to look like a piece of crap.

Stained, worn gray linoleum, and I know it's real linoleum because the same stuff was on the floor of every kitchen in Walkers Pasture. Two sofas face each other, covered in a dirty beige-and-brown tweed, perfect for showing off spills and stains. Yep, these two couches have more stains on them than a menu at a greasy diner. Jesus. This dump is a pharma company. If this were the only place that manufactured aspirin, I'd just as soon keep my headache.

Behind a long metal table—not unlike the metal dining tables in the residents' cafeteria at GUH that the NYPD used—sit two classic "big guys." They wear identical white short-sleeved shirts with black clip-on ties.

"Yes, ma'am?" the larger of the two says to me. His attitude is neither pleasant nor rude, merely robotic.

Nervously, of course, I say, "Is this GIH Pharma and Research?"

He ignores my question. He looks at his colleague. They both smile as if they just heard a lame joke. Maybe they have.

After the very uncomfortable pause the second guy finally says, "How can we help you?"

"Like I asked your friend, is this GIH Pharma?"

The first guy speaks. "Are you here to see someone?"

"I'm here to see Mr. Eagleburg." My mouth is so dry that I'm amazed I can even speak.

"Eagleburg?" the guy says. "Did you mean Eagleton?"

Oh, Mom. I wish you would've remembered the right name. This could get me thrown out before I even begin. But there's no going back now.

"Yes, I'm sorry. I'm exhausted from all the driving to get here. Yes, Mr. Eagleton."

Another pause, and the second guy taps something into his laptop. After a few moments, he says, "They're expecting you."

I can't help myself for spitting out, "They're *expecting* me?"

"Ms. Ryuan?" the guy says.

"Uh, yes."

Now my mind and heart are truly flooded with worry and confusion. I should have listened to Troy. I should have called Blumenthal. I should have stayed home today. I should have gone to law school. I should have...

The second guy comes out from behind the table. He gently takes me by the elbow. "Come along, Ms. Ryuan. General Infant Health extends to you a warm and hearty welcome. Keep calm."

"I am calm," I say, not at all convincingly.

To him. To myself.

"Good," the guy says. "Now I'll take you back."

CHAPTER 73

THE SECURITY ESCORT AND I stand at a metal door that leads out of the reception area. He punches a very long code into the electronic lock near the door-knob. Then urges me forward again by my elbow as he opens the door. It was hardly worth the time or trouble for him to touch my elbow. As soon as the door opens, we take two steps, and we are then standing in a room about the size of a small walk-in closet, no larger than four feet by four feet, with another door on the opposite wall.

My escort and I practically fill the entire space. There is a very creepy sense of intimacy. It is at once frightening. I could be killed here—he could molest me, abuse me, rape me. All of those things, some of those things.

Within a few seconds I realize there is a small window in the little room, too. A pretty young blond woman is looking at us. She smiles at the guard; he smiles at her. Then she nods and mouths the word *okay*. The guard holds a small plastic card up to a minuscule black dot on the new door. As expected, the door opens. A tall, dark-haired woman stands in a slightly larger room.

She speaks to the guard. "Thank you, Carl."

"She's all yours now, Nina," the guard says.

Nina—I am stunned. I try to get a closer look at this woman. Of course this is not the Nina from the video or the cemetery or the surveillance photos.

I think for a nanosecond that perhaps the original Nina has been transformed by plastic surgery and hair coloring, or…*Oh, what the hell is wrong with you, Lucy?*

The guard leaves, and New Nina opens another door behind her. There's no electronic code or card needed to open it.

When the door opens, our little space is flooded with light, pouring in from the new room. We step into that room, which is big and so stunningly bright that my eyes require some blinking and rubbing in order to adjust. Within a few seconds I see that everything is painted a traditional office color—a soft pale blue. The ceilings have industrial white cork. The floors are black-and-gray spattered white tiles. Of course it looks just like a hospital. In fact, with a few minor adjustments of space and color it could be the maternity floor of GUH.

New Nina and I stand in front of a huge glass viewing window. Behind the window, at the far wall are two women and a man. Their backs are to us. The three of them are wearing blue hospital scrubs, and all three are bent over a PC that seems to be fascinating them. Of even more intense interest to me are the many other human beings in the room. The babies. Babies and babies and babies.

I estimate roughly fifty high-tech-type cribs. It looks as if each crib holds a baby.

Even more fascinating and frightening are the

wires and tubes and electronic monitors that run in and out of all these cribs. These wires seem to feed into some wall monitors displaying charts and numbers and letters and graphs.

New Nina suddenly raps hard with her knuckles on the vast glass nursery window. One of the women—a doctor, nurse, biochemist? —turns toward New Nina and nods, a wisp of annoyance on her face. That annoyance immediately disappears when New Nina gestures in my direction. The woman says something to her colleagues. I think at first she is walking toward the door to meet me, but instead she stops at one of the cribs near the window. With her back to me she removes a syringe from her pocket. It looks like she's about to thrust it into the infant's stomach. Then she hesitates and seems to change her mind. She looks flustered, nervous.

The second woman turns and looks at her colleague. In a voice loud enough that I can hear it through the window, she says, "Oh, for Chrissake, Bobbie. I'll get the sample myself," and she marches sternly toward the first woman. This tough-acting woman grabs the syringe from Bobbie.

I look away from the scene, and New Nina seems to sense my discomfort. "You obviously find watching this very upsetting," she says. "We have a room where you can wait for your host. You'll be better off there."

In what seems to be a standard GIH technique, she takes my elbow to lead me. Her grip is a bit stronger than the guard who brought me in.

"Not so tight," I say.

"I apologize, but I want you to go quickly. For your own sake. It will only be a moment," she says.

I turn a bit and look back through the nursery window. Now all three of the people in blue scrubs — the two women and the man — are leaning over the crib. The first woman, Bobbie, who failed to take the sample, lifts the infant from the crib. She holds the infant while the other woman pierces the baby's little belly with the syringe. I turn away again. When I look back, the woman with the loaded syringe is walking toward one of the doors, which she opens. In a moment the first woman places the screaming baby back into the crib and rushes to the door herself.

The two women are suddenly standing with me and my escort. Back inside, the man leaning over the crib seems to be poking around in it. A few seconds pass. Then the man looks up from the crib. He turns and faces the glass window.

I see his face. I pull my elbow away from my escort. I push quickly past the other two women and rush through the open door. I move toward the man. He smiles at me. I know him.

The man is Dr. Rudra Sarkar.

CHAPTER 74

AN ERUPTION IN MY brain. An explosion of confusion and anger and fear. I can almost feel my mind clicking madly, trying to sort out what I am seeing, and what it all means.

Sarkar. Rudra Sarkar. Dr. Sarkar.

Then comes an extraordinary surprise. Something else explodes inside me. Along with my rage I experience something completely shocking: I feel my heart breaking. At what? The horror of what surrounds me? The screaming of the innocents? The jungle of tubes and wires and monitors? Yes, of course, and also the astounding betrayal, from, of all people, Dr. Sarkar. This is a man who delivers life, and he is now standing before me, a monster, even beyond a monster. Who the hell is this guy? The devil himself.

"This had to happen, Lucy. It was only a matter of time before your nimble mind figured it all out. I knew that one day you'd find it." The voice is the warm, reassuring voice I have always liked, the voice that soothed so many expectant mothers.

"But I never dreamed I'd find you here, Dr. Sarkar. Never. It absolutely never crossed my mind."

Sarkar's charm has not at all disappeared. He smiles. His eyelashes flutter. "This is simply the arrival of the inevitable," he says.

"No. No. This was never inevitable," I say.

"Let me tell you something wonderful, Lucy." A pause, a smile. Then, "Your visit could not have occurred at a better time. Only last week I had to dismiss my assistant, Nina. I believe you knew her."

I am stunned, now speechless.

Sarkar continues to talk. "Because, you see...Well, Lucy, this might be a wonderful opportunity for you. This might..."

Yes, I am shaking, but I am also hoping that deep inside I will find the strength to confront this horror.

The explosion travels from my brain to my lips. "Stop! Stop talking!"

"Lucy, please. This is a professional space," he says.

"You are a fucking madman," I yell, as if this observation was a revelation.

He laughs, then turns deadly serious. "No, I am a pioneer. What we are doing will aid, no, *cure* infants with congenital heart problems. We are isolating those genes that—"

"Don't talk anymore," I yell.

Our argument seems to have woken every infant in the nursery. The wailing is almost overwhelming. Sarkar and I stand alone together in the nursery.

His eyes twinkle, but it is a watery, distant, peculiar twinkle.

"Let me explain the procedure. Tell me if you don't see the value," Sarkar says, as if we are two colleagues chatting over a cup of coffee.

The babies continue screaming. I glance at the door to see if the women will return.

Where is Troy? Swimming in the river? Where is anyone?

I say, "When I thought the babies were being harvested for childless couples, I thought it was disgusting. The word itself, *harvested,* is awful. But I thought at least the babies would have homes, probably good homes, probably good parents, advantages. But this. This is kidnapping and murder rolled into one. And the pain. The infants are suffering, being tortured."

I move closer to Sarkar, who continues to smile in a hateful, condescending manner.

I intend to continue yelling. I don't know when I'll stop, when I'll run out of words that reach beyond anger.

Then I look down into the crib beside me.

A tiny baby, wearing a tiny plastic brace on his tiny shoulders. The baby has lots of beautiful dark hair.

It is, of course, the Morabito baby, the very infant who only a few hours ago Dr. Sarkar helped deliver.

Then I hear a voice. "What the hell is going on in here?"

The door has opened. The two women who'd left a few minutes ago have returned.

I begin to reach into the crib.

"I'll handle this," Sarkar shouts at the women. "Get out. Get the hell out."

The two women scurry back through the door and close it behind them. As soon as I hear the door click, I hear a loud sound, a human grunt.

Suddenly rough hands grab me by both my shoulders. I'm thrown to the ground. My head hits the floor. Hard.

I am lying on my back. Sarkar is on top of me. He is

like a schoolboy who has won a schoolyard fight. His knees have pinned down my shoulders. A punch to my right cheek, followed by a harder punch to my other cheek. The teeth in the back of my mouth crackle.

I taste the blood filling my mouth.

Sarkar gets up from me quickly. Standing over me, he looks a mile tall. Then he—I don't believe this—kicks me. Over and over and over.

I am screaming.

I think I'm going to pass out. And then…

I hear a gunshot.

I move my aching, bleeding head ever so slightly. I see it all happen. I see Sarkar's feet stumble and hesitate and stumble again.

He falls. He falls to his knees. Then he completes his collapse. He's on the floor. On his back right next to me.

We must look just like a boyfriend and girlfriend sleeping on a blanket at the beach.

I do not know what makes me move. I do not know what motivates me. I do not know why anything is happening the way it is happening. I find the strength to kneel. I look at Sarkar's face. His eyes are open, but they look like the eyes in a corpse. I push him onto his stomach. Blood is soaking his blue scrubs. Nothing will stop the flow of blood here. What makes me want to try to save him? Who would want to save the devil?

I find the strength to push Sarkar onto his back again. I push hard on his chest. Compression. Exertion. I lean in and hold his chin with one hand, his nose with the other hand. I put my lips on his lips and try to breathe life into him.

"Take a deep breath, and just push, one big push, just

give me a short breath and then a big push." That is what I am thinking or hearing or saying. I am in a great confusion. Is this birth or is this death?

"Lucy, it's no use," I hear. It is Leon Blumenthal who is speaking.

I am still hearing the word *push*. If I could only get Sarkar to give one good push.

Hands reach down and touch my shoulders and arms. The hands must be those of Leon Blumenthal.

Those hands lift me gently, and I am forced to remove my lips from Rudi Sarkar's lips.

CHAPTER 75

NEW JERSEY STATE POLICE. FBI. Harrison Police.

Officers and more officers and more officers.

Blaring sirens and flashing red lights.

Vehicles. Helicopters overhead.

Medics and sharpshooters and doctors and nurses.

It is the whole rich crazy symphony of fear and noise and general bullshit that accompanies something so awful and huge and shocking.

"Get her into the ambulance right now," I hear.

Blumenthal? Wait. Of course not. No, I guessed wrong. They weren't his hands. It can't be. Blumenthal was never called. I said don't call him. I was arrogant. I didn't need him.

Troy. Of course it was Troy. Troy called Blumenthal. Troy ignored my orders. *Thank you, Troy. Thank you, God.*

"Don't move, miss," says a police medic. "Don't move. You're injured."

"No, I'm not. But thanks for caring," I say, and I start to stand. I'm up. I'm good. I'm better. I feel the bulky bandage that encircles my head. Then I hear a voice.

"I had to do it, Lucy. I had to call Blumenthal

and Cilia," Troy says. We hug like two siblings who haven't seen each other for years.

"Well, of course you had to call. That's exactly what I told you to do," I say.

"No. You specifically said not…" And then he smiles. "You are a lying bitch. Always have been. Always will be."

"No, buddy. It's just my compulsion to always be right," I say. And we hug again.

The medic makes one more attempt with me. "You really should be checked by a doctor, miss."

"Doctor?" I say. "I've seen all the doctors I wanna see today. I've got doctors on the ceilings and the floors."

I look around the crazy, noisy nursery. Pediatric nurses and doctors, probably from the nearest hospitals, are spreading out among the cribs. Infants are being disengaged from tubes and monitors and wires. Infants are being handed from one medical person to another. Some are being rushed out of the room, presumably to emergency stations. Other babies are simply held and patted and soothed and fed and changed.

It's a mess, but as my mother used to say every Christmas and Thanksgiving, surrounded by her noisy, sloppy relatives, *"Yes, it's a mess. But it's a joyful mess."*

Then I see Blumenthal approaching me. He's barking into his cell phone. He's shooting orders at police officers. He looks stern as he comes near me. But in only a moment I can tell that his anger is all pretend. He tries hard not to melt into someone gentle. But he manages to keep the angry face.

"You did everything wrong. You did exactly what I told you *not* to do."

"Yes, that's true. I guess I'm sorry, but I'm not really

sorry," I say. Then, full of arrogance and sarcasm and peace, I add, "Listen, Detective. You had the right town. Unfortunately, you had the wrong state. But you came close. I just had to step in."

Then he says, "And everything turned out all right. Thank you. Thank you, Lucy."

With that, we throw our arms around each other and hug. And it is then that I begin sobbing. Loud. Relentless. Uncontrollable.

"Goddamnit," I say. "I'm the biggest baby in the room."

"No, you're not. You're the smartest grown-up in this room. *And* you're the best person I've ever met."

Blumenthal tilts his head back and looks at me. He shakes his head back and forth. He holds my shoulders. We hug again, and then, after a few moments, he says, "We've figured out a lot in the last half hour, Lucy." And he explains—in that concise, brief, logical way of his. He explains that Dr. Barrett Katz was framed, set up by Sarkar. Sarkar falsified records and invoices. Sarkar thought the Katz scandal would be a distraction from the kidnapping scandal. Katz's insistence that he was innocent was absolutely true.

"I guess I should be happy that Katz isn't going to prison for thirty years," I say.

"Yes, you should be. Katz is a good man."

"Okay, I'll try to be happy about it. But I'm not predicting my success at that. Once an asshole al—" I begin. But my voice is drowned out. Sirens and shouting and screaming babies.

A few seconds later, above the din, I hear a woman's voice.

"Leon," the voice calls. "Leon." The voice shows up with a very pretty woman attached to it. "Detective,

I'm going down to the Harrison police station. Then I'm heading to Newark's Children's Hospital. Most of the babies are being taken there. Then…"

The woman looks at me, and with genuine warmth and enthusiasm in her voice says, "Oh, my God. It's you. It's Lucy. You're the hero of the year. God bless you."

Blumenthal says, "Lucy, this is Barbara Holt."

Of course! This is the flashy woman with the fancy shoes who spoke to me so casually, so intimately about "Leon." I didn't recognize her without a floral sundress and nine-hundred-dollar Louboutin heels. Barbara Holt. The girlfriend.

"Barbara is a new UC. UC means—"

"I know, Detective," I say. "UC means undercover."

What I don't know is where she gets the money to buy those shoes.

"Sorry," he says. "I just wanted to introduce the two of you."

Barbara and I look at each other and smile a smile that says, *I know what you're thinking.* Then we laugh.

She walks quickly toward the door. And I survey the room. It is still a noisy madhouse. The room seems twice as crowded as it did fifteen minutes ago. What I'm guessing are media helicopters can be heard hovering outside, invading like a sloppy army. The babies who have not been rushed off to medical facilities seem to have turned up their volume to a deafening decibel. A few well-dressed politicians are being allowed into what must be considered a crime scene. Mr. Mayor. Ms. Police Commissioner. A woman introduces herself to me and Blumenthal as the "lieutenant governor." More officers. More doctors. The sirens don't stop.

Yes, Mom. I know. A joyful mess.

CHAPTER 76

FORTY-FIVE MINUTES LATER, a new group of four NYPD police cars pulls into the dirt parking lot of the pharma facility. Blumenthal and Troy and I watch them from an office window. Men and women pour out of the cars and rush toward the building.

"It's the mothers, the fathers!" Troy shouts. "I recognize some of 'em."

I do, too. I see Katra. I see Katra's father. Bella and Marco Morabito are rushing closer as well. A blur of familiar faces and not-so-familiar faces.

"This is wonderful," says Troy. I agree.

"Wonderful for some," says Blumenthal, who has been reading the screen of his iPhone. "We're allowing in only the parents of the babies who made it through alive. Other moms and dads will have their hearts broken."

Silence. Then we take a collective deep breath and go to meet the parents. The lucky ones.

EPILOGUE

DR. KATZ AGREED TO my taking a one-month leave of absence with salary.

He's such a softie.

When I first asked for four weeks he responded, "Does it really have to be quite so long, Ms. Ryuan?" Then he rushed to add, "Well, I suppose you deserve it."

And I, of course, responded, *"Suppose? You suppose I deserve it?"*

So I can't say that Dr. Barrett Katz is a changed man, but like so many of us at GUH, once he absorbed the enormity of the horror that had happened, things seemed much better. We will never forget the nightmare, but somehow the air seems clearer, the mood seems happier, more peaceful.

One hopeful sign of change in Katz is that he told the GUH staff, "Please don't call me Barrett anymore. It's too formal. Call me Barry."

Okay, Barry, what a loosey-goosey guy you've become.

In that one month of paid leave, I spent a lot of good time with Willie, The Duke, Sabryna, Devan, and the baby. Sabryna is now calling the infant Olivia. Why? "Because it is a beautiful name," she says. "Why should she only have one name when so many people love her?"

Oh, okay, whatever. It makes sense, if you don't think too hard about it.

The fact is, no matter what Sabryna calls the baby, she is just about the cutest little being I ever delivered, and that's saying a lot. We know that one of these days her mother, Valerina, will be ready to take her home, but until that day arrives, we are joyful to have little Anna Tyonna Olivia Gomez with us. Almost as joyful as the Kovacs, and all the other families whose babies were recovered.

I also spent some of my time off with Leon Blumenthal and the ADA assigned to the case follow-up.

Yes, I know, Leon. ADA stands for "assistant district attorney."

We recorded any details we remembered from the case—the cemetery, the lucky arrest of Orlov in Queens, and of course the events that led to the discovery and death of Rudra Sarkar and his laboratory of terror.

Finding Tracy Anne wasn't much of a challenge for the FBI. She grew up in Menasha, Wisconsin, a little town on Lake Winnebago. She was not-too-cleverly "hiding out" there with her mother and father. One amusing little tidbit. The Town of Menasha is located right next to a little town called Neenah.

Yep, it's pronounced exactly the way you think it is.

The greatest tragedies of Sarkar and Orlov's living nightmare was of course the awful harm done to the innocent babies and their parents. No doubt about that. The case goes down in medical history as one of the most bizarre, and certainly one of the most horrid.

But there was one other personal tragedy. Orlov

and Sarkar had bullied and threatened Nina incessantly. Orlov had forced her into her role—he even admitted that to the police. Nina Kozlova truly had wanted to escape from the gang, and she found only one way to do that.

The NYPD found her dead in the bathroom of a Days Inn hotel in the Bronx. Nina had shot herself in the heart.

If Leon Blumenthal had not asked Social Services to arrange a funeral for Nina, she would have been buried on Hart Island, New York City's potter's field. Social Services even found a Russian Orthodox priest to preside over the graveside ceremony.

Blumenthal thought we should attend the service. And so he and I did. To my way of thinking, it was a perfect day for the funeral of a sad Ukrainian woman. The weather wasn't quite rainy, but it wasn't quite clear. A warm mist showed up on a warm day to make everything even warmer and more humid. The sky was a flat blanket of gray—no clouds, no light, nothing but gray.

The only bright spot in the entire area was the Russian priest, an old man with a very long white beard. His religious vestments were bright red and white with long threads of gold running through. He held a golden crucifix with a golden image of the dying Christ on the cross. The priest was the only ray of lightness, brightness, and sunshine on that dead and dreary day.

"I'll wait a few more minutes," the priest said to Blumenthal and me. "Then I must leave. I have other commitments."

The priest spoke to us because, sadly, we were the only people at the service. Two cemetery workers stood smoking at a respectful distance from our tiny group. I assumed that once the ceremony was over these two guys would put Nina in the ground and cover her with dirt. And that would be that.

"I'll begin," said the priest.

He said some prayers in Russian, or maybe in Ukrainian. He blessed the coffin. He held his right hand on the coffin itself and continued to speak softly in the foreign tongue. When he finished that prayer, he asked that Blumenthal and I touch the coffin. We did, holding our hands on the coffin precisely as the priest had.

I said the Hail Mary. Blumenthal said something in Hebrew. The entire program took no longer than fifteen minutes, maybe not even that. The priest gave the final blessing:

> *Have compassion on me, the work of your hands, O Lord.*
> *Cleanse me through your loving-kindness.*

And that was it. It was over, all over.

I couldn't help but think in police terms: the terror, the horror, the tragedy, all finished, solved and resolved. Case closed.

Both Leon Blumenthal and I said good-bye to the priest and walked to our car.

As we walked away, Leon Blumenthal turned to me and said, "That was pretty sad." Then he took my hand and held it gently. "So what do you think about all this, Lucy?" he asked as we walked.

I looked up at him, and I considered, as always, telling him exactly what I was thinking. "You really want to know what I think?" I asked.

"Yes," he said. "I really do."

"I think we just had a helluva first date."

ACKNOWLEDGMENTS

Thanks to the two splendid midwives who helped birth this book, Lizzie Witten and Eileen Conde.

ABOUT THE AUTHORS

JAMES PATTERSON is the world's bestselling author and most trusted storyteller. He has created many enduring fictional characters and series, including Alex Cross, the Women's Murder Club, Michael Bennett, Maximum Ride, Middle School, and I Funny. Among his notable literary collaborations are *The President Is Missing,* with President Bill Clinton, and the Max Einstein series, produced in partnership with the Albert Einstein Estate. Patterson's writing career is characterized by a single mission: to prove that there is no such thing as a person who "doesn't like to read," only people who haven't found the right book. He's given over three million books to schoolkids and the military, donated more than seventy million dollars to support education, and endowed over five thousand college scholarships for teachers. For his prodigious imagination and championship of literacy in America, Patterson was awarded the 2019 National Humanities Medal. The National Book Foundation presented him with the Literarian Award for Outstanding Service to the American Literary Community, and he is also the recipient of an Edgar Award and nine Emmy Awards. He lives in Florida with his family.

RICHARD DiLALLO is a former advertising executive. He lives in Manhattan with his wife.

READ ON FOR A
SNEAK PEEK OF
*THE PRESIDENT'S
DAUGHTER*
BY JAMES PATTERSON
AND BILL CLINTON.

COMING IN JUNE 2021.

LAKE MARIE

New Hampshire

An hour or so after my daughter, Mel, leaves, I've showered, had my second cup of coffee, and read the newspapers—just skimming them, really, for it's a sad state of affairs when you eventually realize just how wrong journalists can be in covering stories. With a handsaw and a set of pruning shears, I head off to the south side of our property.

It's a special place, even though my wife, Samantha, has spent less than a month here in all her visits. Most of the land in the area is conservation land, never to be built upon, and of the people who do live here, almost all follow the old New Hampshire tradition of never bothering their neighbors or gossiping about them to visitors or news reporters.

Out on the lake is a white Boston Whaler with two men supposedly fishing, although they are Secret Service. Last year the *Union Leader* newspaper did a little piece about the agents stationed aboard the boat—calling them the unluckiest fishermen in the state—but since then, they've been pretty much left alone.

As I'm chopping, cutting, and piling brush, I think back to two famed fellow POTUS brush cutters—Ronald Reagan and George W. Bush— and how their exertions never quite made sense to a lot of people. They thought, *Hey, you've been at the pinnacle of fame and power, why go out and get your hands dirty?*

I saw at a stubborn pine sapling that's near an old stone wall on the property, and think, *Because it helps. It keeps your mind occupied, your thoughts busy, so you don't continually flash back to memories of your presidential term.*

The long and fruitless meetings with Congressional leaders from both sides of the aisle, talking with them, arguing with them, and sometimes pleading with them, at one point saying, "Damn it, we're all Americans here—isn't there anything we can work on to move our country forward?"

And constantly getting the same smug, superior answers. "Don't blame us, Mr. President. Blame *them*."

The late nights in the Oval Office, signing letters of condolence to the families of the best of us, men and women who had died for the idea of America, not the squabbling and revenge-minded nation we have become. And three times running across the names of men I knew and fought with, back when I was younger, fitter, and with the teams.

And other late nights as well, reviewing what was called—in typical innocuous, bureaucratic fashion—the Disposition Matrix database, prepared by the National Counterterrorism Center, but was really known as the "kill list." Months of work, research, surveillance, and intelligence intercepts resulting in a list of known terrorists who were a clear and present danger to the United States. And there I was, sitting by myself, and like a Roman emperor of old, I put a check mark next to those I decided were going to be killed in the next few days.

The sapling finally comes down.

Mission accomplished.

I look up and see something odd flying in the distance.

I stop, shade my eyes. Since moving here, I've gotten used to the different kinds of birds moving in and around Lake Marie, including the loons, whose night calls sound like someone's being throttled, but I don't recognize what's flying over there now.

I watch for a few seconds, and then it disappears behind the far tree line.

And I get back to work, something suddenly bothering me, something I can't quite figure out.

BASE OF THE
HUNTSMEN TRAIL

Mount Rollins, New Hampshire

I n the front seat of a black Cadillac Escalade, the older man rubs at his clean-shaven chin and looks at the video display from the laptop set up on top of the center console. Sitting next to him in the passenger seat, the younger man has a rectangular control system in his hand, with two small joysticks and other switches. He is controlling a drone with a video system, and they've just watched the home of former president Matthew Keating disappear from view.

It pleases the older man to see the West's famed drone technology turned against them. For years he's done the same thing with their wireless networks and cell phones, triggering devices and creating the bombs that shattered so many bodies and sowed so much terror.

And the Internet—which promised so much when it came out to bind the world as one—ended up turning into a well-used and safe communications network for him and his warriors.

The Cadillac they're sitting in was stolen this morning from a young couple and their infant in northern Vermont, after the two men abandoned their stolen pickup truck. There's still a bit of blood spatter and brain matter on the dashboard in front of them. An empty baby's seat is in the rear, along with a flowered cloth bag stuffed with toys and other childish things.

"Next?" the older man asks.

"We find the girl," he says. "It shouldn't take long."

"Do it," the older man says, watching with quiet envy and fascination as the younger man manipulates the controls of the complex machine while the drone's camera-made images appear on the computer screen.

"There. There she is."

From a bird's-eye view, he thinks, staring at the screen. A red sedan moves along the narrow paved roads.

He says, "And you are sure that the Americans, that they are not tracking you?"

"Impossible," the younger man next to him says in confidence. "There are thousands of such drones at play across this country right now. The officials who control the airspace, they have rules about where drones can go, and how high and low they can go, but most people ignore the rules."

"But their Secret Service…"

"Once President Matthew Keating left office, his daughter was no longer due the Secret Service protection. It's the law, if you can believe it. Under special circumstances, it can be requested, but no, not with her. The daughter wants to be on her own, going to school, without armed guards near her."

He murmurs, "A brave girl, then."

"And foolish," comes the reply.

And a stupid father, he thinks, to let his daughter roam at will like this, with no guards, no security.

The camera in the air follows the vehicle with no difficulty, and the older man shakes his head, again looking around him at the rich land and forests. Such an impossibly plentiful and gifted country, but why in Allah's name do they persist in meddling and interfering and being colonialists around the world?

A flash of anger sears through him.

If only they would stay home, how many innocents would still be alive?

"There," his companion says. "As I earlier learned…they are stopping here. At the beginning of the trail called Sherman's Path."

The vehicle on screen pulls into a dirt lot still visible from the air. Again, the older man is stunned at how easy it was to find the girl's schedule by looking at websites and bulletin boards from her college, from something called the Dartmouth Outing Club. Less than an hour's work and research has brought him here, looking down at her, like some blessed, all-seeing spirit.

He stares at the screen once more. Other vehicles are parked in the lot, and the girl and the boy get out. Both retrieve knapsacks from the rear of the vehicle. There's an embrace, a kiss, and then they walk away from the vehicles and disappear into the woods.

"Satisfied?" his companion asks.

For years, he thinks in satisfaction, the West has used these drones to rain down hellfire upon his friends, his fighters, and, yes, his family and other families. Fat and comfortable men (and women!) sipping their sugary drinks in comfortable chairs in safety, killing from thousands of kilometers away, seeing the silent explosions but not once hearing them, or hearing the shrieking and crying of the wounded and dying, and then driving home without a care in the world.

Now, it's his turn.

His turn to look from the sky.

Like a falcon on the hunt, he thinks.

Patiently and quietly waiting to strike.

SHERMAN'S PATH

Mount Rollins, New Hampshire

I t's a clear, cool, and gorgeous day on Sherman's Path, and Mel Keating is enjoying this climb up to Mount Rollins, where she and her boyfriend, Nick Kenyon, will spend the night with other members of the Dartmouth Outing Club at a small hut the club owns near the summit. She stops for a moment on a granite outcropping and puts her thumbs through her knapsack's straps.

Nick emerges from the trail and surrounding scrub brush, smiling, face a bit sweaty, bright blue knapsack on his back, and he takes her extended hand as he reaches her. "Damn nice view, Mel," he says.

She kisses him. "I've got a better view ahead."

"Where?"

"Just you wait."

She lets go of his hand and gazes at the rolling peaks of the White Mountains and the deep green of the forests, and notices the way some of the trees look a darker shade of green from the overhead clouds gently scudding by. Out beyond the trees is the Connecticut River and the mountains of Vermont.

Mel takes a deep, cleansing breath.

Just her and Nick and nobody else.

She lowers her glasses, and everything instantly turns to muddled shapes of green and blue. Nothing to see, nothing to spot. She remembers the boring times at state dinners back at the White House, when she'd be sitting with Mom and Dad, and she'd lower her glasses so all she could see were colored blobs. That made the time pass, when she really didn't want to be there, didn't really want to see all those well-dressed men and women pretending to like Dad and be his friend so they could get something in return.

Mel slides the glasses back up, and everything comes into view.

That's what she likes.

Being ignored and seeing only what she wants to see.

Nick reaches between the knapsack and rubs her neck. "What are you looking at?"

"Nothing."

"Oh, that doesn't sound good."

Mel laughs. "Silly man, it's the best! No staff, no news reporters, no cameras, no television correspondents, no Secret Service agents standing like dark-suited statues in the corner. Nobody! Just you and me."

"Sounds lonely," Nick says.

She slaps his butt. "Don't you get it? There's nobody keeping an eye on me, and I'm loving every second of it. Come along, let's get moving."

Some minutes later, Nick is sitting at the edge of a small mountainside pool, ringed with boulders and saplings and shrubs, letting his feet soak, enjoying the sun on his back, thinking of how damn lucky he is.

He had been shy at first when meeting Mel last semester in an African history seminar—everyone on the Dartmouth campus knew who she was, so that was no secret—and he had no interest in trying to even talk to her until Mel started getting crap thrown at her one day in class. She had said something about the importance of microloans in Africa, and a few loudmouths started hammering her about being ignorant of the real world, being privileged, and not having an authentic life.

When the loudmouths took a moment to catch their respective breaths, Nick surprised himself by saying, "I grew up in a third-floor apartment in Southie. My Dad was a lineman for the electric company, my Mom worked cleaning other people's homes and clipped coupons to go grocery shopping, and man, I'd trade that authentic life for privilege any day of the week."

A bunch of the students laughed. Mel caught his eye with a smile and he asked her after class to get a coffee or something at Lou's Bakery, and that's how it started.

Him, a scholarship student, dating the daughter of President Matt Keating.

What a world.

What a life.

Sitting on a moss-colored boulder, Mel nudges him and says, "How's your feet?"

"Feeling cold and fine."

"Then let's do the whole thing," she says, standing up, tugging off her gray Dartmouth sweatshirt. "Feel like a swim?"

He smiles. "Mel...someone could see us!"

She smiles right back, wearing just a tan sports bra under the sweatshirt, as she starts lowering her shorts. "Here? In the middle of a national forest? Lighten up, sweetie. Nobody's around for miles."

After she strips, Mel yelps out as she jumps into the pool, keeping her head and glasses above water. The water is cold and sharp. Poor Nick takes his time, wading in, shifting his weight as he tries to keep his footing on the slippery rocks, and he yowls like a hurt puppy when the cold mountain water reaches just below his waist.

The pond is small, and Mel reaches the other side with three strong strokes, and she swims back, the cold water now bracing, making her heart race, everything tingling. She tilts her head back, looking up past the tall pines and seeing the bright, bare blue patch of sky. Nothing. Nobody watching her, following her, recording her.

Bliss.

Another yelp from Nick, and she turns her head to him. Nick had wanted to go Navy ROTC, but a bad set of lungs prevented him from doing so, and even though she knows Dad wishes he'd get a haircut, his Southie background and interest in the Navy scored Nick in the plus side of the boyfriend column with Dad.

Nick lowers himself farther into the water, until it reaches his strong shoulders. "Did you see the sign-up list for the overnight at the cabin?" he asks. "Sorry to say, Cam Carlucci is coming."

"I know," she says, treading water, leaning back, letting her hair soak, looking up at the sharp blue and empty sky.

"You know he's going to want you to—"

Mel looks back at Nick. "Yeah. He and his buds

want to go to the Seabrook nuclear plant this Labor Day weekend, occupy it, and shut it down."

Poor Nick's lips seem to be turning blue. "They sure want you there."

In a mocking tone, Mel imitates Cam and says, "'Oh, Mel, you can make such an impact if you get arrested. Think of the headlines. Think of your influence.' To hell with him. They don't want me there as me. They want a puppet they can prop up to get coverage."

Nick laughs. "You going to tell him that tonight?"

"Nah," she says. "He's not worth it. I'll tell him I have plans for Labor Day weekend instead."

Her boyfriend looks puzzled. "You do?"

She swims to him and gives him a kiss, hands on his shoulders. "Dopey boy, yes, with you."

His hands move through the water to her waist, and she's enjoying the touch—just as she hears voices and looks up.

For the first time in a long time she's frightened.

LAKE MARIE

New Hampshire

After getting out of the shower for the second time today (the first after taking a spectacular tumble in a muddy patch of dirt) and drying off, I idly play the which-body-scar-goes-to-which-op when my iPhone rings. I wrap a towel around me, picking up the phone, knowing only about twenty people in the world have this number. Occasionally, though, a call comes in from "John" in Mumbai pretending to be a Microsoft employee in Redmond, Washington. I've been tempted to tell John who he's really talking to, but I've resisted the urge.

This time, however, the number is blocked, and puzzled, I answer the phone.

"Keating," I say.

A strong woman's voice comes through. "Mr. President? This is Sarah Palumbo, calling from the NSC."

The name quickly pops up in my mind. Sarah's been the deputy national security advisor for the National Security Council since my term, and she should have gotten the director's position when Melissa Powell retired to go back to academia. But someone to whom President Barnes owed a favor got the position. A former Army brigadier general and deputy director at the CIA, Sarah knows her stuff, from the annual output of Russian oilfields to the status of Colombian cartel smuggling submarines.

"Sarah, good to hear from you," I say, still dripping some water onto the bathroom's tile floor. "How're your mom and dad doing? Enjoying the snowbird life in Florida?"

Sarah and her family grew up in Buffalo, where lake effect winter storms can dump up to four feet of snow in an afternoon. She chuckles and says, "They're loving every warm second of it. Sir, do you have a moment?"

"My day is full of moments," I reply. "What's going on?"

"Sir...," and the tone of her voice instantly changes, worrying me. "Sir, this is unofficial, but I wanted to let you know what I learned this morning. Sometimes the bureaucracy takes too long to respond to emerging developments, and I don't want that to happen here. It's too important."

I say, "Go on."

She says, "I was sitting in for the director at today's threat-assessment meeting, going over the President's Daily Brief and other interagency reports."

With those words of jargon, I'm instantly transported back to being POTUS, and I'm not sure I like it.

"What's going on, Sarah?"

The briefest of pauses. "Sir, we've noticed an uptick in chatter from various terrorist cells in the Mideast, Europe, and Canada. Nothing we can specifically attach a name or a date to, but something is on the horizon, something bad, something that will generate a lot of attention."

Shit, I think. "All right," I say. "Terrorists are keying themselves up to strike. Why are you calling me? Who are they after?"

"Mr. President," she says, "they're coming after you."

JAMES
PATTERSON
RECOMMENDS

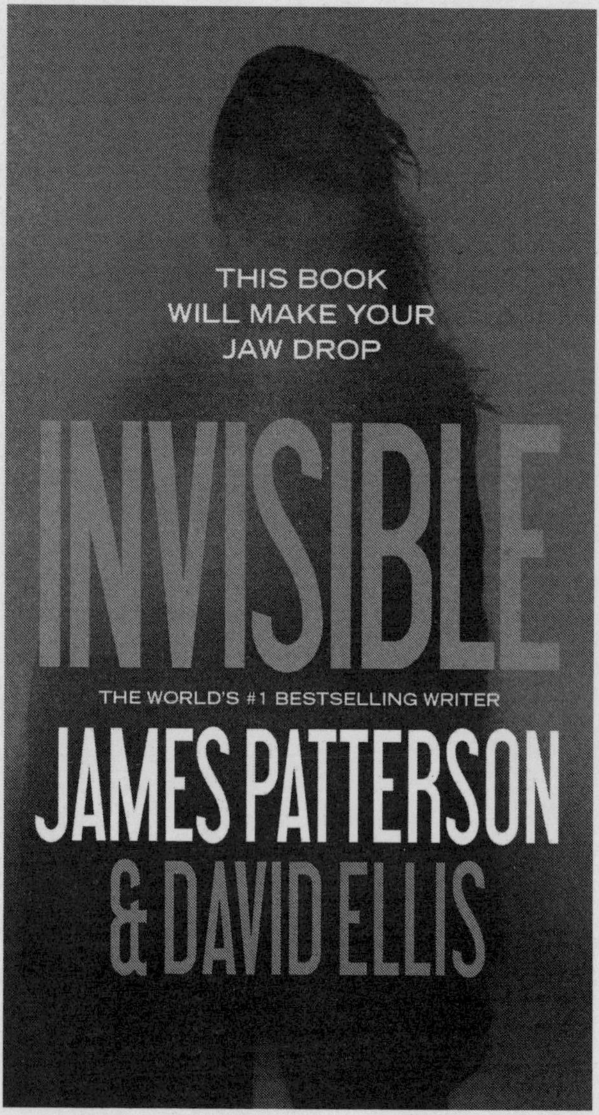
THIS BOOK
WILL MAKE YOUR
JAW DROP
INVISIBLE
THE WORLD'S #1 BESTSELLING WRITER
JAMES PATTERSON
& DAVID ELLIS

INVISIBLE

When I started writing *Invisible,* it seemed like every other TV network was telling the same kinds of police stories, with similar robberies and crime twists. So I wanted to tell a different kind of suspense story, one that would really make your jaw drop. In the novel, Emmy Dockery is a researcher for the FBI who believes she has stumbled on one of the deadliest serial killers in history. There's only one problem: he's invisible. The mysterious killer leaves no trace. There are no weapons, no evidence, no motive. But when the killer strikes close to home, Emmy must crack an impossible case before anyone else dies. Prepare to be blindsided, because the most terrifying threat is the one you don't see coming—the one that's invisible.

And don't miss Emmy Dockery's second mystery, *Unsolved,* available now.

THE FIRST LADY

The US government is at the forefront of everyone's mind these days, and I've become incredibly fascinated by the idea that one secret can bring it all down. What if that secret is a US president's affair that results in a nightmarish outcome? Sally Grissom, leader of the Presidential Protection Division, is summoned to a private meeting with the president and his chief of staff to discuss the disappearance of the first lady. What begins as an escape to a safe haven to get away from the revelation of her husband's indiscretion becomes a kidnapping when a ransom note arrives along with what could be the first lady's finger. It's a race against the clock to collect the evidence, which all leads to one troubling question: Could the kidnappers be from inside the White House?

JAMES PATTERSON

AND BRENDAN DUBOIS

*Her family is missing.
She'll do whatever
it takes to bring
them home.*

THE CORNWALLS VANISH

PREVIOUSLY PUBLISHED AS *THE CORNWALLS ARE GONE*

THE CORNWALLS VANISH

There's nothing more terrifying than coming home and knowing that something is wrong. Army intelligence officer Amy Cornwall experiences that when she finishes a tour filled with haunting sights and walks in the front door to find her home empty. She receives a phone call with very specific instructions— failure to complete them will mean the death of her husband and ten-year-old daughter. Now Amy has to defy Army Command and use every lethal skill they've taught her to save her family. There's no boundary that she won't cross in order to find them, because without her family, she might as well be dead.

NEVER

NEVER

JAMES
PATTERSON

CANDICE FOX

NEVER NEVER

As tough as Alex Cross. As smart as the Women's Murder Club. The brilliant, fierce Detective Harriet Blue. She's a resilient woman who can hunt down any man in a hardscrabble continent half a world away. My newest detective, Harry, is her department's top Sex Crimes investigator, and she'll need to use all her skills when her own brother is arrested for the murder of three beautiful women. And clearing her brother's name under the watchful eye of her new "partner" is anything but easy. She has to delve into deep, dark secrets, and failure to solve the mystery may mean she never makes it back.

For a complete list of books by

JAMES PATTERSON

VISIT
JamesPatterson.com

Follow James Patterson on Facebook
@JamesPatterson

Follow James Patterson on Twitter
@JP_Books

Follow James Patterson on Instagram
@jamespattersonbooks